Quade's Quest

Ahead of them, Quade saw a young woman leave the store. As she did, many of the soldiers watched her intently. He was certain they had thoughts about her that were anything but honorable.

"Well, lookey over there. Good Day Miss Hannah," Simon said, as he touched the brim of his hat in greeting.

The woman nodded in their direction but kept walking, as though she wanted nothing to do with either of them.

"Uppity Bitch. You'd think she was the Queen of Sheba instead of just old Horace's adopted daughter. Every man on this post gets hard just lookin' at her and she won't give any of them the time of day. Don't know where she got them 'better than anyone else' ways about her, but one day she'll find out what it's like to be with a man. If I have my way I'll be that man."

Quade studied the young woman until they drove passed her. He didn't want to appear nosey, so he did not turn back to stare at her the way he wanted to do. She was indeed a beautiful young woman, but there was no way that she was white. He'd seen enough Indian women to know that Hannah Whitfield had to have some Indian blood in her. Perhaps she was an orphan that the missionary and his wife had adopted.

"Did you hear what I said?" Simon asked when Quade made no comment on the man's statement.

"I heard you. I'm afraid that if you think you're going to have anything to do with the lovely Miss Whitfield, you have another think coming. Just by the way she looked at you I could see that she wasn't interested in anything you have to offer her."

Other Works From The Pen Of

Sherry Derr-Wille

Becky's Rebel

North battles South as Joe Kemmerman fights Becky Larson's Yankee brothers for the right to make Becky his own.

Coffee Tea or Love

In the first of the stories surrounding those gals from Minter, WI, Lane Allerton is faced with the man who got her pregnant thirty-five years ago. Is Grant Price her dream lover or a nightmare?

Transplanted Love

Lori Carter is reluctant to tell the new man in her life about her kidney transplant. For one night she wants to be like everyone else and not the bionic woman.

A Precious Jewel

Julie Weston thought she had the perfect marriage, until she learned the truth about the man she's been mourning for a year. Wanting to be loved if only for one night turns her life upside down when Devan Yates enters her life as well as her heart.

Bosslady

Nineteen years after Joe claimed Becky as his own, their daughter, BJ, is returning to Texas to claim what is rightfully hers. When she runs into Whit, the foreman of her ranch, she finds the fight is going to be tougher than she ever thought.

Her Tenant

Dee Williams has a duplex to rent but Bryce Devlin isn't her idea of the perfect tenant. He is so handsome that he tempts her and at the same time he is far too available to fight her attraction to him.

Kate Armstrong: Over-The-Hill Coed

Kate needs to get the three credits she is short in order to get her degree but going back to school after over thirty years is hard. Even harder is finding that the jerky jock who gave her fits in high school is now her professor, Denny Bostian.

Hello, Do You Know Me?

Jerry Fellows went to Vietnam and returned in a body bag, or did he? Matt Bratzman returned to the states with no memory of his past. When uninvited memories flood his mind, he can't help but wonder if he is Matt or Jerry. Only a trip to Minter, WI will unlock the past and solve the mystery.

Quade's Quest

by

Sherry Derr-Wille

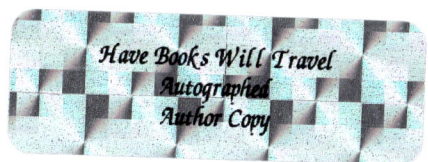

A Wings ePress, Inc.

Western Historical Romance Novel

HEDBERG PUBLIC LIBRARY
316 SOUTH MAIN STREET
JANESVILLE, WI 53545

Wings ePress, Inc.

Edited by:Leslie Hodges
Copy Edited by: Elizabeth Struble
Senior Editor: Leslie Hodges
Executive Editor: Lorraine Stephens
Cover Artist: Christine Poe

All rights reserved

Names, characters and incidents depicted in this book are products of the author's imagination or are used fictitiously. Any resemblance to actual events, locales, organizations, or persons, living or dead, is entirely coincidental and beyond the intent of the author or the publisher.

No part of this book may be reproduced or transmitted in any form or by any means, electronic or mechanical, including photocopying, recording, or by any information storage and retrieval system, without permission in writing from the publisher.

Wings ePress Books
http://www.wings-press.com

Copyright © 2007 by Sherry Derr-Wille
ISBN 978-1-59705-761-5

Published In the United States Of America

May 2007

Wings ePress Inc.
403 Wallace Court
Richmond, KY 40475

Dedication

I would like to dedicate this book to my editor, Leslie Hodges. When I first started writing this for someone else, she said she wanted it. When the pain of rejection was still at the forefront, she asked to see it. Without her respect and all the wonderful edits she's done for me, this book might never have found a suitable home.

Prologue

Montana Territory—1870

Horses thundered through the village, gunfire and screams permeated the air. Even though Little Hummingbird clutched her mother's hand, fear filled her mind. She wished her father were with them as well as her older brothers. They had been gone for many days hunting and were not expected back for many more days. Ahead of her stood the fringes of the forest. She knew within their dark recesses she would be safe from the blue-coated soldiers who had ridden into the village before the sun barely crested the horizon.

"Hide, Little Hummingbird," her mother instructed as she pushed the child toward the trees. "No matter what happens do not come out until it is safe."

Always one to obey without question, Little Hummingbird ran until she could run no more. Where she stopped stood a hollow tree with an opening just large enough for her to squeeze inside.

In the distance the gunfire continued. After what seemed like forever it ceased and she relaxed. The songs of the birds of the forest returned and were comforting, for while the gunfire had been the loudest, they had not sung.

Surely now that everything is safe, my mother will come and find me. Willing to wait until her mother arrived, she curled into a tight ball and fell asleep.

~ * ~

The hooting of an owl woke her. Outside of her hiding place the darkness of night had fallen. The hunger that growled in her small stomach prompted her to leave the security of her tree and make her way to her village. When the soldiers had ridden into camp her mother was just beginning to prepare the morning meal. With all of the rush to get away from the village, there had been no time to eat.

The fact that her mother had not found her came as no surprise. Little Hummingbird had always been able to hide where her friends could not find her. It was possible that her mother had searched, perhaps walked right past the tree and had not seen her. What joy there would be when she returned to her mother's arms?

Walking slowly through the forest, she realized how far she had actually run in her frightened flight. The moon was already dropping toward the western horizon when the trees finally began to thin.

As she stepped out into the clearing where she had last seen her mother, she tripped over a fallen log, hidden by the darkness. As she got to her feet, her hand touched the log, only to realize it was a body.

In the weak light of the predawn moon, she looked more closely at the body that had impeded her return to her mother. From the dress, she could tell it was a woman. In the light of dawning, she recognized the design of the quillwork on the bodice of the dress. Tears stung her eyes as she forced herself to look into the face of the woman. The look of horror and shock was frozen upon her mother's once beautiful face.

Blood streaked across her throat as an ugly gash ran from ear to ear. Her long black hair had been taken as a trophy, just as the men of her village took the scalps of the white invaders of their land.

She looked away from the grizzly sight, realizing for the first time that her mother's leggings had been pulled off and cast aside. Her legs were spread wide. Had the blue-coated soldiers who came to her village done to her mother what her father did in the dark of night in the sleeping furs? If so, it was wrong. Even at five winters of age, she knew it was wrong. A man only shared night pleasures with his wife, be it his first, second or third wife. It did not happen between people who were not committed to each other.

Not knowing what to do, she continued to sit beside the body of her mother. She remembered when her mother had given birth to a baby who could not get his breath. At the time the people sang a funeral song. Little Hummingbird did not know the words for such a song, but she knew she must sing them so her mother's soul could walk with the ancestors.

Out of desperation, she made up words for such a song. She sang of her mother's beauty, her loving touch and her virtues. Over and over again, she sang the words until her voice was no longer audible. Then and only then did she cry and pray that her father and brothers would arrive and comfort her in their loving arms.

In the distance, she heard a rumble that sounded like thunder. She glanced up, surprised to see a beautiful blue sky dotted with fluffy white clouds and bright sunlight.

Before she could run back into the forest, she saw a white man's wagon bearing down on her. A woman drove the team, while a man ran toward her.

"Hurry, Martha," the man shouted words that meant nothing to Little Hummingbird. "I've found another one with a child. Praise the Lord the child is alive."

Fear clutched at Little Hummingbird's entire being. As it

did, the words of the song that echoed in her mind turned from one for her mother to her own funeral song. With the words repeated over and over again, she closed her eyes and waited for the death that would reunite her with her mother. *Please, Great Spirit, allow me to be with Mother this day. Do not let these whites see my fear of death.*

Instead of the bite of the man's knife or the sting of a bullet, she felt herself being lifted into his arms. Once he held her protectively, he handed her to the woman. When she finally allowed herself to open her eyes, she saw that the woman who cradled her and stroked her hair had tears running down her cheeks.

"You poor baby," the woman crooned.

Even though Little Hummingbird did not understand the words, they were soothing. Instinctively she knew she would come to no harm from these people.

"Oh, Horace, the woman must be this poor child's mother. We cannot leave her here alone. They're all dead. She'd never survive."

"Don't worry, Martha, we'll take her with us. We will not continue on to the mission with the Cheyenne. Instead we will go to the south and find a mission there. In that area, no one will know us. We will tell people that we rescued her from an orphanage and adopted her. She will become our daughter."

Little Hummingbird's tears flowed down her cheeks as she watched the man bury her mother so that the wild animals would not feast upon her flesh. While the man worked, the woman built a fire and put a pot, that looked like the one Little Hummingbird's mother had gotten from the white trader who came to the village, on to heat.

The smell of a savory stew made Little Hummingbird's stomach growl in anticipation. It had been so long since she had last eaten that her body cried for the nourishment the stew represented.

When at last the woman handed her a bowl of steaming stew, she ate it hungrily. By eating so quickly, her empty stomach rebelled. The woman held her head while she lost the precious food she had just eaten. With nothing more to lose, the woman helped her to drink a sip of water, and then gave her a spoonful of the stew that had tasted so good earlier. By eating small amounts, the food soon filled her empty stomach and did not disagree with her.

These people were kind. She could feel it. Even though they were white, like the men who had killed her mother as well as others from the village, she instinctively knew that they would protect her from the evils of the world.

Quade's Quest   Sherry Derr-Wille

One

Nevada—1885

"Lieutenant McPherson, your conduct will not be tolerated at this fort. Do I make myself clear?"

Quade wondered what Major Walters meant. He'd done nothing other than his duties, so what was his new commanding officer babbling about? "I'm sorry, Sir, I don't understand any of this. What have I done?"

"Are you as stupid as you look? My wife told me all about your advances. Such a thing will not be tolerated. I was told you were an honorable man, but I can see that it was an exaggeration. Are you trying to get back at me for losing your position as the assistant to the commanding officer of this post?"

Quade remembered his encounter with Mrs. Walters the day before in town. She was struggling with an armload of packages from one of the stores. At the time it seemed the courteous thing for him to take them from her and carry them to her carriage. Her driver had helped her to step up and she had thanked Quade for his assistance. How could anything like that be considered improper?

"Don't just stand there, Lieutenant, as of this moment you are confined to your quarters. Your new orders will be arriving within the week."

Quade saluted sharply, too stunned to react to his commanding officer's accusation. Instead he turned and left the office where he had served for so long.

On his way to his quarters, he met several people he knew, but didn't stop to talk to anyone. Once there he picked up his journal to read what he had written about his chance encounter with Grace Walters the day before.

He thumbed through the handwritten pages until he came to yesterday's entry.

> *Went into town to meet with the marshal regarding one of my men who was being held following a brawl at the Gilded Lilly on Saturday evening. Private Jenkins will be free as soon as he serves five days in jail, since he cannot pay his fine. When he returns to the fort, a military court will deal with him. As I was leaving the marshal's office, I saw Mrs. Walters struggling with her purchases. After I carried them to her carriage, I returned to the fort and reported my findings regarding Private Jenkins to Major Walters.*

A light rap on his door drew his attention away from the journal he held in his hands. When he opened the door, Grace Walters stood in the doorway of his quarters.

"I—I just want to apologize for any trouble I may have caused for you," she said her bottom lip trembling and tears running down her cheeks.

Quade's first thought was to slam the door in her face, but he needed to know exactly what this woman had told her husband about him. "You and I know what happened in town yesterday, so exactly what was it you told your husband?"

"He was being so—so—well... he wasn't paying any

saw a mixture of disbelief, pity and condemnation reflected.

Major Walters sat at his desk as he had less than a week earlier at the beginning of this nightmare.

"I hope your confinement has given you time to think on the wrong you have done me. I have your transfer here. As much as I wanted to have you demoted, that punishment did not fit your crime. I can only hope you will be more careful at your next post. Many men such as myself bring their wives with them. I would hate to have you dishonor yet another woman."

Quade could hold his tongue no longer. "I have but one thing to say to you, Sir. I am innocent of these charges. I did nothing more than assist your wife with her packages, as I would have assisted any woman who was struggling with such a load. Perhaps you should speak to your wife concerning this matter."

"I know that Grace came to your quarters. After that she came home and recanted everything she said. I did not believe her then, nor do I believe *you* now. This envelope contains your orders along with a train ticket. Your train leaves for Montana Territory this evening. I assume you have packing to do. You are dismissed."

The words *Montana Territory* rang in Quade's ears as he took the papers from Major Walters, saluted and left the office. The door slamming behind him told him that any comforts he had enjoyed over the past four years were gone forever. He had heard stories of the Indian raids on the frontier and wanted no more encounters with a people who were only fighting for the land that had been theirs since the beginning of time.

His four-man guard waited for him outside the major's office and escorted him back to his quarters to retrieve his gear. Once that was done a wagon with the same guards took him to the railroad station in town and waited until he had boarded the train heading east.

It had surprised him that he had been allowed to take his horse with him. Being Army issue he had suspected that Major Walters would have insisted that he leave the gelding at the fort. Of course, being sent to a post in the middle of nowhere meant he would need a horse and this one had been with him since before he left Arizona territory.

He walked about halfway through the passenger car until he came to an empty seat. It pleased him to see that the seat next to him was not occupied. He would have a bit of solitude in which to contemplate his future with the Army. He thought of writing to his folks, but since he hadn't written to them in almost nine years he didn't see much point in telling them of his disgrace.

"Is this seat taken?"

He immediately recognized the voice of Grace Walters. Before he could reply she seated herself next to him. He turned to look at her and was shocked by her appearance. The bruise he had seen days earlier had been replaced by many more, including a nasty looking black eye. If he didn't know better he would think she had been involved in a bar room brawl and gotten the worst of it.

"My husband is sending me east with instructions to get a divorce as soon as I arrive. I only wanted him to love me. I thought if I told him that other men found me attractive he would want me again. I was wrong and now we are both suffering, Can you ever forgive me?"

Quade could only stare in disbelief at the woman who had ruined his career. How could she ask him for forgiveness? She was the one who had told the lie and he was paying the price.

"I don't think so. What I worked so hard to build up over the past nine years you destroyed with one lie. Forgiveness is for ministers and priests. It's not something I'm comfortable doing. Now, if you will excuse me I'll find another place to sit. We have a long trip ahead of us and I doubt either of us would be attention to me so I told him that if he didn't find me interesting you did. Then one lie led to another until I—I told him that we had been..."

"You told him we were lovers? It's no wonder I'm confined to quarters and waiting orders for relocation. Do you have any idea how hard I worked to be assigned to this fort? How could you do such a thing?"

"I—I..."

"Don't stammer woman, just get away from me. The damage is done. I hope it was worth it to you."

As she turned to leave, he noticed the bruise on her left cheek. She too had suffered because of her lie. Even though he didn't want to see a woman mistreated, he refused to show her compassion. He'd worked hard to reach the rank of lieutenant and because of her lies all of it was for nothing.

After closing the door, Quade lay down on his bed and reviewed his career. Nine years ago he'd been but sixteen when he ran away from his father's farm in Missouri to join the army. He'd been sent to the Arizona Territory to fight Apaches. There his field promotions came quickly. After five years he'd reached the rank of sergeant. Tired of fighting Indians, he had asked for a transfer to quieter duty.

Virginia City, Nevada had been a good move for him. It was there he met Major Cass Eaton. Within the first month, Major Eaton had put Quade in for a promotion to lieutenant so he could act as the major's personal assistant. Major Eaton had been his commanding officer for almost four years—until two months ago when he died suddenly in his sleep.

Just a month ago Major Walters came to Virginia City to take Major Eaton's place. With him had come his own personal assistant, leaving Quade to begin a new phase in his military career. He'd been thrust into the role of leadership that his battlefield promotions had not prepared him for. Until today he thought he had adjusted well. Now with his future uncertain, he had misgivings.

~ * ~

Almost a week passed before Quade saw anyone other than the private who brought him his meals.

The knock on his door at nine in the morning startled him. When he went to see who could be calling, he was not surprised to find his visitor to be Major Walter's personal assistant. "Major Walters asked me to bring you to his office," the man said.

Quade couldn't help but wonder if this particular request bothered the man. He was certain everyone at the fort knew why he was being confined to quarters.

As much as the expression on the man's face denoted concern, his own uneasiness built as he grabbed his hat and prepared to follow the man. He couldn't help but remember the number of times he had brought prisoners to Major Eaton's office using the same words of explanation.

Never in his wildest dreams had he expected the same request be made of him. In anticipation of the visit he had packed his belongings. He glanced at the bag that contained his uniforms and riding boots. It was a certainty that he would not be allowed to take his horse with him.

As soon as he stepped out into the bright Nevada sunlight, he saw the four-man guard waiting to escort him to Major Walter's office. To make matters worse, it was made up of men from his own company. He knew such a guard was acceptable when the prisoner was a dangerous man, but he had done nothing wrong.

From every area of the fort men stopped their work to watch him walk the three hundred yards from his quarters to the office where he had served as assistant to the major for four years. He tried not to make eye contact with anyone, but when he did he comfortable sitting next to each other."

"Please, Lieutenant McPherson, don't leave me alone. Take me with you to whatever fort it is that you are going to be assigned to."

"I would rather take a snake with me, Mrs. Walters."

The woman's tears began to flow down her cheeks. The one thing he could not stand was to see a woman cry.

"I—I came out here as a mail order bride. I have nowhere to go," she pleaded.

Quade began to soften a bit. "You must have somewhere to go. Where does your ticket say you're headed?"

"Back to Ohio. My parents are there, but how can I ever tell them that—that the man who sent for me has sent me back."

"The same way you just told me. Parents are forgiving. They will welcome you with open arms."

That said, Quade got up and moved to another seat. All the talk about parents and forgiveness did not set well with him at this moment.

After pulling his hat down over his eyes and propping his feet up on the vacant seat across from him, he tried to sleep, but his mind was filled with thoughts of the home and parents he'd left behind in Missouri.

His father and brother had been hardworking farmers, but when he had no desire for the vocation, he felt the sting of his father's belt on his backside. The last beating he'd taken at the hands of his father had prompted his departure from the farm. For the first time in his life he had fought back. When his father didn't get up he was afraid he had killed him. It had been his twin brother Quinton who had insisted he should leave that night. Even though he hadn't killed his father he had injured him badly and for that the old man would surely kill him when he was up and around again.

Quade had wasted no time in packing his belongings and

riding out. He had ridden to the first fort he could find and enlisted. Since fighting was what he was good at, it was best that he fight Indians rather than his own father.

From the night he left home, he had not written to his parents and had no idea what had become of his brother. For the past nine years he had been on his own and done quite well—at least he thought he had until Grace Walters made her accusations and ruined what future he might have had in Virginia City.

~ * ~

The trip was long, hot and dusty. Quade took the time to think about home more than he wanted. It didn't take long for him to take pencil and paper from his bag and compose a letter. As he did, he felt the burden lift. Perhaps it was him and not his parents that were at fault.

Dear Quint,

It's been nine years since I left home and so much has happened. I'd write this to Pa but I know he can't read and I don't know if he's alive or if I killed him on the night I left.

I joined the Army and spent five years in the Arizona Territory. By the time I left I had made the rank of sergeant. From there I was sent to Virginia City, Nevada. I was promoted to lieutenant and served as the personal assistant to Major Eaton until his death. Major Walters replaced him and brought along his own assistant.

I am now being reassigned to a fort in Montana. This is not something I asked for as I have had my fill of fighting the Indians that populate that area. It was the reason I asked for the transfer to Virginia City. I no longer had the stomach for killing men, women and children who had done nothing but be born with red skin instead of white.

If you would like to write to me I will be stationed at Fort Banner, in Montana. Until then I remain your brother—Quade.

Two

The station that the train pulled into was, as far as Quade was concerned, in the middle of nowhere. The area sported a covered platform where people could wait for the train, a water tower and a saloon. It certainly wasn't the civilized city he'd left behind when he stepped onto the train in Virginia City.

As he waited for his horse and gear to be unloaded he saw Grace Walters press her face against the window of the train. If she hadn't ruined his life with her false accusations, he could almost feel sorry for her.

From the car directly behind the one for passengers, he saw his horse being unloaded and went to retrieve him before going to the saloon for a drink and directions to the fort. Blaze, as he had named the horse, seemed glad to see him and immediately settled down. It was evident that this horse was not used to train travel. He stood holding the reins until the train pulled out of the station, in order to keep the animal calm.

Once he stood alone in the vast wilderness that surrounded him, he turned back to the saloon. To his horror, Grace Walters stood on the platform with him.

"Just what are you doing here?" he exploded. A variety of curse words burned to be spoken, but he was in the presence of a lady and had been taught better than to offend the weaker sex.

"I want to go with you," she said, her eyes pleading for him to understand her reluctance to return to Ohio.

"Well, you can't. How would I get you anywhere?"

"But I thought someone would meet you and..."

"And what? We aren't in Virginia City. The post may not have accommodations for you and as you can see there is nothing here."

"Can't you take me with you on your horse?"

Quade glanced at his horse. It would be tempting to have her pressing against him as they rode double, but highly impractical. The fort could be hours away by horseback and riding double that far was out of the question. Instead of agreeing to her harebrained idea, he grabbed Grace's arm and started leading her toward the saloon.

"Where are you taking me?" she asked indignantly.

"To the saloon."

"But—but I don't drink."

"Well, I do and in case you haven't noticed, that's the only building where we can get out of the sun."

"I am a lady. It would not be fitting for me to go into a saloon."

Quade shrugged his shoulders. "Suit yourself," he said, releasing his grip on her arm. "It's hot out here and I need a drink. What you do is of no concern to me." Without looking back, he started to cross the tracks to get to the saloon.

"You don't plan to leave me here do you?"

"Look, lady, I want a drink and some directions to the fort. If you don't want to come with me, I guess you can stand on this platform until the next train arrives. It probably won't be going to Ohio, but I gather that isn't where you want to go anyway."

She started to take a step toward him, then stopped. "What about my things? I can't leave them out here with no one to watch them."

"They ain't goin' nowhere," he replied. It surprised him that he had slipped back into the uneducated voice he always used with his pa. With his position in the army, he had learned to speak in a more cultured tone.

"Someone might take them," she whined.

Quade looked around the deserted station. "Unless the prairie dogs are stronger than they look, I think your belongings will be safe."

He turned back toward the saloon. From behind him, he could hear her heels clicking on the boards of the station platform. The thought of her hurrying to cross the dusty street brought a smile to his lips. He doubted that a lady like her had ever crossed a street without an escort in her entire life.

He held open the batwing doors of the saloon to allow Grace to enter ahead of him. The inside was dark compared to the bright sunlight outside. One look at the windows told him that the dust that had settled on them from the street was too thick to allow any light to penetrate.

Once his eyes adjusted to the dim interior, he saw a heavyset man behind the bar and a scantily clad woman standing with one foot on the bottom rail, making conversation with the bartender. The man spat a stream of tobacco juice to the floor before he addressed them.

"Just come in on the train?" he asked.

Quade thought the question a stupid one, for where else would they come from? "Yes, sir," Quade replied. "I could use a beer and the lady would like—"

"A beer," Grace interrupted.

"I thought you didn't drink," he hissed when the bartender turned to fill their glasses.

"I don't drink hard liquor, but of course beer and wine are not considered to be hard liquor in Ohio. My father made the best of both in the entire county back home."

Quade shook his head. He didn't even want to try to start to understand this woman. Instead he turned his attention to the bartender. "How far is it to the fort?"

The man sat the mugs of beer down in front of them. "It's too late in the day to ride out there now. It will take you the better part of the day. There are just too many renegades around to make the ride at night. Crooked Snake and his bunch are too smart to attack during the day when they might get caught."

"Indians?" Grace gasped. "Are they dangerous?"

"Not if you stay in town, Ma'am."

"You call this a town?" she retorted.

"It's as close as you'll get. Behind those curtains is the store. The tame Injuns from the village get their supplies here when they have things to trade."

"They're allowed off the reservation?" Quade asked.

"Hell, this is in the heart of the reservation. Them Injuns come to me for flour and blankets and such, but like I say, that's only when they have something to trade. The agent comes by here once a week. Usually he's sniffin' tail around that there missionary and his daughter. That one's a real looker. If I didn't know her pa so well, I'd say she was an Injun herself."

Quade thought about his options. He could stay the night and start fresh in the morning or he could take his chances with Crooked Snake. Neither of them appealed to him, but at least a soft bed was preferable to being scalped. "Do you have accommodations for us for the night?" he finally inquired.

"For you and the missus it's four bits a night."

The man's implication outraged Quade. "She's not my wife. She thought she was at a different stop. She'll need a place to stay until the next train comes through."

"Next train ain't for a week. At two bits a day that comes to a dollar seventy five and that don't include meals."

Quade could see tears forming in Grace's hazel eyes.

"I don't have that kind of money," she cried.

"Can you cook?" the man asked. "My cook done took up with a squaw about a week ago. Ain't heard from him since. Shirl here has been trying, but cookin' ain't her best talent, if you get my meaning."

"Can you cook?" Quade asked.

"Of course I can cook. My biscuits won blue ribbons at the county fair every year."

"You're hired. The job pays two bits a day and room and board. If I'm lucky, by the time the next eastbound train comes through you won't want to leave. Shirl and me, well, we're real easy to get along with and the work ain't hard. When you ain't cooking you can sit in here and socialize with us."

"Would I have to..." she glanced toward Shirl.

"Not on your life, honey," Shirl said, speaking for the first time, her voice laced with a southern drawl. "I'm the only whore here and I like it that way. Red, you go out and get the lady's things. I'll show her around."

For the first time Quade noticed that the bartender was indeed a redhead. "I'll take a room for the night, but what about my horse?"

"Barn's out back. Come with me and I'll show you where to put him. I get two bits for the horse, but he gets good feed."

Quade followed Red back out of the saloon. "Do you really have need of a cook? I mean, this place looks downright desolate."

"Wait 'til tonight. There's a lot of ranches around and we do a good business. If we had to depend on the Injuns we'd starve, but we do get a right good crowd in here, especially when the weather is this hot. Them cowhands work up a powerful thirst and we've got the beer and whiskey to quench it. 'Course along with the drinks they usually work up an appetite. Besides, Shirl and me have to eat and so does Clem, he runs the store, and Sam, the piano player. We're sort of like family. The little lady will fit in right well."

Quade shook his head. It was hard to imagine Grace Walters fitting in with a tobacco chewing bartender, an aging whore, a piano player and the shopkeeper who ran this godforsaken outpost in the middle of an Indian reservation. Of course, anything was possible and she certainly didn't want to return to Ohio and her family.

After taking Blaze to the barn, Quade went to help Red with Grace's trunks. "Just what is your connection to the lady?" Red asked once they took everything to one of the upstairs rooms.

Without going into great detail Quade outlined his history with Grace.

"Did she really think you'd take her with you?"

"Guess so. I'm indebted to you for taking her off my hands. What can I expect when I get to the fort?"

"Not much. It ain't big. Got a stockade, which is more than I can say for most of the ones around here. Inside there's the barracks, officers' quarters, the house for the missionary and his daughter and a store. Guess you could say you'd be comfortable enough. Ain't much to do, though. The only trouble you'll have will be with Crooked Snake. He gets riled up a couple of times a year. It's funny, I haven't heard much about him this year, but you can bet he's back. He hightails it back to Canada in the winter and only comes down to bother the soldiers in the summer. Otherwise you'll be looking after the tame ones and kowtowing to that agent. He's an arrogant son of a bitch. Luckily, I don't have to deal with him much. He comes in once a week to get his itch scratched, if you understand what I'm saying."

Quade knew all too well what Red meant. He came in to get

his fill of whiskey and Shirl. In return, he made certain Red and Shirl were well taken care of. Like so many of his kind, he had no respect for the people he was sent to care for.

Quade found the room above the saloon to be adequate. The bedsprings were shot but the room was clean and that was all that mattered. After stowing his gear he lay down and in time fell asleep. The new country he'd come to dominated his dreams. He'd had his fill of fighting Indians, so what was he doing in the middle of a reservation with a renegade like Crooked Snake hell bent on causing trouble for him?

~ * ~

From the shadows that crossed his room Quade knew he had slept most of the afternoon away. His stomach growled making him wonder if Grace or Shirl was manning the stove in the kitchen behind the saloon. Before he went down to the main floor, he splashed his face with the tepid water from the pitcher.

As soon as he opened his door the sound of someone playing the piano drifted up the stairs. To his surprise, he found Grace playing songs a lady like her had no business knowing, and Sam watching her with a grin as wide as the Grand Canyon on his face. The room was filled with cowboys and smoke. A card game was in progress and a well-dressed man, who looked completely out of place, stood at the bar with his arm around Shirl.

"Grace has stew on the stove in the kitchen," Red greeted him. "It's two bits, help yourself. The biscuits are the best I've ever had and she even found some cherries and made pie. Sure do hope she doesn't leave on that train that's coming next week. Oh yeah, there's someone here asking about you."

The fact that Red was able to string so many words together without a breath came as a surprise to Quade. Even more of a surprise was that someone, anyone, would be asking about him. "About me? Why?"

"See that guy over there with Shirl? He's the Injun Agent. He'll be riding out to the fort with you in the morning. Sorry about Shirl, but he has priority since he pays real good. She'll be here the next time you come in, though. Said she'd give it to you on the house with you having to wait and all. Damn agent ain't even supposed to be due in till next Monday. Shirl was damn put out about him coming in early and all. She really wanted to show you a good time tonight."

The thought of being with Shirl turned his stomach. He'd had one paid companion and knew such pleasures were not for him.

"You must be the new lieutenant that's coming out to the fort," someone behind him said.

Quade turned to see the Indian Agent standing close enough that if he'd been an enemy, Quade would have been dead by now. It made him realize that he needed to hone his skills of perception. The time he'd spent in Virginia City had made him lose his edge.

"I'm Simon Leary, Indian Agent for the reservation. Red tells me you're going out to the fort in the morning. It will be good to have company for a change."

Quade scrutinized the man in front of him. His black suit, string tie and white shirt looked out of place and his appearance reminded Quade of a weasel that was about to raid the hen house back on his father's farm in Missouri.

"It should prove interesting," Quade commented, all the time hoping to get the words out without showing his disgust. "I have several questions about the post. That should pass the time."

The man smiled, then turned back to where Shirl waited for him. Quade watched Simon put his hand down the front of Shirl's dress and fondle her ample breast. The very act sickened Quade. It also made him wonder if ample breasts were a prerequisite for being a whore. If they were, Grace would never make it in that profession. It wasn't hard to notice that she was rather small in that department.

Instead of watching Simon and Shirl any longer, he turned toward the kitchen to fill his plate and ease the hunger that gnawed at his stomach.

He marveled at the quality of the meat and vegetables in the stew. It was evident that it was made from food stores that were sent from Washington to the Indians. He knew it was a common practice, but it still didn't make it right or gain his approval.

After eating his fill of biscuits and stew, he cut himself a piece of pie. He knew if Grace continued to cook here, Red would certainly raise his prices. In Virginia City he could have charged twice that much for such a meal.

When Quade returned to the saloon, Red handed him a beer. He was glad he had planned to leave in the morning. If he stayed much longer, not only would his money be depleted, but also he could easily turn into a drunk. He'd watched the menfolk back home do just that when crops failed and he wanted no part of it.

He selected a table at the far side of the room to sit and watch the patrons as the conversations became louder and the card game more intense.

"Mind if I join you?" Grace asked, as she pulled out a chair and sat down.

"It's a free country," he replied after taking a long drink of the warm beer. Damn but he missed Virginia City and the ice from the mountains that kept the beer cold.

"Did you get something to eat?"

Quade nodded. "You're a good cook. It should help pass the time until the next train comes through."

"Red and I have been talking about that. They're really good people. I think I'll like cooking here. There's nothing for me in Ohio. At least here I can make some money and not be under my father's roof. I told Red we could easily raise our prices and if we can get the Indians to hunt for us we could feature venison and buffalo steaks as well. We could each make some money."

"Don't count on the Indians hunting for you. There isn't much game around for them, to say nothing of it for anyone else. Where do you think that meat comes from?"

"It's not what you think. Red buys his meat from the ranchers and has his vegetables shipped in from San Francisco on the train. He told me that the Indian Agent offered him the same stuff and a lot cheaper too, but he told him no. Red really likes the Indians on the reservation. He certainly doesn't want to take the food out of the mouths of their children."

Quade nodded. His opinion of Red had certainly been raised with that piece of information. He also realized there was more to Grace Walters than what he saw on the surface. Some of the things she'd said since their arrival told him she wasn't the well-bred woman she wanted people to think she was. Somewhere in her background was a businesswoman's training. She knew too much about profit and loss to think otherwise.

"So how is it that you know so much about running a restaurant and making money?" he finally asked.

"Back home, my pa did make the best beer and wine in the county, but it certainly wasn't to sell and make money for his family. He was a drunk and he beat us at every opportunity. If it hadn't been for Ma working in the restaurant her father left her, we would have starved. I started cooking for her when I was ten. It kept me away from Pa and the way he acted when he was drunk. As soon as I was old enough, I put an ad in the paper to become a mail order bride. I wanted everything that Miles said he would give me. At first it wasn't bad, but once we moved to Virginia City, he became like Pa. When he wasn't working, he was drinking, and when he came home he hit me. I can't, I won't go back to a life like that."

Quade couldn't believe that he was starting to feel sorry for this woman. It was best if he left in the morning. If he didn't she could easily draw him into her web and he'd be caught forever. She certainly was lovely to look at and if he gave her half a chance he knew she would willingly share his bed.

Three

A knock on the door to his room brought Quade to full awareness. Outside his window the first rays of morning were streaking the eastern sky. Instinctively he reached for his gun before he realized that anyone intent on doing him harm wouldn't knock.

After putting his gun back in its holster, he pulled on his britches and opened the door. It surprised him to see Simon Leary standing in the hallway.

"It's a long trip to the fort. I thought you would like to get an early start," Simon greeted him. "Red told me that his new cook would have breakfast ready for us by six. It's best if we get started before the heat of the day sets in."

Quade pulled his watch from his pocket, flipped open the case, and checked the time. In the dim light from the kerosene lantern that burned outside his door he could see that it was already five. He wondered how Grace liked getting out of bed at this ungodly hour.

"That will give me time to get cleaned up and ready to go."

After Simon left, Quade lit the lamp in his room and poured water into the basin. After shaving, he took a fresh uniform from his gear and dressed for the day.

Grace greeted him when he walked into the saloon. "Just

need to know how you like your eggs and I can get your breakfast finished."

"Sunny side up is fine with me. Sorry to get you up so early."

"Don't be. This is the first time since I left home that I've felt needed. Miles only wanted one thing from me and it certainly wasn't good meals."

She disappeared into the kitchen. Before she returned, Simon came in from outside. "I've got my horse hitched to my buggy and your horse tied on the back. Did you tell that new cook how you like your eggs?"

Before Quade could reply, Grace brought out plates with bacon, eggs, fried potatoes and biscuits from the kitchen. "I'll be right back with your coffee," she said once she sat the food in front of them.

"That woman is a damn good cook," Simon commented. "Between her and Shirl, my visits here will be a real pleasure."

Quade made no response. Instead he concentrated on the food in front of him. After what Grace had told him, he knew that it didn't come from Simon. At least that was one point in Red's favor. He wondered if he had misjudged the man who sat across the table from him. If he had, the trip to the fort could prove to be quite interesting.

~ * ~

Hannah walked the short distance from the house to the store. As usual, several soldiers were congregated at the entrance, discussing the affairs of the fort.

"I hear they're sending a new lieutenant out here," one of the men said.

"What in the hell did the poor bastard do to get sent here?"

The first man glanced in her direction before answering. She recognized Private Zimmer as one of the few men who had any regard for her whatsoever.

"Don't know," he finally replied, "but it must be pretty bad. None of us are here because it was our choice. From what I gather, he fought Indians in the Arizona Territory before he transferred to Virginia City. Can't say I'd willingly trade that post for a place like this."

Hannah pretended not to be listening to the conversation as she stepped around the man to enter the store.

"Morning, ma'am," the first soldier said as he touched the brim of his hat.

"Good morning," she replied, as sweetly as she could. She hurried inside, her mind swimming with the overheard conversation. If this new lieutenant was a seasoned Indian fighter, her father, Crooked Snake, as well as her brothers, Growling Bear and Tall Elk could be in danger. As renegades, she often heard their names mentioned around the fort. She had only been five when she lost her mother and since then had only heard about her father from others.

She was certain he, like her brothers, thought she had been killed in the raid that took the lives of everyone else in the village. It was best that way. Her life revolved around Horace and Martha and the children at the reservation. She could not imagine living the life she would have been destined to live if the massacre had not occurred. As Horace and Martha's daughter she was able to help her people.

"Don't know how old Horace got such a looker for a daughter," she heard the more crude of the two soldiers say. "I'd sure like a poke with her."

"Well, it ain't gonna happen. She's too good for the likes of you and me. She's polite and all, but if I ever heard that anyone here touched her, I wouldn't be held responsible for my actions."

She smiled at the response from Private Zimmer. She knew he'd been sent here because he'd been caught drinking on duty.

That didn't matter to her. Maybe if she was a man and in the army she'd drink, too. At least he treated her with respect. She wondered how much respect she would get if any of them knew her father was Crooked Snake.

"What can I get you today, Hannah?" Bill Edwards, the shopkeeper, asked.

"Papa is feeling poorly. He needs more of that medicine you gave him last time. It helped him so much. I also need the things on this list." She handed the list to Bill. While her filled her order, she looked at the yard goods. Her father could use some new shirts and the white broadcloth would be perfect. She had just picked up the bolt of cloth when she noticed the piece of cloth next to it. The pale blue would be ideal for a dress for her. After calculating the cost of such an extravagant purchase, she decided that she could afford it. As a teacher her salary was meager, but so were her needs. The dress would take much of her money, but it would be worth it. She picked up both pieces of fabric and put them on the counter.

"Are you going to be doing some sewing, Hannah?" Bill asked, as he picked up the fabric.

"Yes, Papa needs some new shirts and I need enough of the white to make them for him."

"Do you need buttons or thread?"

"No, I'll cut the buttons off his old shirts and I have thread."

"Is the blue for you?"

"Yes, I think it will make a lovely dress."

Bill measured out the fabric while she counted out the two dollars to pay for her purchases.

"This is a wise choice," Bill said as he handed her the brown paper wrapped packages. "The blue will suit you well. Do you plan on having it done for the dance next week?"

"I'd forgotten about the dance," Hannah said. She flashed a brilliant smile at Bill. "Of course I'll have it finished by then.

With school out for the summer, Papa only goes out to the village twice a week. I should have plenty of time to finish it. Thank you so very much for reminding me."

After paying for her purchases, she left the store. As she did, she saw Simon Leary. She wished she had been home before he came back to the fort. Just seeing him made her uneasy. Not only did he look at her as though she was a choice cut of meat waiting to be eaten, but also she knew how he treated the Cheyenne. Many times the flour he took to them was bug infested and often the meat was rotten. At first she had thought he was taking it to Red to serve in his saloon, but after meeting with the man, she learned that although Simon had tried selling him the rations, he had declined. For all the coarseness the man represented, he truly liked the Indians who came to the store to trade. He was also one of the few men in the territory who refused to sell them whiskey.

She had no idea where the meat and other provisions were going, but she did know that more than once her father had spent his own money to buy supplies for the Indians so that the children would not starve.

"Good day, Miss Hannah," Simon called as he drove past her kicking up a cloud of dust.

She nodded her greeting and kept walking. She noticed a horse trailing behind the carriage and took a second look at the man who sat next to Simon. She judged his age at less than thirty and by the uniform he wore, she knew he must be the new lieutenant she had heard the men talking about. Waiting for the carriage to pass, she again looked at the stranger. It was hard to tell much from behind, but she could see that he had broad shoulders and his hair was a light brown in color.

He'll be stationed at the fort, Hannah, her inner voice sounded in her head. *You will have many opportunities to see him without Simon leering at you. Besides, he's an Indian fighter. It's best if you don't get too close.*

~ * ~

Quade was relieved when the fort finally came into view. Within ten minutes of leaving Red's saloon, he knew Simon Leary was a self-centered bore. After five hours of listening to the man degrade the once proud people he was supposed to protect, Quade wanted to be sick. The trip would have taken less time if the man didn't stop to relieve himself at every tree and bush he saw. Quade knew dogs that stopped less when they were marking their territory.

A sentry, standing on the catwalk, saw them approach and had someone open the gate for them. The buildings within the stockade all needed attention. The only one that looked decent was a small house with a flower garden that sat just inside the gate.

"That house you're so interested in belongs to Horace Whitfield," Simon advised him. "He's the missionary that caters to those no good Indians at the reservation."

"You mean the ones you were sent here to care for?" Quade asked.

"It's my job to be the Indian Agent here. I never said it was something I wanted to do. The bucks are only interested in whiskey and the squaws are little more than breeding stock. You'd think they would hunt or something."

"If you recall, we just drove the length of the reservation. I didn't see any game for them *to* hunt. Besides, I've been in the army long enough to know that these people aren't even given weapons."

"I should have known you were one of those Indian lovers. Well, you can get that notion out of your head. I've been here for two years and there's nothing worth loving about any of them."

Ahead of them, Quade saw a young woman leave the store.

As she did, many of the soldiers watched her intently. He was certain they had thoughts about her that were anything but honorable.

"Well, lookey over there. Good Day, Miss Hannah," Simon said, as he touched the brim of his hat in greeting.

The woman nodded in their direction but kept walking, as though she wanted nothing to do with either of them.

"Uppity Bitch. You'd think she was the Queen of Sheba instead of just old Horace's adopted daughter. Every man on this post gets hard just lookin' at her and she won't give any of them the time of day. Don't know where she got them 'better than anyone else' ways about her, but one day she'll find out what it's like to be with a man. If I have my way, I'll be that man."

Quade studied the young woman until they drove past her. He didn't want to appear nosey, so he did not turn back to stare at her the way he wanted to do. She was indeed a beautiful young woman, but there was no way that she was white. He'd seen enough Indian women to know that Hannah Whitfield had to have some Indian blood in her. Perhaps she was an orphan that the missionary and his wife had adopted.

"Did you hear what I said?" Simon asked when Quade made no comment on the man's statement.

"I heard you. I'm afraid that if you think you're going to have anything to do with the lovely Miss Whitfield, you have another thing coming. Just by the way she looked at you I could see that she wasn't interested in anything you have to offer her."

"And I suppose you think she'll take an interest in you? Well, my young friend, I'm afraid you're sadly mistaken. She's the prettiest thing this side of the saloon and don't you think she doesn't know it. She won't give anyone at this fort more than a smile and a nod and that's just because she's polite."

Quade tended to agree with Simon. He couldn't help but wonder what kind of a future this young woman could expect.

Simon pulled on the reins to stop the carriage in front of what Quade decided could only be the office of the commanding officer of this fort. When he got out of the carriage, Quade untied his horse and took his gear from the back.

"I'm obliged for the ride from the saloon to here," he said to Simon. "I'm certain that we'll be seeing more of each other in the future."

"Don't count on it. I don't spend much time here. Just stop by the office to make a report now and then and to check on the supplies that have arrived. Mostly I'm out among the savages trying to make certain the young bucks don't get it in their heads to take off with the renegades whenever they show up. I'll be staying for a couple of days, since I hear Crooked Snake is in the area. I ran into him once and don't intend to do it again. He's one mean son of a bitch."

Quade merely shook his head in disgust. He'd grown up on a farm with a father who thought nothing of swearing up a storm every time he got drunk on a Saturday night. He hadn't liked it then and he cared less for it now. He knew the soldiers did their fair share of cussing, but as Major Eaton's aide, Quade had learned that he could get his point across just as easily by not using offensive language.

After tying his horse to the railing, he left his gear outside and went in to report to his new commanding officer.

"Lieutenant Quade McPherson, reporting for duty, Sir." He stood stiffly at attention as he waited for the captain behind the desk to acknowledge him.

While he waited for the man to look up, Quade silently assessed the man who was to be his new commanding officer. His uniform was far from the crisp ones Quade was used to seeing in Virginia City. His hair was way too long and had more gray than black among the strands. He couldn't help but wonder if this man was too old for the post or if the post had aged him far beyond his years.

"At ease, Lieutenant, we aren't all that formal here. I'm Captain Rolland VanEtt. From the wire I received from Virginia City, I assume you know your way around an Indian fight."

"I've fought my share of Apaches down in the Arizona Territory. Can't say it was to my liking, but I've done it."

"I'm afraid you'd better hone your skills if you plan to stay at this post. Every once in a while, Crooked Snake gets the young bucks on the reservation riled up and then there's hell to pay."

"I've heard a lot about this Crooked Snake since I arrived, Sir. Just who is he?"

"You'd better take a seat, this is a long story. Do you mind if I call you Quade? We're quite informal here. At least among the officers, of which there is just you and me. I'd prefer you call me Rollie when we're alone."

Quade nodded his agreement. This certainly didn't strike him as the spit and polish stick by the rules post Virginia City had been.

"Crooked Snake's story goes back about fifteen years, well before that mess with Custer and the Seventh. Back then, some gung ho captain decided to make a name for himself by wiping out Crooked Snake once and for all. He and his men attacked the village just after dawn. The problem was, he didn't find Crooked Snake there. Instead he managed to wipe out a village of women, children and old men. By the time Crooked Snake came back some missionaries had buried the dead. I don't blame the poor bastard for turning renegade. He fought at the Little Big Horn, or so the story goes, but when they were rounding all the Indians up to go to the reservation, he went to Canada. Now it's anyone's guess as to where he hangs his hat. I do know that he raises hell around here with great regularity. I'd like to capture him, but he's true to his name. Once I get him in my sights he disappears back into his hole."

"I've heard stories about such massacres. As much as I wanted to believe they didn't happen, I know that history can't be altered. How many men does this Crooked Snake have with him?"

"Usually it's just his sons, Growling Bear and Tall Elk, but on occasion they get a few of the young bucks to join them. That's when the trouble really starts."

"What about the Indian Agent, Leary, can't he tell the people that siding with Crooked Snake will only get them in more trouble with the army?"

Rollie laughed at Quade's question. "The only thing Leary is interested in is how much money he can make from the supplies he gets for the Indians. I can't say for certain where he peddles them, though I have a feeling it's to the ranchers. I know that Red over at the railhead told him what he could do with his supplies and he hoped they fit. Red gets on well with the Indians on the reservation. Even hires some of them to help him out. As much as they would like for him to give them whiskey, he refuses. I think the elders respect him for that."

Quade shook his head. This was going to be one interesting post. The only good thing he'd seen so far was the daughter of the missionary. With any luck, he would get to know her better.

Four

"Did you get everything you needed?" Horace asked when Hannah returned home.

"Yes, Papa, and I found some material to make new shirts for you."

Her father looked at her disapprovingly. "You shouldn't be spending your precious time working on shirts for an old man. It has been far too long since you have had a new dress."

Hannah kissed his cheek. "Oh, Papa, you are too good to me. You will be happy to know that I purchased a length of cloth for a dress for the dance they are having at the post a week from Saturday night."

"Has one of the young men asked to be your escort?"

It was all Hannah could do to keep from crying. Although her father asked the question he already knew the answer. The men on this post were not God-fearing Christians. These were men with a past who were more interested in bedding a woman than courting her.

"I already have the best escort—that is, unless you have decided not to accompany me."

"I thought perhaps you met the new lieutenant that I have heard is coming."

Hannah felt herself blushing at her father's statement. "I saw him arrive. He was with the Indian Agent. Apparently they met at the railhead. At least that was where Simon said he was going, as though I care that he visits that woman up there."

"He tells you those things only to make you jealous. He wants to court you; at least that is what he tells me. Why do you have such contempt for him?"

"He's not the kind of man I have any interest in. You haven't heard the way he talks about the Indians when you aren't around. He despises them and is here only to make money from selling the supplies that are sent for the reservation. His love is for Simon and perhaps that woman he goes to see. If he knew who I really am he would have me put in the stockade in order to get my father to turn himself in and collect the reward money that the army is offering."

Horace pulled her into his embrace. "Crooked Snake doesn't even know you're alive and no one here thinks of you as anyone but my daughter."

She relaxed in his embrace. To him she was the daughter he and Martha had always wanted, when in reality her father was the most hated renegade in the area. It should be enough for her, but for some unexplained reason she longed to see her father and brothers at least once before they were killed. The thought of their deaths devastated her as much as if it were Horace she was thinking of. She had been but a child of five winters when her mother was killed, but even at such a young age she knew the names of her father and brothers. They were the names she repeated every night as she prayed to the Great Spirit to protect them. As she learned of the God of Horace's Christian faith, she knew that He was all-powerful and would watch over her father even though Crooked Snake didn't believe in Him.

Rather than dwell on things she could not change she went about preparing dinner for her and her father. The stew that she had made early this morning simmered on the stove so all she had to do was cut thick slices of bread and set the table.

"Gracious God, Bless this food and the hands that prepared it," Horace began once he sat down at the table.

Hanna bowed her head, thankful for the lengthy prayer that would follow since it would give her time to reflect on the thoughts that had crowded her mind since she returned from the store. *Will I ever see my father and brothers or will I live my life in denial of my heritage?*

~ * ~

Quade found his quarters less desirable than the ones he had left in Virginia City. The floor was filthy. Before he did anything else, he knew he had to evict the resident rat. The next thing he had to do was get rid of the family of mice that had made a home in the pile of dirty clothes, left by the former occupant of the room.

He spent most of his first day at the post patching holes, washing the floor as well as the windows and chasing the varmints back outside where they belonged. He was just dumping the last pail of dirty water when he noticed several soldiers watching him intently.

"Ain't goin' to do you no good," a tall lanky soldier said, as he lounged against the hitching rail. "'Round here we just learn to live with the critters to say nothing of the dust and dirt."

"What is your name, Soldier?" Quade inquired.

The man straightened at the authoritative sound of Quade's voice. "Private Matthews, Sir."

"There is no excuse for filth, Private. It wouldn't hurt any of you to grab a bucket and clean out your own quarters. Since I know what a monumental task that will be, I will give you three days before I come in to inspect your work."

"Inspect?" Private Matthews questioned. "You ain't at no fancy pants post, Lieutenant. This post is, well, more laid back than most. Don't mean we ain't ready to fight if necessary, but..."

"But nothing. There is no excuse for living in filth. I will speak to Captain VanEtt about this tomorrow morning. I am certain he will agree with me. Now do as I say or I will see that you enjoy the hospitality of the stockade."

The young man gave him a sloppy salute and hurried toward the barracks. He knew it would be only a matter of time before the entire fort knew that he was a hard ass who didn't take slovenly behavior or filth well.

Quade began to whistle as he continued to make his quarters livable. When the floors were as clean as he could get them, he took the mattress and blankets out to the pile of filthy clothing he had started making earlier, he returned to his quarters to tighten the ropes on the bed and to scrub down the wooden frame.

When he finished he walked over to the store to purchase fresh blankets as well as a new mattress. Since he had no way of getting the ones on his bed clean, he knew that new ones would be the best solution to the problem. As for the mattress, it was probably as flea and tick infested as the blankets. He didn't relish waking up in the morning bit up by the vermin that were crawling in his bedding and mattress.

The sun was already sinking in the west when he arrived at the store. He'd have just enough time to make his purchases and add them to his bed before he went to eat supper with the men.

"Good afternoon, Lieutenant," the storekeeper greeted him. "I heard you were coming. The name is Edwards, Bill Edwards."

Quade shook the man's hand in greeting. "McPherson, Quade McPherson, it's good to meet you. I was hoping I could buy some new blankets and a new mattress for my quarters as well as some towels and soap. The last man to use these quarters must have taken the soap and left the bedding and towels in a terrible condition."

Bill laughed heartily. "Other than the captain, you're the first man who has ever come in here for soap. I hope I see some changes around here for the better, but don't count on it. As I recall, the captain tried to clean this place up when he first came, but as you can see, it didn't happen."

"Well, between the two of us I think we'll be able to change that. If this is like most posts, you know everything that goes on."

Bill winked. "Guess I do. What do you want to know?"

"What can you tell me about Simon Leary?"

"Nothin' fit for polite company, if you get my drift. That son of a bitch tried to sell me the supplies meant for the Indians over at the reservation. When I wouldn't have any of it, he went to Red up at the railhead. Guess you already know what happened up there. Red's a good man, he told Leary that he could come there to buy whiskey and have a go at Shirl when he needed it, but he wouldn't deprive women and children of proper supplies."

"So what does he do with the supplies he gets for the Indians?"

"There's plenty of ranchers around here who pay his price. It's still cheaper than having the goods shipped in or going all the way to Red's place to get them. They could come here, but why travel any distance when Leary delivers everything they need right to their door?"

"Just who are these ranchers? I'd like to talk to them."

"You'll meet them all soon enough. There's a dance a week from this Saturday night."

"A dance? I didn't think there would be that many women on a post as remote as this one."

"It all started when my wife and I came here. Elizabeth is from the east and was used to dances and such. She wanted to have a dance every Saturday night, but there were no young ladies here to attend. When Bessie VanEtt arrived the two of them got their heads together and decided to have a dance once a month and invite the ranchers. Guess they all thought it would be a good idea. Of course they enlisted the help of Hannah and the rest—well, as they say, that's history. The ranchers will all be comin' and bringing their wives and daughters. Elizabeth says it gives the girls a chance to see other young men than the men who work for their fathers. Don't know why they would want to associate with this mangy lot, but to each his own I guess."

"Do the men—ah—clean up for this dance?"

"Like I told you, I don't sell much soap. I've seen 'em dunk themselves in the horse trough but that's with their clothes on. Can't rightly say any of them are much on cleanin' up, as you call it."

"They will be. How much soap do you have on hand? Is there enough for a bar for each soldier at the fort?"

Bill laughed. "More than enough, but I can't see you gettin' any of them to use it."

"They will. Fill up a box with the soap and add it to my bill.

I'd appreciate it if you would deliver it tomorrow while I'm meeting with Captain VanEtt. As for the blankets and mattress I'll take them with me."

A wide grin filled Bill's face. "If you don't want the men to catch wind of what you're planning, why don't you leave by the back door. Elizabeth can take over for me here and I'll bring the mattress for you. Otherwise it will be a lot for you to be carrying by yourself. I know the captain tried to make these changes when he first came here, but nothing ever came of it. I'm sure you can enlist him to help and between the two of you, you might just make this fort a place to be proud of."

Quade nodded his agreement, and after picking up the lighter of the purchases he helped Bill to carry the mattress out the back door of the store and into the back door of his quarters.

Once inside, Bill let out a low whistle. "Didn't think this place could be so, well you know, so clean. The only way you're going to get rid of the stench, the fleas or the ticks, is to burn that mess I saw out back."

"All in due time. I have a feeling that tomorrow there will be a lot more blankets and mattresses to add to that pile."

"I have to tell you, I don't have that many mattresses in stock. I could come up with at least one blanket for each man, but otherwise where will they sleep?"

"The weather is warm enough for them to sleep in tents until we can get what we need from Denver."

Bill shook Quade's hand again and slapped him on the back. "By God, I think you'll turn this post around after all. More power to you, Son, more power to you."

By the time his bed was made, Quade was ready for supper. It would be his first meal and first real contact with the men of this post. The thought was one that terrified him. In Virginia

City he had eaten in the officers' mess, but here he was the only officer. He certainly couldn't count Rollie, since having his wife here meant he didn't plan to take meals with the men.

Quade arrived early and chose a table in the corner where, with his back to the wall, he could watch the men of his new post as they entered the hall. The cook put a slab of beef on his plate along with mashed potatoes and a biscuit. He would have enjoyed a vegetable, but he knew these men were not the type who wanted anything to do with vegetables with their meals.

He, on the other hand, liked vegetables. Having grown up on the farm, summer was his favorite time of the year. His mother always grew a large garden when it was the time for fresh vegetables. Due to the overabundance she also did a lot of canning for winter use.

The first bite he took of the biscuit told him that he wished Grace were doing the cooking here. This one certainly didn't have the flaky texture and delicious taste of the ones he had enjoyed last night at Red's saloon. The meat was also not to his liking. It was burned on the outside and raw and stringy on the inside. The only edible thing on his plate were the potatoes and they were filled with lumps. He knew that in time he would get used to such meals, but he certainly missed Virginia City and the food he had enjoyed in the officers' mess.

"That's him," he heard Private Matthew's say in a voice loud enough to be heard throughout the room. "He's the new Lieutenant. He's the one that told me we had to clean out the barracks."

"We'll see how long that lasts," another man said. "Remember when VanEtt first came here? It didn't take long for him to realize that this place don't deserve cleaning."

Quade added nothing to the conversation. He would enlist

the help of his superior officer and together they would make a difference on this post. It was no wonder the Indians called the white men filthy. These men were. He'd been around the savages long enough to know that most of them bathed daily and it was the bear grease that they used to ward away the biting insects in the summer that caused the stench most soldiers talked about when they referred to them.

After choking down the last of the biscuit and coffee, Quade returned to his quarters. He would have his work cut out for him in the next couple of days, and he knew he would need a good night's rest in order to start the process in the morning.

Five

The sound of the bugle brought Quade to full attention. He'd had a good night's sleep without the worry of becoming flea bitten as well as tick infested by morning. After shaving and washing up for the day, he donned a clean uniform and left for breakfast. Surely the cook would do a better job of making bacon and eggs than he had last night's supper.

When he arrived at the mess hall, he noticed that the men were already swilling down the coffee. Just the thought of if was enough to make Quade vow to stop drinking the vile brew until he could get a chance to talk to the cook and teach him the proper way to make a decent pot of coffee.

As he made his way to the corner table that he had occupied the night before, he nodded his acknowledgment to the men. Those who did look up immediately turned back to their conversations without so much as an attempt to be civil to him.

After eating a solitary, less than satisfying meal, he made his way to Rollie's office.

"You did what?" Rollie asked when Quade told him about buying the soap and his plans to have Bill deliver it to the men.

"I bought the soap and I intend for the men to use it. Now, do you have a vacant building that we could use for a bath house?"

"I actually had a bath house built, but I could never get the men to use it. How do you plan to bring about this change?"

"Oh, I thought a threat of latrine duty or perhaps a visit to the stockade might be an incentive. I threatened Private Matthew's with the stockade and it looked like he took it seriously. At least when I left the store yesterday afternoon he was making an effort to sweep out the barracks."

"By God, I think you're just what we need around here. A real breath of fresh air. When I first came here, I tried to bring order to this place, but there was no one to back me up. The Lieutenant was just as lazy as them men."

"That's what I gathered from talking to Bill Edwards. He tells me there's to be a dance a week from Saturday night. I trust the ranchers and their families will find the men more presentable by then."

"That damnable dance. It was the idea of my wife and Elizabeth Edwards. They thought they could bring culture to this godforsaken place. I know the womenfolk look forward to it, but to me it's more a nuisance than a help. The men look forward to it because they think they can have their way with the women who come. It usually ends up in a fight, but the women all look forward to showing off their cooking abilities and having a night away so they can enjoy the music."

"So where do you find music way out here?"

"Harlan Knopes from the Bar K is good on the fiddle and Red closes up his saloon and comes down with his piano player, Sam, and Shirl and anyone else he can round up from that place. We get some right fine music between the two of them. It also gives me a chance to talk to Red about what's going on at that end of the reservation. He knows everything there is to know about the Indians."

"Isn't that a long way to come just for a dance?"

"Not if you're riding with Red. He's not like Leary. I'm

certain that old fox brought you in the most round about way and stopped at every tree and bush to do it. If you follow the river it only takes about two hours. Of course, they all spend the night here and return on Sunday morning after church services. It's the only time they get to church so it's quite an event for them. Simon tells me there's a new woman up there. Says she's doing the cooking and is much better at it than Ike ever was."

"Her name is Grace Walters," Quade said filling in the blanks for Rollie.

"Walters, that name is certainly familiar."

"It should be, her husband was my former commanding officer, Miles Walters. He's the one who sent me here."

"I see, then you know this Grace Walters *very* well."

"Not as well as you think. She made the whole story up to get attention from her husband. What she did cost me my reputation as well as put a mark on my military career that will follow me until the day I either retire or die."

Rollie nodded his head sagely. It was evident that he had known the sting of a false accusation. Why else would he be in a godforsaken place like this post?

Quade decided it was time to change the subject. "From the little I've heard, Leary is selling the supplies for the Indians for his own profit. Any idea who is buying them? Bill seems to think that it's the ranchers that are getting those supplies."

"I tend to agree with him. I just haven't had any luck finding out which ones are sincere in the way they denounce Leary, and which ones are just saying what they think is right and proper."

"Since they don't know me from Adam, I'll do a little nosing around at the dance. Getting information from people who don't want to give it is something I'm good at. I guess that's why I ended up with the position of personal assistant to Major Eaton in Virginia City. Of course, all that changed when

Major Walters took over."

"Well, all I can say is you'll have an interesting time at the dance. Once the ranchers have some of the punch that we keep in the back for the men, they'll open up. They get to talking about anything and everything. The language can get mighty blue. The wives all have a fit and that ends the night."

"Well, let's hope I can get to them before their wives do. I sure would like to know where Leary is selling the rations that are meant for the people at the reservation."

Quade left Rollie's office and started back toward his own quarters. As he did, he noticed a group of soldiers standing in his way.

"So," the corporal who had addressed him at supper the previous evening said, as he blocked the plank sidewalk, "they tell me you're the son of a bitch who ordered that soap to be delivered to the barracks."

"You've got the right man, but it's Lieutenant Son of a Bitch to you. Do you have a problem with cleaning your barracks, to say nothing of yourself?"

"You're damn well right I have a problem. This ain't no sissy post like the one they kicked you out of. You ain't no better than the rest of us, if you know what I mean. Some folks just ain't too bright. Did you think that screwing the wife of your commanding officer would remain a secret?"

"I see no reason to defend myself to you. I do see a reason why you should follow orders."

"Well, I don't. With all the whores around a fort like the one you were at, you were a fool to take on the one woman who could get you sent out here to ten miles past hell."

"I'll say this once and only once. I never touched the major's wife. She made up the story to make her husband jealous. As for following my orders, I outrank you in more ways than one. I've given you the soap as well as two days to get the job done. If in that amount of time I don't see some improvement around here, I'll be forced to see you to the stockade."

The corporal laughed, then drew back his big fist and landed the first punch squarely on Quade's jaw. He stumbled backwards from the force of the blow, but didn't lose his balance. Instead, he lunged at the man, catching him completely off guard. Without so much as a punch, he pushed him to the ground and pinned him there with only a slight amount of pressure at a strategic place on the man's neck.

"What is going on out here?" Rollie demanded as he neared the place where Quade and the corporal were sprawled on the ground.

Quade looked up to see one of the men give the captain a sloppy salute. "It was the damnedest thing I ever saw," the man said. "The lieutenant pinned him down and never even threw a punch. He just touched Collins on the neck and the next thing you know he was out cold."

"How did you do that, Lieutenant?" Rollie inquired as the men took Collins to the stockade.

"It's just a little something I learned when I was a kid. The kids at school were both older and bigger than me and they used that to their advantage more than once. I was in the first grade when they took after me in school. I was the one who had to stay after and I really didn't think it was fair. Once everyone went home, the teacher, his name was Mr. Baldwin, told me that he was the younger brother and his father had taught him how to get the upper hand. He said it was best to tackle the person who wanted to fight and then pin him to the ground. Once that was done just apply pressure to a certain place on the neck and your opponent would go unconscious. It works every time. I only had to do it to those older kids twice and that was the end of them wanting to fight."

The explanation brought laughter from everyone. When it finally died down, Quade assessed the men who stood before him. They were all there because they were the bad apples in the barrel at their former posts. Here it was going to be different. Between him and Rollie, they would give the men something that had been taken from them, self-respect.

"Where would you like us to start, Sir?" Private Zimmer asked.

Quade looked down at his uniform. It was dusty from the fight with Collins. Since it would need laundering, he saw no problem in helping the men do something that they hadn't done before.

"You get some buckets of water and I'll go over to the store for some scrub brushes. We'll start on the floor of the barracks and work our way up."

By the time he returned from the store, Quade was surprised to see the sparse furnishings of the barracks strewn across the grass that grew on the side of the building. Once he entered the building, he saw the men sweeping the dirt and mouse droppings from the wide boards of the plank floor.

While two men worked on scrubbing the floor, the others took their bedding along with the blankets and mattress Quade had removed from his quarters the day before. It only took a few minutes for them to set the whole pile ablaze in the middle of the parade grounds. Quade knew it would cost the army dearly to replace the blankets and mattresses but he also understood that it would be the only way to rid the barracks of the flea and lice infected bedding.

With the blaze burning brightly, the men scrubbed down the bed frames and tightened the ropes that would hold the new bedding. He was glad that the weather was warm, because the men would have to sleep in tents until the new bedding was sent out from Denver. In the meantime, it wouldn't hurt any of them to paint the buildings and make this fort look presentable.

By evening, the men were taken down to the river and instructed to wash the stink from their bodies with the harsh soap Quade had purchased earlier in the day. It was only a temporary solution until the bathhouse could be made useable, but it was one that Quade knew would work well. Once they were dressed in clean uniforms, he marched them back to the fort and started to cut their hair.

"My pa was a barber," Private Kanter said. "I can help you with the cuttin'. I used to help my pa a lot in the shop. Then he got shot and well, Ma and me we headed West. When she took sick and died, I joined the army. Been here ever since."

Quade smiled at the young man's offer and brought out another chair. It was just getting dark, when the last of the men had received haircuts and decent shaves.

Even though Quade had eaten dinner with the men, he still found that he was hungry as well as tired. He equated the feeling with the fact that he had done more physical labor today than he had on any day since arriving in Virginia City. Looking around the post, he was proud of what had been accomplished. The only man who hadn't been bathed and received a haircut had been Corporal Collins and when his week in the stockade was over he, too, would be made presentable just like the rest of them.

~ * ~

Hannah was just putting the bread dough in the oven when she heard a commotion from the fort. Standing on tiptoe, she looked out the kitchen window in time to see Corporal Collins strike the new lieutenant. She put her hand to her mouth in horror but soon used it to hide the smile that crossed her lips when the victim became the aggressor and pinned Collins to the ground.

"Serves him right," she said aloud.

"What did you say?" her father asked when he entered the kitchen.

"I heard a commotion and looked to see what was going on. That terrible Corporal Collins hit the new lieutenant. I was afraid that Collins was going to beat him up the way he did the last lieutenant we had here. Instead, somehow this new man got the upper hand and they took Collins to the stockade."

Horace looked at her with many questions in his eyes. "I take it that you and Corporal Collins have exchanged words before. Why is it that I have not heard of it?"

"It was nothing to bother you with, Papa. The man is always making lewd suggestions about what he would do with me in bed. I ignore him and refuse to comment on the things that he says. I do have to admit that I am frightened of him, but usually Private Matthews or Private Zimmer intervenes and Corporal Collins doesn't touch me."

"And it's a good thing that he doesn't. I think I will take a walk over to Captain VanEtt's office and tell him of this behavior. It may get your friend a few more days in the stockade."

"Please, Papa, don't do such a thing. I have handled this in my own way and know how to avoid the man. Let's just leave it at that."

Although Horace agreed, Hannah knew that as soon as he left the house, he would be in the Captain's office. To him she was his daughter even though they both knew that she was little more than the little Indian girl who they had thought was without parents and had taken into their home.

She continued her work in the kitchen. When everything sparkled, she made her way to the parlor where she began to cut out the pieces that would soon be not only her father's shirts but also her new dress. As she worked on the blue print material, she envisioned herself in the arms of the handsome lieutenant who just arrived at the fort. He would make a wonderful beau, at least until the time came that she had to tell him who her father and brothers were. Then it would all be different.

The clock was just striking twelve when she heard her father return home. How the morning had gotten away from her was beyond her comprehension. As soon as the door slammed, she got to her feet and went to the kitchen to ladle out bowls of the soup she had set to simmer right after breakfast. After cutting slices of the still warm bread she set the table for dinner.

"Your mother would say that you are spoiling me in my old age," her father teased.

"Then she spoiled you as well, for I do not remember a time when she didn't have dinner on the table for you when you came home."

"How right you are. I did talk to the captain and he invited us to his home for supper tonight. He said that he thought you and Bessie would enjoy having time to talk about the dance that is being held a week from Saturday."

"You don't fool me, Papa. Who else is going to be at their home this evening?"

"Come to think of it, he did mention inviting Lieutenant McPherson. He thought it would be good for that young man to meet someone other than that surly lot of men who are stationed here."

The answer she received was far from unexpected and yet it terrified her. Everyone here accepted her as the daughter of the missionary. Would this new lieutenant question her heritage? Would he want to use her to flush out Crooked Snake? No matter what happened, she knew she could never allow him to know the truth about her parentage.

"That will be nice," she said, the tone of her voice less than enthusiastic. Luckily her father didn't notice it or he question it.

Instead, he took his place at the head of the table and bowed his head to say grace for the meal she had just set before him.

~ * ~

Quade wanted nothing more than to return to his quarters and sleep after a day of working with the men. Instead, he was obligated to attend the dinner party Mrs. VanEtt was giving to introduce him to Horace Whitfield and his daughter, Hannah.

The prospect of spending the evening with the woman who had dominated his thoughts ever since his arrival at the fort was a pleasant one. He hoped she would be receptive to him. It was time he settled down, and courting the lovely Miss Whitfield might lead to something more.

Over the years his twin brother had probably married and started a family. Undoubtedly he was running the family farm and was well settled.

That was the kind of life Quade wanted. He'd had enough of being a single officer. He wanted the companionship of someone he didn't have to pay to be with. He also wanted out of the military, but without a wife, there was no use in putting down roots. For a single man, the army was the best solution. At least it was for him.

As soon as he finished helping to erect the city of tents that would house the men until new mattresses could arrive, Quade made his way to the river. The bathhouse would not be useable for at least another few days. If he wanted to bathe for tonight's party, the river was his only option.

Being alone, he stayed in the shallows, close to his gun, in case Crooked Snake or any other of the renegades he had heard of ambushed him. Earlier, there had been safety in numbers, but now he was alone and a much easier target.

"Thought we'd find you here," he heard someone say.

Quade had been so caught up in his thoughts he hadn't heard the intruder arrive. *Some alert officer I am,* he silently lamented as he looked up to see Private Matthews and Private Zimmer standing on the shore, their rifles in hand.

"What do you boys want?" Quade asked, knowing he was at the disadvantage. He was naked in the river and his clothing was stacked close to where the two young men stood.

"We saw you head off this way," Private Zimmer said. "Figured you were going to take a bath. It ain't safe for anyone to be outside the fort alone, so we decided to tag along in order to watch over you. We know it ain't easy to bathe and keep watch for old Crooked Snake at the same time. I'm not ashamed to say I'd like to get that sly devil in my sights. Face it, Lieutenant, you didn't hear us get here. If we can sneak up on you, I figure you wouldn't hear him and his renegades either."

Quade couldn't help the smile that crossed his lips. This morning there would have been no one who would have come out to keep watch while he took his bath. By defeating Corporal Collins and helping the men with the work he had insisted they do, he had gained at least two friends within the ranks of the troops he was expected to lead.

"Much obliged. It shouldn't take me long here. We all did a good day's work, but such work can make a body dirty."

"Don't fret none, Lieutenant, the rest of the men are planning to come down here again after we finish with supper. None of them want to end up in the stockade like Collins. Besides, they did a good day's work and everyone admits they enjoyed getting clean this morning."

Quade made no comment. With Matthews and Zimmer watching his back, he waded out further into the river and dove beneath the surface to immerse his entire body in the cool refreshing water.

Once he was clean, he walked toward the shore. While Matthews held his rifle protectively, Zimmer handed him a clean towel. When his body was dry, he reached for his dress uniform that he had hung on a low bush when he first arrived at the river. He was buttoning the last button on his shirt when he saw a glint of sunlight reflected off the barrel of a rifle high in the hills on the far bank of the river.

"I think it's time to go back to the fort," he observed.

"Couldn't agree more," Matthews replied. "After what I saw just now, I don't think the men will be comin' down to the river tonight. That way that rifle caught the sunlight a few minutes ago you can bet we aren't the only ones who were watching you take your bath. We'll make it back to the fort safely. If Crooked Snake wanted us dead, we wouldn't have seen anything. He would have been on us before we knew it. He's lookin' you over and seein' if you're worth killin'."

Quade made no comment. He knew Indians. At least he thought he knew Indians. He'd fought the Apache and heard about other tribes. As far as he knew none of them sized a white man up to see if he was worth killing. They killed and asked no questions about the man. What kind of a man was this Crooked Snake? Why did he not take the chance to murder the three of them when it was open to him?

He knew that his questions would not be answered any time soon. Until they were, he would discreetly ask questions and hopefully get the answers that he was looking to find.

~ * ~

Hannah stood in front of the mirror in her bedroom. Her reflection told her that she had spent far too much time primping for supper with Bessie and Rollie. They were friends and had seen her at her worst, so why was she taking such pains with her appearance for tonight's supper? She knew the answer all too well. The new lieutenant would be there and she wanted to make a good impression on him.

The yellow dress that had always been reserved for summer

dances, and would soon be replaced by the new dress she was working on, complemented her coloring well. She smiled as she ran the brush through her long black hair one more time. Usually she wore it braided, and the braid wound into a halo around the top of her head. For parties, she preferred to wear it down and pulled away from her face. The ribbon that secured it was of the same material as the dress.

When people had commented on her hair color and skin tone, her father had always told them that her mother had been Chippewa but had died, leaving Hannah in an orphanage. Of course, Hannah knew it was a lie. She remembered vividly the day that her whole world had changed, the day that the soldiers had massacred not only her mother but also everyone else she had ever know in the village. On that day, she had learned that not all whites were like the soldiers. Martha and Horace had treated her as though she was their treasured child. She remembered the long hours they spent teaching her English and the proper way for the daughter of a missionary to act. Horace, not Crooked Snake, was the man she called Father, the man she loved above all others.

"Are you ready to leave?" Horace called from the front room of the house.

"Almost, Papa." Before leaving her bedroom, she pinched her cheeks and moistened her lips with her tongue. Since her father frowned upon cosmetics, like the ones Bessie VanEtt used, this was the only way she could enhance her natural beauty.

When she stepped into the kitchen, she saw the look of approval in her father's eyes. In his hands was the pie she had baked earlier in the day. It had been meant for their supper but with Bessie's invitation she knew it would be the perfect gift to take to her hostess.

"You look beautiful, Daughter. Unless that new lieutenant is blind he should be quite taken with you."

"I know you want to see me settled, Papa, but a soldier is not going to be taken with me for long. Once he knows of my heritage he will hate me as much as he does the Indians on the reservation. I am resigned to that. When the time comes, I will return to my people and live as they live. I have the skills to teach them—not only to read and write, but also about our Lord. It is quite possible that one of the young men will ask me to be his wife and I will be proud to..." She left the rest of her sentence unspoken. This was the fate she knew would be hers and yet it was one she dreaded. After living in this fine home, she didn't know if she could ever go back to the life of her real people and if she did, she would have none of the skills she should have learned from her mother in order to survive.

~ * ~

Crooked Snake lay flattened out against a rock, watching the new lieutenant who was bathing in the stream.

"I could easily kill him," his oldest son, Growling Bear said. "What kind of a fool bathes in the stream without protection?"

"This man is no fool," Tall Elk commented. "See, his guards just arrived."

"Then we could kill them all," Growling Bear suggested.

"Enough of this talk. I have known of this man since before we returned to our people with the meat for them to survive. Both your mother and the Great Spirit came to me in dreams and told me of his coming. This man is a warrior, a man who has fought our brothers the Apache. He is a brave man. To kill him from ambush would anger the Great Spirit. When it is his time to die, it will be in battle. This man deserves to see the men who will take his life. Besides, I have told you the time for killing has ended. We have come here to bring meat to our people. The taking of white lives will not bring back your mother and sister."

"I think you grow soft in your old age, Father," Tall Elk said. "I say we should kill all the whites. When the time is right, this man will be mine for the taking."

His sons continued to grumble about their father's decision, while Crooked Snake studied the young lieutenant. *His bravery is evident by the fact he comes to the stream alone. Surely he has heard that my sons and I have returned to our people. Even though I no longer seek revenge, my sons are young and the anger still burns hot in their blood.*

::He is, indeed brave, my husband,:: his wife's voice whispered in his mind. *::His coming could prove to be very interesting for our people. Be careful, my husband. As much as I yearn to have you join me, the time is not right. There is much for you to learn before you leave the life you cherish so highly.::*

~ * ~

Quade heard the conversation coming from the Edwards' house long before he stepped foot on the porch. He recognized the voices of both Bill Edwards and Rollie VanEtt, but the voice of the third man was foreign to him.

"Quade, we were beginning to get worried about you," Rollie greeted him. "We thought you weren't coming."

"Since the bathhouse isn't ready to be used yet, I went down to the river. I was foolish enough to go alone, but luckily two of the men saw me leave and followed to keep watch."

"Hopefully, you didn't have any trouble," Bill said.

"Not really. We did see the glint of sunlight off the barrel of a rifle but it was way up in the hills. The men were certain it was Crooked Snake. At least he didn't keep me from coming tonight."

At the mention of Crooked Snake the third man seemed to tense. Looking at him closer, Quade realized it was the missionary. He couldn't help but wonder why the mention of the renegade bothered him. From what he had heard, everyone at the fort knew about Crooked Snake. The man's name was enough to bring fear into the eyes of every man he met, but this man reacted differently. He was certainly afraid of Crooked Snake, but not because he could lose his life to him. Something else about the man raised Horace Whitfield's hackles, but Quade had no idea what that something else was.

Before Quade had time to ponder the silent questions that filled his mind, Mrs. VanEtt called them in for supper. The sight of roasted chicken on the table set his mouth to watering. He had learned that she kept a well-tended garden in the back of the house along with a pen of chickens. Just looking at the platter of finely roasted chicken made his thoughts return to Sunday dinner when he lived at home. At this time of year there was fresh lettuce with a light cream and vinegar dressing, green beans and mashed potatoes drenched in chicken gravy. He was pleased to see his favorite meal recreated by his hostess.

To his delight, Hannah Whitfield was seated next to him.

"You're in for a treat, Lieutenant," Elizabeth Edwards commented, once grace was said and the food was being passed around the table. "Hannah baked us one of her famous wild berry pies. Her crusts are the flakiest ones I have ever eaten."

"You're embarrassing, Hannah, Elizabeth," Bill warned.

"Not at all," Hannah said.

It was the first time that Quade had heard her speak. To him, her voice sounded like that of an angel.

"It was just something that Mama taught me before she died. Her pies were the talk of every place we ever lived."

"It's a shame these people never got to know your dear mother," Horace said, a sad smile crossing his lips. "My Martha was one of the finest women God ever created."

"It's obvious that you carry Indian blood, Hannah," Rollie said. "Just who were your mother's people?"

"They were Chippewa," Horace said, almost too quickly. It seemed as though he felt the need to make the statement and then change the topic of conversation. "My wife was barren and wanted children so badly that when we decided to go West she insisted on adopting a child from the orphanage in town. Hannah is a delight and neither of us could have asked for a better daughter."

Quade looked at Hannah intently. He knew Indians, and Hannah Whitfield was definitely not from one of the Eastern tribes. It was more than likely she originally came from one of the plains tribes, maybe even the Cheyenne who populated the reservation close to the fort.

"You're embarrassing me, Father. I no longer consider my heritage as Indian. I have been raised as your daughter all my life. I am honored to have the chance to teach the children of the reservation and have such wonderful friends. With all this talking, I am certain that Elizabeth's dinner will get cold. I, for one, do not relish eating cold food."

Everyone at the table laughed. Although Quade joined them, he did so as a measure not to be different. He wasn't nearly as interested in the food his hostess was serving as he was in the woman sitting beside him. He enjoyed being so close to Hannah. From the way she spoke the words, he knew English was not her first language. Somewhere in this woman's past, she spoke another language fluently.

"You said you teach at the reservation, Hanna," he said, instigating a conversation with the captivating woman seated beside him. "Isn't it difficult without knowing their language?"

Hannah seemed to tense but immediately regained her composure. "My father has worked with many of the tribes. When we decided to come here, he studied the language of the Cheyenne. It was only natural that I learn it as well. It has been so with each assignment he has taken in the past. My mother and I have always learned the language of the people we have come to serve."

Quade nodded. "It's a shame that a lovely girl like you is stuck in a place like this. Have you ever thought about teaching in a large city?"

She looked at him as though horrified by his suggestion. "These children need me. The life their parents have always known has been torn from them. It is exciting to open their minds to the world of reading and writing."

Quade agreed. He remembered how he had taken to the book learning his pa called a waste of time. He'd found learning exciting, especially since he had a teacher who saw his potential and fanned the flames of education.

"What about you, Lieutenant?" Horace questioned. "What terrible thing brought you to this place?"

"What do you mean?"

"My father and I have been here only a year, but it has been enough time to realize that the men who are sent here are done so for punishment. Did you get caught drinking on duty or deserting?"

Quade thought of Grace and the lie she told her husband that brought him here. "My commanding officer's wife tried to make him jealous by saying I had taken liberties with her. He wouldn't listen when I denied it." He wondered if anyone at the table believed him. It didn't matter. Even though he didn't do the terrible things he'd been accused of, his sins were worse. He would always live with the guilt of wanting to kill his own father on the day he left the farm.

"Are you planning to attend the dance a week from Saturday?" Elizabeth asked.

"Of course he is," Horace replied before Quade had a chance to answer. "If he's as smart as he looks, he'll be taking my Hannah to the dance."

"Papa!" Hanna exclaimed.

"It would be my pleasure, Reverend Whitfield, but only if it is all right with Hannah. Would you go to the dance with me?" It pleased him to see how flustered she was by his request.

"I've never considered having an escort. It's never seemed important, but yes, I'd be honored to have you escort me."

Quade noticed the smiles that graced the faces of the two older women. It was evident this party had been their idea of matchmaking. It always puzzled him as to why women always hated to see one of their sex without a man in their lives.

The table talk turned to more neutral conversation, leaving Quade to his own private thoughts. Just thinking about holding Hannah in his arms while dancing made him smile with anticipation. He wished the dance wasn't so far away. Perhaps he could call on the lovely Miss Whitfield before the dance.

"That was a fine meal, Elizabeth," Rollie declared once they finished eating.

"Indeed it was, my dear," Bill said. "We'll leave you ladies to your girl talk, and adjourn to the parlor for brandy and cigars."

Elizabeth beamed at the compliment and nodded her approval at the men leaving the table.

Once they were in the parlor, the conversation turned to the fort and the changes that were being made. "I ordered those mattresses and extra bedding," Bill commented. "I received a wire back saying that they would be sent with the supplies for the reservation."

"Supplies the Cheyenne will never see," Horace spat. "They will come and Simon will make a big production of loading them in his wagon before leaving the fort. He won't return for several days, and when he does he will have left the Cheyenne with buggy flour and rotten meat. It's a disgrace. I'm ashamed to even go out to the reservation after his deplorable behavior."

"I've heard the same thing from Red at the railhead," Quade agreed. "What does the man do with the supplies?"

"It's beyond me," Bill commented. "I've asked the ranchers and none of them are buying from him."

"Rollie and I have been talking about this very thing," Quade said. "Would it be possible to have him followed once he leaves the fort?"

"Followed?" Rollie questioned. "How? This is such open country he'd spot anyone following him a mile away."

"He'd spot the soldiers, but would he see the Indians? They know this country. If we could get their help with this, we could find out where he goes and who buys their supplies."

"And take matters into their own hands," Rollie declared.

"Not necessarily," Horace added, joining the conversation. "I could talk to the elders. They are as concerned about what he is doing as we are. I think they would be agreeable to such a plan, if it was presented properly. I'm going out there tomorrow. Let me talk to them and at least give them the option of helping. We do have a few days before the supplies will be arriving."

Quade was surprised when Horace offered his help, but what better person to approach the people? He had their trust which was something neither the soldiers nor Simon had been able to gain. Perhaps this idea of his would take root and bring an end to Simon's dishonest dealings.

Six

Hannah's mind spun with the memory of sitting next to Quade at Elizabeth's dinner party. She was so preoccupied with her own thoughts she almost burned her father's eggs.

"Is something wrong?" Horace asked.

"I don't know what has gotten into me this morning," Hannah replied. "I'm having trouble concentrating."

Horace smiled and then laughed out loud. "Have we sheltered you so much that you do not understand the pull between a man and a woman, especially when the man could become special to you? It is the new lieutenant who has you so confused. Even though I'm an old man, I can still see that you interest him and he interests you. There is nothing wrong with your feelings."

"How can you say that? You and I both know who and what my father is. I love you dearly, but it was Crooked Snake's seed that gave me life and everyone knows of him."

Horace reached across the table and took her hand in his. "I, like you, have heard the stories the soldiers tell about your father as well as your brothers. I think it is time for you to go to the reservation with me and ask questions about the man they know so well and see in an entirely different light. After hearing both stories, perhaps you will be able to find the actual truth."

Hannah said nothing. Instead, she concentrated on her breakfast. As she did, she remembered the dream that had come so often. In it, her father was loving, her brothers protective. None of them were ruthless killers. Even if that was what they had become, they certainly had good reason.

With breakfast finished, Hannah hurried to clean her kitchen so she could go to the reservation with her father. She dreaded the ride out there in the open carriage. The summer sun was already cresting the eastern horizon and promising another hot day.

Outside, her father waited for her by the carriage. "I'm pleased you decided to accompany me this morning. We must hurry, for our presence is needed among the Cheyenne."

Hannah allowed her father to help her climb into the carriage and watched as he slapped the reins against the back of the horse.

"Before we reach the reservation, there is something you must know. Last evening Lieutenant McPherson asked me to request the help of the Cheyenne to find out what Simon is doing with the supplies for the people."

"He is asking the Cheyenne for help? Why? None of the soldiers we have ever known has trusted the Indians before. What make this man so different?"

"He cares. He told me he fought the Apache in the Arizona Territory. He asked to be transferred from there to Virginia City because he was tired of fighting a people he considered a proud race. He knows the Cheyenne can follow Simon when he leaves here with the supplies without being detected. With Crooked Snake in the area, no one will be concerned if a few braves leave the reservation. They will think the men have gone to join the renegades."

"Is he a renegade? Is my father as terrible as the soldiers

say?"

"As I said earlier, you should listen to both sides of this debate and come to your own decisions. It is the reason I wanted you to come to the reservation with me today. The women have much meat to preserve for the winter. You should not only ask the questions that so burn on your mind, but you should also learn the ways of your people. They will need many hands to have it preserved before Simon comes to the reservation to question where it came from."

Hannah thought for a moment. She, too, wondered where the Cheyenne got the meat they were preserving. She knew the hunting around the reservation was far from good. Even if it were better, the weapons needed to hunt had been taken from them. *How had they obtained the meat?* From the look on her father's face she knew he had said all he intended to say on the subject. It was evident he wanted her to learn the truth from the people rather than that which he would be only repeating.

The smell of the village's fires hung in the air creating a haze in the heat of high summer. Children she knew from her classes ran to greet them. Since they had been at this reservation for more than a year, she knew each child by name and loved all of them dearly. It was the adults she hardly knew. They were her father's students. To them she was an outsider.

As much as she wanted to go be with the children, she stayed with her father until they reached the area where the women were working with piles of fresh meat. Although she knew animals were slaughtered for food, she'd never seen so much red meat in one place before. The sight of it, as well as the blood from the animals, was enough to turn her stomach. Instead of turning away from the grizzly sight, she swallowed down the bile and prepared to join the women who would have been her friends if her entire village had not been destroyed.

Her father got down from the carriage and came around to

assist her to do the same. Immediately, the women looked at her with apprehension in their eyes.

"Owl Woman," her father said in Cheyenne. "This is my daughter, Hannah. She is the one who teaches the children. She wants to help with the meat and learn of your ways."

"Can we trust her?" one of the women asked.

"We trust her with the minds of our children, why shouldn't we trust her in other matters?" Owl Woman replied, her answer becoming yet another question.

"You are right, but we are not children. What will happen to us if she tells the Indian Agent where we have gotten this meat? If he knows..."

"He will not know. I give you my word. Hannah will help you while I speak with the elders."

The name of Owl Woman brought back memories Hannah thought were long dead. Owl Woman was her mother's sister. On the morning of the massacre, she was with the hunters. She and several of the other unmarried women went with the hunters to help with the butchering of the meat. Did her father know that the woman he'd instructed to teach her was, of all people, her aunt? She doubted it.

"Come and sit with me," Owl Woman said. "Have you ever butchered and prepared meat for winter before?"

Hannah shook her head no. "I have not been trained in your ways. My parents adopted me in the east before they came to the frontier to begin their ministry. I had no chance to learn the ways of my people."

"Who are your people?" one of the other women asked.

"My father tells me I was an orphan of the Chippewa. Surely you know of orphans among your people."

"We do, but none that would be given to the whites. The Chippewa must not value family. An orphan here would be taken in by the people and raised with love."

"Do you have children, Owl Woman?"

"My sons, Little Hawk and Red Sky, are students at your school and my daughter, Bright Dawn, is married to a fine young brave. My nephews are the ones who have brought us the meat. They and their father come down from Canada in the summers. This year they have come to bring us meat so that we can survive the winter."

"Are you talking of the renegade, Crooked Snake and his sons, Growling Bear and Tall Elk?" Hannah asked.

"That is what the soldiers call my sister's husband and sons. When the soldiers killed my sister and niece, he extracted revenge by killing whites. It took a long time for him to realize it would not bring Babbling Brook and Little Hummingbird back to him. After the battle with Custer, he knew our way of life was ending. That was when he and his sons went to Canada. For many years they came back for the revenge they felt belonged to them. After this past winter things were different. When he returned he promised there would be no more killing. For this summer his killing has been of the animals needed for our people to survive."

"But when he is in the area, there is violence surrounding the reservation. People say it is Crooked Snake who does the killing.'

"Crooked Snake's sons talk to the young braves. Many of them rebel when it can be blamed on someone else. It saddens Crooked Snake, especially since many times his own sons go with the young rebels. We have had many long talks about how to stop these things from happening."

Hannah could feel tears forming in her eyes. Never had she heard her father referred to as a compassionate man. Owl Woman's description of him gave credence to the dream Hannah had so often experienced.

The morning passed quickly. Before Hannah knew it, the

sun was overhead, but the women made no move to prepare a midday meal. She knew that the children brought food to school for the noon meal, but these women seemed oblivious to the time of day.

Just looking at the raw meat made any appetite she may have had disappear. Even so, she wondered if these women, who were used to the work, were hungry.

From behind her, she heard singing and turned to see several young girls coming toward them bringing platters of food. The women washed the blood from their hands and sat down to a meal of cooked meat, berries and fry bread.

With the midday meal finished, Hannah went back to work, helping the women as they cut strips of meat for the drying racks. As the afternoon wore on, she kept glancing toward the men, in the hopes of seeing her father or brothers. She knew she would recognize her father but over the years her brothers had grown from boys to me. If her calculations were right, they would be over thirty by now. Were they married? Did they have children? Would they even remember her?

It was well into the afternoon when Hannah found herself working alone with Owl Woman. "What do you know of your people?" the older woman asked.

"Not much, really. My mother died when I was very young and my father..." she allowed the rest of what she knew of the truth to die on her tongue. If she said too much, Owl Woman might guess at her identity and question why she called a white man father. It was hard not to blurt out the truth, but she knew to say more would jeopardize her standing in the white world.

"Perhaps your father is a renegade," Owl Woman said. "I would have to be blind not to see your mother in your smile and your father in your eyes. I do not know how or why the Great Spirit has brought you back to us, but I am indeed blessed that he has."

"On the day my mother and the others were killed, I hid in the forest." Saying the words brought back the memory of the day when life as she had always known it disappeared. "When I left my hiding place, they were all dead. All but my mother were buried. That was when Horace and Martha found me and..."

"And took you away from the smell of death and the horror of what the soldiers had done. Your white father is a good man, and I understand why he wanted to keep your identity a secret. I rejoice in the fact that you are alive. Your mother would be so proud of you. As much as I want to, I will say nothing to your father or brothers until you are ready to tell them yourself."

"Did my... Horace tell you?"

"He said nothing. You must remember, I am of your family. I knew you the moment you stepped from the carriage. As for your white father, never hesitate to call him father again. He has raised and loved you when everyone you knew and loved was lost to you. It was he and his wife who comforted you when you cried and calmed your fears when the Great Spirit sent bad dreams to your sleep time. Never forget their love."

Before Hannah could say anything more to her aunt, several other women joined them. Only the smile on Owl Woman's face told Hannah her family would forever love her.

The lengthening afternoon shadows cast themselves across the drying racks when Horace came to pick Hannah up for the return trip to the fort. "Did you learn of your people?" he asked, once they left the village.

"Yes, Papa. I learned the way of the people and so much more. Owl Woman is my mother's sister."

"I know. That is why I brought you to her. Did she recognize you?"

Hannah nodded. "She said she saw my mother in my smile and my father in my eyes. How did you know who she was?"

"When we first found you, Martha and I were afraid the soldiers would guess your identity, so we made certain we didn't settle in the area where you were found. As you know, we have been at many forts, but never any this far to the north. One of the last things she asked of me was to find your people. That is why we came to this fort. I had hoped someone would have recognized you when you were teaching the children. When that didn't happen, I started asking questions about Crooked Snake. That was how I learned that Owl Woman was your aunt I am pleased that she recognized you. The next step is to reunite you with your father and brothers."

Tears stung Hannah's eyes. "It is enough to have found Owl Woman. I learned much about my father today, but it is not the time for me to find him. He has done the killings the soldiers talk about. Even my brothers have extracted revenge and still do. It goes against your teachings and everything I hold dear. I know with age my father has mellowed, but meeting him is something that will have to wait."

"Your decision pleases me, for I am not ready to lose my daughter to her true people just yet."

Hannah leaned over to hug Horace. "You will always be my father. Owl Woman made me see that even though Crooked Snake gave me life you have given me love. If you had not rescued me, I would have died before my father and the others returned to our village."

They drove on in silence for many minutes, each trying to cope with their emotions. It was Hannah who finally broke the silence between them. "Were the men responsive to your proposal?"

"Not at first. They distrust the soldiers and with good cause. I finally convinced them that the new lieutenant is different. When I explained that they would be following Simon so that the soldiers could deal with him and bring in an honest man to fill his job, they relented. Their hatred for Simon outweighed their distrust of the soldiers. I told them that when the supplies are delivered, I will come and let them know so that they can be ready to follow Simon when he leaves the fort."

"What if they decide to deal with Simon in their own way?"

"They have agreed to allow the army to handle things. The elders are fed up with the treatment they received from Simon. They also realize this is the first time the soldiers have ever asked for their help. It will not be the young men who follow Simon. Their minds are on the wrong things and they have not learned the tracking skills the older men possess. The elders understand the need for cooperation."

~ * ~

Crooked Snake watched as the missionary and the lovely young girl with him left the village. He had heard good things about Horace Whitfield, even if he didn't believe in the God this man professed to be the one true God. When he had voiced his opinions to Owl Woman, Babbling Brook's sister, she had told him that Horace knew many of the people still clung to the old ways, but he still came to minister to them. If nothing else, the man was very brave.

He had watched the missionary many times in the past, but today was different. Today he had a young woman with him. She was beautiful and even from this distance he could tell she had no white blood.

A lump formed in his throat as he thought of his beloved Babbling Brook and his daughter, Little Hummingbird. They were lost to him. He decided that is she had lived Little Hummingbird would be about the same age as the woman who shared the missionary's carriage. Now that they were no longer in the village, he would go and talk to Owl Woman and see what she knew about the girl.

With the white missionary gone, those in the village

welcomed him. He immediately sought out his sister-in-law to question her about those who had just left. He found Owl Woman cleansing her hands from working with the meat all day.

"Who was the woman who came with the missionary?" he asked once he seated himself at Owl Woman's fire.

"She is the daughter of the missionary."

"She is not white, how can that be?"

"She is an orphan and was adopted by the missionary and his wife. They have raised her as their own. She is the one who comes to teach the children."

"What manner of people would allow a white man to adopt an Indian child?"

"You must understand that the ways of the Cheyenne are not the ways of all of the people. She is of the Chippewa tribe who lives far to the east. Without parents she had no one. They have lived among the whites longer than we have. It is possible that they felt they were doing what was best for the girl."

Crooked Snake shook his head. "How could anyone think it best for a child to be raised by the whites? What manner of people are these Chippewa? Have they no morals?"

"Just remember there are good and bad in all people. The missionary is a good man. He has given Hannah the love she could not receive from her own parents. Do not judge him too harshly. He did bring her to me so that she could learn of our ways."

"Trust of the white man does not come easily for me, but Babbling Brook has appeared to me in a dream and told me that the time for revenge and fighting is past. I am trying to bring my sons to the same conclusion, but it is hard. I am glad Babbling Brook and Little Hummingbird did not live to see the humiliation our people suffer at the hands of the whites."

~ * ~

Quade paced Rollie's office, nervously. "Horace should have returned by now. What if they Cheyenne have turned on the old man?"

"Would you sit down, Quade?" Rollie asked. "Pacing won't bring Horace to this office any sooner. Even though I don't think the Cheyenne will go for this harebrained idea of yours, it's doubtful they'll do any harm to Horace."

"It's not harebrained, Rollie!" Quade shouted. "If we don't follow Simon, we'll never know where he takes the supplies or who he sells them to. You know as well as well as I do that the only ones who can pull this off without being noticed are the Cheyenne."

"And what happens if they agree to this then decide to take matters into their own hands and kill Simon? What will I be expected to tell the Department of Indian Affairs? How can I tell Washington that I allowed the Cheyenne to leave the reservation to follow a government agent, only to have him murdered?"

"You can blame me. For what he's doing to these people, I'd be tempted to murder him myself if I thought I could get away with it. He's selling the supplies that are meant for the Indians and bringing them spoiled meat and buggy flour. The only thing that bastard thinks about is lining his pockets and having a poke at Shirl when he's done. He certainly doesn't give a damn about the people he's been sent here to protect."

A knock at the door interrupted Quade's ranting. "May I come in?" Horace asked before entering the room.

"Of course, Horace," Rollie replied. "We've been waiting for you. What did the Cheyenne have to say?"

Horace seated himself in one of the chairs opposite Rollie's desk. "At first they were skeptical, but they understand the need to see where Simon is going with the supplies. It was the decision of the council that the older men will follow Simon since the younger men might be tempted to take matters into their own hands. No one other than the council will know what is going on."

"Thank you, Horace," Quade said, extending his hand to the older man. "I realize these people have no reason to trust us to keep our word. I have you to thank for getting the Cheyenne to help us."

"We all tend to underestimate these noble savages, Lieutenant," Horace said. "I've preached the Gospel to these people most of my life. They never cease to amaze me. When Martha and I first came west, it was to convert the heathen savages. I soon learned they are a very spiritual people. Many of them have converted to Christianity, but only because it is a new God and what they consider the proper thing to do. If the truth be known, many of them give lip service to our God while they pray to the Great Spirit. Because I turn a blind eye to their choice of worship, they trust me."

Seven

Hannah took her sewing to the porch in order to catch any breeze that might be blowing. Just prior to the noon meal, the supply wagon had arrived. As soon as Horace finished eating, he left for the reservation. Although she begged to go with him, he told her that this wasn't the time for her to be socializing with Owl Woman. This trip was not a social one, since he would be meeting with the elders. The supplies had arrived and the Cheyenne needed to be prepared to follow Simon when he went out with the supplies tomorrow morning.

Hannah worried about the plan. If you could believe what he said, Simon was a crack shot and would relish any opportunity to shoot any of the Cheyenne who ventured off the reservation if they crossed his path. She prayed the elders would remain hidden from his view so that they could report to Quade and Rollie as to where he went.

She turned her thoughts to the length of fabric that lay in her lap. It would take several hours for her to finish the dress for the dance. As she worked on it, she daydreamed about being swept across the dance floor by Quade. Even though his duties had kept him busy, the memory of his touch and the smell of his cologne on the night of Elizabeth's dinner party lingered in her mind. Hannah prayed he would think she was pretty in her new dress.

"Good afternoon, Miss Hannah." Simon's voice seemed to come out of nowhere to shatter her mental ramblings.

"Good afternoon to you, too, Mr. Leary."

Almost before she could say more, Simon mounted the steps to the porch and stood in front of her as he leaned against the railing. "I thought we agreed that you would call me Simon."

"I know you told me that was what you preferred. I guess I forgot, Simon."

"I saw your father leave. Was he going to the reservation?"

Hannah knew she had to think quickly. "Yesterday while we were at church, there were several members of the council who wanted to meet with him. The meeting was set for this afternoon. He left as soon as he finished his lunch. He told me not to worry if he didn't return until tomorrow morning. He often stays at the reservation overnight since they maintain a house for his use."

"What a shame that he would leave you here alone and unprotected. Anything could happen to a lovely young thing like you while he's gone."

"I'm quite capable of taking care of myself, Simon. I've done it many times in the past. When meetings such as these come up, there is nothing for me to do, especially during the summer when the children are not in school. I have plenty of work to do around the house to keep me busy."

Simon reached over to finger the material of the dress she was working on. "Is this for the dance on Saturday?" he asked.

She didn't like the look in his eyes. For the first time in more years than she cared to remember, she was actually frightened of a man. "Yes, it is for the dance. I decided it was high time I made myself a new dress. I've been so busy with the classes for the children at the reservation as well as keeping Papa's house clean and making him shirts, I haven't had time to make anything new for myself. This seemed like the perfect opportunity." She knew she'd said far too much. Unfortunately, the words had gushed from her mouth. She knew it was due to her nervousness at having him so close that she could smell the cheap cologne he usually doused himself in.

"I'd be honored if you would allow me to escort you to the dance," he said, leaning even closer to her.

"That won't be necessary," Quade said before she had a chance to speak. "She's going to the dance with me."

Silently, she thanked Quade for his intrusion. Just having him stand up to Simon made her hands stop shaking and her stomach settle.

"I should have known. Guess the right officer had to come along. Well, I hope you're prepared for a chilly evening. From what I can tell, she's one cold bitch. I, on the other hand, will be quite cozy with Shirl. They always come to the dances, you know. What will your little playmate, Grace Walters, have to say about that?"

Hannah held her breath in anticipation of the confrontation that was about to happen. Instead, Quade stepped up onto the porch to face Simon.

"What I do and who I do it with is none of your business. If I'm not mistaken, you have supplies to get loaded to take to the reservation tomorrow. I suggest you see to your duties and leave Miss Whitfield alone."

Without another word, Simon left the porch and hurried across the parade grounds to where his wagon was waiting to be loaded.

"Thank you," Hannah said when Quade turned to face her. "I'm certain he watched my father leave and took advantage of the situation. I'm afraid I made a terrible mistake by telling him my father might not return until morning."

Quade glanced in the direction that Simon had gone. "I'm afraid you might have. Leary is not someone to make mad and I'm certain we both angered him. I doubt that he'll do anything foolish, but just in case I'll post a guard here tonight. I saw Simon heading this way after your father left. Is he meeting with the council this afternoon?"

"Yes, and I do believe the meeting will go far into the night. From what Papa learned yesterday, some of the elders are very much against this plan. I can only pray that they go along with it. Can I get you something cool to drink?"

"No thank you. I'm on duty. Of course, one of my duties was to invite you to the VanEttes for dinner this evening. The invitation was for you and your father, but since he may not return, I would be more than happy to stop by, at say five, and escort you to dinner."

Hannah smiled. Of course she wanted Quade to escort her to dinner. She wanted him in her life, but she knew it was impossible. Sooner or later, he would learn that her father was Crooked Snake. When that happened, she and her white father would, more than likely, be forced to move. The people here would, undoubtedly, accuse her of the things her father and brother had done over the years. She hated the thought of leaving not only Quade, but also her family behind. "I would be honored, Lieutenant McPherson. Until tonight."

Quade put his fingers to his cap in mock salute. "Until tonight, lovely lady." With that, he turned and walked down the steps to the porch.

As much as Hannah wanted to stay out on the porch to continue her sewing, she didn't want Simon to see what she was doing. Even though he worked on the other side of the fort, she could feel him staring at her. The fear she had felt earlier was threatening to reappear. Being in the house with the door securely locked would at least keep the wolf from the door but would make the heat of high summer almost insufferable.

~ * ~

Quade turned in time to see Hannah go back into the house. It worried him that Simon had such a bad effect on her. At least after tomorrow morning he would be gone.

He thought about the coming morning. Hannah said that the council had doubts about the plan. He certainly hoped that Horace could change their minds. If Simon weren't followed, they wouldn't be able to prove that he was cheating the Indians.

He heard a shout go up from the men and realized that the mattresses and bedding had been shipped with the supplies. Considering that clouds were forming in the west, there was a good chance that a summer storm could hit, breaking the heat that had held the area in its grip for the past several days.

After leaving Hannah's house, Quade went to where the men were unloading the bedding. Before he reached the wagon, Simon approached him.

"You'll be one sorry son of a bitch that you had any truck with that woman," Simon said. "It's evident that she's got Injun blood in her. What will happen when you find yourself fighting her people?"

"The extensive Indian wars are over, Simon. There would

be no trouble if people like you didn't continue to cheat the Indians. Think about it. With Crooked Snake back in the area, you could easily lose your hair if you aren't careful."

"I'll remember that, Lieutenant. I'll also remember that these people are dependent on me. If I get killed who knows what Washington will do in retaliation. Now, I have work to do if I plan to leave in the morning."

Quade turned from Simon, disgusted by his holier than thou attitude. Who did he think he was fooling? It certainly wasn't anyone at the reservation or anyone at the fort for that matter. Wherever he was selling these supplies, he was doing so at a fat profit. His pockets were being lined quite handsomely, while the Cheyenne were suffering. If this plan didn't work, Quade was ready to write to Washington and tell them just what kind of a man was representing them in Montana.

~ * ~

It was apparent to everyone that Bessie VanEtt's home was sparse in comparison to the one she enjoyed describing when she talked about her youth. Hannah knew it bothered her that she didn't live in luxury, but not so much that she refused to entertain. When she did, she used the china and crystal she'd brought with her from the east.

At times Hannah envied Bessie her beautiful possessions, even though she knew envy was a sin. Even though she did her share of entertaining, she also knew her table never looked this elegant. Her tablecloths were made of the cotton fabric that her mother had so lovingly stitched so long ago. She knew they were getting shabby, to say the least, and that they should be replaced. Instead she found that everyday needs like new shirts for her father and occasionally a new dress for herself took precedence.

"Is there anything I can help you with?" Hannah asked Bessie when she came from the kitchen with yet another platter of food.

"Everything is under control. I just want you to enjoy yourself this evening. Rollie told me about your run in with Simon this afternoon. I wish that horrible little man would be called back to Washington."

Bessie disappeared back into the kitchen, leaving Hannah with her thoughts. *How could Quade spread the gossip about what had transpired on the porch? Was nothing sacred to these people?*

"I'm sorry if you're upset about what Bessie just said," Quade whispered as he put his hand on her shoulder. "I had to make a report to Rollie, I just didn't think he would repeat what I told him to his wife."

Hannah took a deep breath. Of course, Quade had to make a report of what had happened. It was his job. It only bothered her because she was so worried about her father being out at the reservation all night and what might happen if Simon decided to take advantage of the situation.

"I shouldn't let it bother me," she replied. "Being on a post like this has to be hard for Bessie and Elizabeth. They're both from the more populated areas in the east where they don't have to scrounge for the gossip they so enjoy."

"I don't see it as gossip," Quade continued. "I think they're as concerned for your safety as I am. I've had a long talk with Rollie about this and he agrees that you should spend the night here. Once Simon leaves in the morning, the worry will be gone. Neither of us likes the idea of you staying alone tonight."

"Well put, Quade," Rollie chimed in. "We were going to wait until after supper to bring up the prospect of Hannah spending the night with us. I don't trust Simon, either in business or in personal ethics. It would be safer if you spent the night in our spare bedroom. That way even if he does come to your home, you won't be in any danger from him."

"But I couldn't," she protested. "I've never run away from problems and neither has my father."

"Simon is more than a mere problem, my dear," Rollie contended. "He is a threat. Just in the way he deals with the Indians, I know what kind of a man he is. I wouldn't put anything past him, especially since he has told every man at the fort that he plans to make you his and his alone. Knowing that Quade is going to be taking you to the dance on Saturday may easily push him over the edge. Since he knows that you will be alone tonight, anything could happen."

Hannah hung her head as Rollie's words renewed her fear of being alone. "I'm ashamed to say that Simon frightened me terribly today. It's been a long time since I've been frightened like that. I realize he's someone who would easily act upon his desires, no matter who gets hurt in the bargain. I'm just not comfortable imposing on you and Bessie tonight. I'm not prepared. I have nothing to wear and..."

"And nothing," Bessie said, joining the conversation. "Anything I have will fit you perfectly and it's only for one night. Tomorrow you will be able to return home. I've already laid out a fresh nightdress for you in the spare bedroom. I will be delighted to have you as our houseguest for tonight."

Hannah smiled weakly. These people were her friends because they thought her to be an orphan befriended by Martha and Horace. If they knew the truth, would they be so eager to open their home to her?

~ * ~

Quade held Hannah's chair. As he did, he enjoyed the fresh scent of her hair. She was indeed a beautiful woman, even with her Indian heritage.

"Your father tells me you went out to the reservation with him a few days ago to help the women while he had council with the elders," Quade said, initiating the conversation.

"Yes. It was my mother who always went out to help the women when we lived at the other posts. I was far too young. With her gone, my father decided it was time I took her place and learned the ways of the people he serves."

"What did you do?" Elizabeth Edwards asked.

"I helped them prepare some food for the winter. We all know that they will not receive the supplies that the government has promised, so they were gathering nuts and berries."

Nuts and berries, my Great Aunt Tillie, Quade thought. *I saw her when she returned and her dress was stained with blood. The people have meat from somewhere. I certainly wish I knew where. Of course, this isn't the time or the place to ask such questions.*

"Did they tell you anything about Crooked Snake?" Bill asked.

Quade noticed that Hannah stiffened at the mention of the renegade who was on the minds of everyone in the area.

"They say that he and his sons return every summer to help the people. The women look on them as saviors of the people rather than ruthless killers."

"What do you think they are?" Rollie pressed.

"I think they have every right to seek justice for what was done to their village. How would you feel if you returned to the fort to find everyone and everything you held dear destroyed?

The story the women tell is that his wife and daughter were among those slaughtered by the soldiers. I realize this is a military post, but senseless murder is never right. My father teaches, 'Thou shalt not kill,' and yet that is exactly what the soldiers did. Killing in a war is one thing, but to attack innocent women and children at the crack of dawn is another. It isn't just Crooked Snake's people who have had such things happen. I have heard similar stories at many of the other forts where we have served."

Quade heard sadness in her voice. It was almost as though she was reliving the events the women had told her about. "I think this is far too delicious a meal to spoil it with talk of senseless killing. I know I saw my share of it in the Arizona territory and am pleased that we have come to a peaceful agreement with the Cheyenne."

"Peaceful!" Rollie declared. "What is peaceful about Crooked Snake coming back here every summer and declaring war on this fort? When he goes back to whatever hole he calls home, things quiet down. It's only when he and his sons return that the pot is stirred and everyone is frightened out of their wits."

"I agree with Quade," Elizabeth said. "I think we should talk about kinder things. I am looking forward to the dance on Saturday night. It will be good to see the ranchers, and yes, even to see Red and everyone from the railhead."

"Even Shirl?" Bill questioned.

"Yes, even Shirl. She is a delight to talk to and while she is here, she is quite the lady. I have no problems with her, as long as she doesn't throw her profession into our faces."

"I agree," Hannah said, the composure returned to her voice. "I think it's a shame that she has to sell her body to make a living, but if you read the Bible, you'll see that women have been doing just that since the beginning of time. Sometimes I think it is the men who are to blame for women like Shirl and not the women themselves."

"Well said!" Rollie declared. "I agree with Elizabeth and Hannah, Shirl is what men have forced her to be. If she enjoys her work, who are we to condemn her. As long as she doesn't ply her trade here at the fort, she is always welcome. Speaking of being welcome, Grace Walters will be coming with them this time. Does that bother you, Quade?"

Quade knew how Hannah had felt only moments earlier. The mention of Grace was enough to set his nerves on edge. "Grace and I have made our peace. I realize she was only trying to get her husband to notice her with those accusations. In the end he noticed her all right, with his fists. After that he ordered her to go back East. I have felt the brunt of that man's anger, but not in the same way as Grace. When I left her at the railhead, she was quite happy to be doing the cooking and everyone there had accepted her."

Is that really the way I feel? I doubt it. Grace is responsible for me being here and I'll never forgive her for putting a black mark on my military record. I know I have to be cordial to her on Saturday night, but it will be difficult.

"What are you making to bring to the dance, Hannah?" Bessie asked, relieving Quade of further reliving the disgrace that brought him here.

"I was looking through Mama's recipes and decided to make a sponge cake. They always go over well. I also thought I would make some ham sandwiches. Papa was able to obtain a nice ham from one of the ranchers and I have been saving it for just such an occasion."

"Of course you will be making the sandwiches with your wonderful rolls," Bill teased. "Really Quade, you haven't tasted rolls until you've eaten the ones Hannah bakes. They are some of the best I've ever eaten."

"And what about my rolls?" Elizabeth teased.

"Your rolls are good, but not nearly as good as your biscuits. They're light as a feather and rival even the ones my mother used to serve when I was but a boy."

The mention of biscuits, brought to mind the ones Grace had made when she took on the job of cooking at the railhead. They were light and once drenched in butter, some of the best he'd ever had. It was no wonder that Red offered her the job of cook.

"Don't you agree?" Rollie's question brought Quade back to the conversation at hand.

"Agree?" he asked.

"Every woman has her specialties. It isn't fair to pit one against another. I've tasted Elizabeth's biscuits and agree they are some of the best I've ever had. Hannah's rolls are equally good. That brings us to my dear wife and when it comes to making cakes and pies it's hard to top her. We are blessed to be surrounded by such wonderful cooks."

"I guess you're right. With my ma, it was her berry cobbler that was the talk of the neighborhood. In the summer it was with the fresh berries that grew wild around our farm. During the winter she used ones she canned over the summer. I can still taste that cobbler. I doubt if I'll ever have one as good."

"I see what you men are doing," Elizabeth said. "We women enjoy being praised for our abilities in the kitchen, just like you men enjoy bragging about how well you shoot a gun and how good you are in the bedroom."

Everyone laughed, except Hannah. As an unmarried woman,

Quade knew such an intimate subject must be embarrassing to her. He wondered how different her life would have been if she would have remained with her native people. He had heard that entire families slept in the same area, leaving no doubt as to what transpired between a man and a woman. At times he thought that was the better idea. If marital relations were not such a mystery, men like Simon wouldn't be so quick to try to satisfy his urges with women who wanted nothing to do with him.

With dinner ended, the men went to enjoy their brandy while the women cleaned up the kitchen. "What kind of a threat did Simon make to Hannah?" Rollie asked.

"It wasn't so much the words but his actions that told me he could be a danger to her. He knows that Horace plans to spend the night at the reservation. From the look in his eyes he wanted her in the same way he wants Shirl. It's not a good time for Horace to be gone overnight. I'm just grateful that she'll be here with you and Bessie tonight. At least I won't be so worried about her. If you hadn't suggested it, I was going to post a guard at her house, but then no man can watch front and back at the same time."

"It's the least we could do. Horace is a good man. I think Hannah intrigues Simon because of her Indian blood. Even though she's from one of the eastern tribes, she's still Indian and as such Simon thinks she's inferior and it's all right to treat her without the respect she's due."

I can't believe these men are so blind they don't see her as being from this area. I knew it the minute I saw her. Quade continued to allow his mind to wander while his friends talked of other things. He liked thinking about Hannah. Saturday night he would enjoy having her in his arms as they danced across the floor and got to know each other better. They would make the most striking couple at the dance.

His thoughts turned to Grace. He wondered if she was still at the railhead or if she would have boarded an eastbound train. From what she said, he doubted if she would be going back to her parents, but was Montana enough distance between her and Miles Walters? He didn't think so. He had a bad feeling about his former commanding officer, one that nagged at his mind whenever he thought about Grace.

~ * ~

Hannah awoke to the sound of an argument coming from outside her window. Usually such things didn't greet her in the morning. It wasn't until she remembered that she'd spent the night at Bessie and Rollie's home that she realized how close to the parade ground she was.

She got out of bed and made her way to the window. Outside, she saw Simon arguing with one of the soldiers about something. As she watched, Quade came to break up the fight. Once he did, Simon climbed onto the wagon seat and slapped the reins against the backs of his horses. The team started moving as Simon cracked the whip against their backsides to make them go faster. She prayed that the gate would be open so that they could be on their way and far from the fort by the time she was ready to return to her own home.

The clothes she'd worn the night before lay folded on the chair where she had placed them before retiring for the night. Once she was dressed, she went downstairs to see if she could help Bessie in the kitchen.

The mantel clock was striking eight when she got to the bottom of the stairs. She sniffed the air and was surprised not to be able to smell coffee or breakfast cooking. The house was quiet and she wondered if Bessie was still sleeping. A check of the kitchen told her that no breakfast has been prepared and that her hostess was still in bed.

It doesn't matter, she told herself. *I'll just go home so that I won't be any bother to Bessie. There's plenty to eat there and I should start preparing a noon meal for Papa.*

As soon as she opened the door to step outside, she saw Quade coming toward the house. "Have you had breakfast yet?" he asked.

"Not yet. Bessie is still sleeping. I thought I'd go home and fix something for myself."

"Rollie thought that was what you were planning. He sent me over here to take you to the mess hall. He told the cook to fix your breakfast when you arrived. I'm afraid it won't be more than bacon and eggs and coffee, though."

"That would be more than enough to satisfy me. I was thinking more along the lines of a cup of coffee and some bread and preserves."

"I refuse to allow you to eat alone," Quade said, as he tucked her hand into the crook of his elbow.

Hannah blessed her darker complexion as it hid the blush that was creeping into her cheeks at his attentions. Never before had she allowed anyone to get close enough to make her heart beat so quickly or her stomach do flip-flops.

Once in the mess hall, she found the breakfast the cook served her to be very good. The eggs were done the exact way she liked them, the bacon was crisp, the bread was lightly browned and coffee just the right strength.

"This bread is delicious. I wonder how he does that. I would have never thought to brown it."

Quade looked at her in surprise. "Haven't you ever had toast before?"

Hannah shook her head. "Mama always just sliced it and put it on a plate for us. This is delicious. The butter has melted just as though it came directly from the oven."

"I've never toasted bread but I'm certain the cook will be glad to show you how it's done."

With the meal completed, Hannah went out to the kitchen to see if she could learn the secret of toasting bread.

"It's something my ma did," the cook told her. He then showed her a long handled implement that he told her held two pieces of bread in a wire cage. "I just hold this over the fire until the bread is lightly browned and then I flip it over. I usually don't make it for the men. It would take too much time, but you're special, Ma'am."

Hannah thanked the man and made a mental note to see if Bill had such a device in the store. It was one purchase she would be pleased to make. She was certain that her father would enjoy having toast with his morning meal.

At last Quade walked her across the parade grounds to her home. As she thought, her father had not yet returned. Without having to clean up breakfast dishes, there would be plenty of time to concentrate on sewing the new dress for Saturday night. With any luck she could have it finished by the time she needed to prepare supper.

As soon as they neared the house, Hannah felt something was terribly wrong. Even before stepping onto the porch, Quade commented that the front door was standing wide open. She was certain it had been securely locked it before she left. If her father had been home and Simon not been so threatening, Hannah wouldn't have thought twice about leaving it unlocked, but yesterday had been different.

"You wait out here," Quade suggested. "I'll go in and make certain no one is waiting to ambush you."

"No one's in there," she said. "This has to be Simon's doing. No one else would kick in the door like this." She ran her hand over the splintered wood and broken lock while Quade went in to search the house.

"I think it's best if you go back over to Rollie and Bessie's place," he said when he returned to the porch.

"What do you mean? What's wrong? Is it Papa? Did he return last night? Is he sick?" Without waiting for answers, she pushed past Quade. The kitchen was a mess, with the table turned over and chairs strewn around the room. In the parlor the dress she'd been working so hard to complete for Saturday night lay in shreds on the floor, her scissors beside them.

"Your father isn't here," Quade said, from behind her. "I don't think you should be here either. I need to report this to Rollie and you..."

"I need to clean up this mess. There's no danger in me staying here, Quade. Simon left the fort this morning and he won't return for several days. By that time I'll have this mess cleaned up and this will be but a bitter memory."

"What's going on here?" Horace demanded.

Hannah turned to see her father enter the room. His face was white with shock when he saw the mess at which she'd just been staring.

"Are you all right, Hannah? Who could have done this thing?"

She allowed Quade to explain about the problems she'd had with Simon and the jealousy that had given birth to such anger.

"Where were you when all this occurred? Did he harm you?"

Hannah crossed the room to embrace her father. "No, Papa, he didn't hurt me. After what happened yesterday afternoon, Bessie and Rollie suggested I spend the night at their house."

"Thank the Lord for such good friends. Where is Simon? I want to have this out with him."

"He left early this morning, Horace," Quade said. "I can only pray that the elders of the Cheyenne will be following him to see where he goes. If they can give us the answers we need, next month my men will be waiting to arrest him."

"And what of this? Shouldn't he be arrested for what he has done to my house, to say nothing of Hannah's new dress?"

"I'll talk to Rollie, but I think it's best if we don't allow him to know that we suspect him in this. We want to stop him from selling the supplies meant for the Indians to others and lining his pockets with the profits. I don't mean to make what he did here sound any less serious, but he will get his punishment if we don't tip our hands so quickly. I'm going to Rollie's office now and report this. Please don't let Hannah clean anything up. I suggested that she go back be with Bessie, but she refuses to leave."

Hannah watched Quade leave her house. Her first thought was of the dress that had been so important to her. Now she would have to wear one of her old dresses, as she didn't have the money to replace the fabric, nor the time to complete it before Saturday night.

As her mind spun with thoughts of what she had lost, Horace sank down into one of the chairs and cradled his head in his hands. "I knew Simon was dishonest, but I never expected him to do anything like this. I am so thankful that you weren't here when he broke in last night."

"I am too, Papa. He must have been very angry when I

locked the house. I was so frightened after he left in the afternoon that I locked myself in until Quade came to take me to dinner at Bessie's place. You were invited, but of course I knew you would be spending the night at the reservation. If you hadn't, we would have both been here and who knows what could have happened to us."

Horace nodded. For the first time he looked very old. She knew he wasn't even sixty, but every one of his fifty-eight years showed in his face and eyes. "Did the council relent? Did the elders follow Simon this morning?"

Horace looked up as though he had forgotten why he went out to the reservation the day before. "Yes, Daughter, they did. I was invited to eat the evening meal with Owl Woman and her family. She asked me many questions about you. When the business with Simon is cleared up and Crooked Snake has returned to Canada, she wants you to come out and spend some time with her. I told her that you would be teaching by then and would, more than likely, want to stay at the house they have for me at the reservation, rather than driving back and forth to the fort every day. She was overjoyed."

Hannah thought of her Cheyenne aunt. More than anything else she wanted to spend time with the woman and learn of her ways. Teaching the children and staying at the mission house would give her the opportunity.

She heard a commotion coming from the kitchen but allowed her father to investigate it. She took a moment to mourn the dress that she would never finish in time for Saturday night's dance.

~ * ~

Quade made his way from Hannah's home to Rollie's office. His mind spun with the mess he'd seen as soon as he entered the house. Simon would have to pay, but not until after they arrested him for selling the supplies to God only knew whom. It was too important to stop him exploiting the Cheyenne to charge him with what he'd done at Horace and Hannah's home.

"Where are you going?" Bill asked when he passed the store. "You look like you have the hounds of hell on your heels."

"I guess I do. Someone broke into Hannah's house last night and destroyed the dress she was working on for the dance in addition to kicking in the door, breaking the lock and ransacking the kitchen. I'm on my way to report it to Rollie."

"Hold up a minute. I'll close up the store and go with you."

Quade had to admit, he was less than pleased with getting Bill involved. Of course, he'd been the one who had told him what was going on. Hopefully, none of the enlisted men would find out. If they did there would be hell to pay when Simon returned to the fort. They might lose any opportunity to charge him with the greater crime of cheating the people he'd come here to serve.

Rollie was just as horrified at Quade's description of the damage done to Hannah's house as Bill. Together the three of them hurried back to the house so that they could see everything for themselves. At Bill's insistence, they stopped so that Elizabeth could accompany them.

At the house, Rollie ran his hand over the shattered lock and wood of the door. "It's evident he kicked it in, but of course we can't be certain it was Simon."

"Why not? Just last night you worried enough about Hannah's safety to have her stay at your house. No one would have worried if it hadn't been for Simon's threats earlier in the day."

"You don't understand, Quade. It would be our word against his. No one saw him break into the house or they would have reported it to me. He could deny it and then where would we be? It's best if we just get the damage repaired and go on as though nothing happened."

"Nothing happened!" Elizabeth declared. "Look at this mess to say nothing of what that monster did to Hannah's new dress."

Quade glanced at Elizabeth and saw that she held a piece of the fabric that Hannah had been working on yesterday in her hands.

"I'm taking Hannah over to my place right now so that we can get started on a new dress for Saturday night."

"Oh, Elizabeth," Hannah said. "I couldn't. I spent most of what I could spare on this fabric. I couldn't begin to consider spending more to buy another length. Besides, I would never have time to finish it."

"Nonsense," Elizabeth replied, taking Hannah's hand in hers. "I have a length of material that I've never made up. I thought I wanted it when it first came in and then I realized the color didn't suit me at all. Before we go back to the house we'll pay a call on Bessie. Between the three of us, we'll have your dress finished in no time."

"Listen to her, Daughter," Horace instructed. "I can clean up things here. I want you to be safely away from this house, even though Simon is no longer at the fort. By this time next month, we'll know where he goes with the supplies and be able to have him arrested and dealt with as the law prescribes."

By the time Hannah left with Elizabeth, Bill had taken the measurements of the door and decided which lock he should install. Feeling rather helpless, Quade spotted a broom in the corner of the kitchen. The least he could do would be sweep up the scraps of fabric that were meant to be a lovely dress for Hannah to wear when he escorted her to the dance on Saturday night.

Eight

By Saturday evening, Elizabeth and Bessie had helped Hannah make the most beautiful dress she had ever seen. The material that Elizabeth said she would never use was a beautiful dusty rose brocade and the pattern she produced was of the highest fashion. Although the neckline was much lower than anything Hannah ever wore before, it fit her perfectly.

To complete her outfit, she added the small gold cross her mother had given her on her sixteenth birthday. Since they had no idea the exact date, they always celebrated on the day that they had found her crying for Babbling Brook, and singing her own death song.

As she stepped into the parlor, the look of approval on her father's face lessened her doubts about the style of the dress. "You look beautiful," Horace declared. "If I were a young man and saw you enter the room, I would fall in love immediately. The color of that dress suits you perfectly."

"Do you think it's too daring?"

"Elizabeth assured me it is the fashion and the young should always be fashionable. God knows what is in your heart and sees how you conduct yourself. He does not look to see how you are dressed, nor does He make judgments by earthly standards. If that were the case, many of the Indian cultures would be forever damned for their practice of taking more than one wife. There is no way that God would ever condemn you for being so beautiful tonight."

Hannah hugged her father. A knock at the door told her that Quade had arrived to take her to the dance. Leaving her father in the parlor, she hurried to answer the door and hopefully see approval in his eyes.

To her surprise, Simon stood on the porch. "S-Simon," she stammered. "I wasn't expecting you."

"I told you I would be escorting you to the dance. I was anxious to see you in the blue dress you were working on when I left. I'm surprised to see you wearing this." He reached out to touch the fabric at the neckline of her dress, his hand dangerously close to her breasts.

"And I told you, I was escorting Hannah," Quade said, as he appeared behind Simon on the porch.

Simon's eyes became dark with anger. "So you did, but I'm certain Hannah would much sooner be seen with a man of means rather than a penniless soldier. Isn't that right, Hannah?" He moved his hand from the neckline of her dress to her arm and he tightened his grip.

"I'm going to the dance with Quade," Hannah said, defiantly.

"Can't you even face me?" Quade asked. "Or are you afraid that if you did, Hannah might turn from you and retreat to the security of the parlor? I'm certain Shirl will be more than willing to be your partner at the dance this evening. The people from the railhead arrived early this afternoon and will be coming with Bill and Elizabeth Edwards. Now, I suggest you let go of Hannah's arm and leave. You certainly aren't welcome here."

Simon loosened his grip, giving Hannah the opportunity to back away from him. "I expect at least one dance this evening,"

Simon said, as he brushed passed Quade.

"I doubt that will happen," Quade commented. "As I recall, her dance card is already full. Perhaps you'll speak to her earlier for the next dance."

Hannah breathed a sigh of relief when Simon stepped down from the porch. He was the last person she'd expected to see at her door this evening.

"Are you all right?' Quade asked.

She looked up, unaware that he'd even stepped into the room. As relief spread through her body, she fought the urge to throw her arms around his neck and allow him to hold her protectively. "I'm more confused than anything. Why would he come here? He must remember what he did in this house before he left with the supplies. Does he think we're stupid not to know he was the one behind the damage?"

"I think he's hiding behind the fact that no one saw what he did here. Who knows what goes on within the confines of his mind? At least you weren't here alone when he broke in. God only knows what he planned to do if he had found you here."

"I don't like to think about it. I've heard stories about men like him and it frightens me. What did he mean that he was a man of means?"

Quade laughed. "More than likely he got a good price for the goods he sold. I saw what was being unloaded from the wagon and it was prime beef. I hope your friends at the reservation were able to follow him. That way we can be waiting for him next month when he goes to see them. I will be interested to see who is buying these things from him. I don't want to believe it's any of the local ranchers."

"Papa says that the elders hadn't returned yet, but Simon arrived with a wagon filled with a few canned goods, some buggy flour and a side of spoiled meat. When he was questioned about it, he said that the trip from Washington to

Denver had taken so long that the food spoiled and the people would have to accept it. Papa said he thought there would be a fight, but the people know how important it is that he is brought to justice, so they said nothing."

"That's good. For this plan to work, we all have to keep quiet about what we know. I've had enough of such talk. Let me say you look beautiful tonight. The color of your dress suits you perfectly."

Hannah laughed. "Just think, if Simon hadn't destroyed my original dress, I would never have had this one. I certainly could have never been able to afford this material. Elizabeth has wonderful taste and Bill has always been one to indulge both her and their children."

"What's going on out here?" Horace asked, as he entered the kitchen. "Did I hear Simon's voice?"

"You did, but I persuaded him to leave and not bother Hannah. For as long as Simon is at the fort, I'll have a guard placed outside your house at night."

~ * ~

Lanterns blazed brightly when they arrived at the mess hall that had been cleared for the dance. There were many ranchers present. It looked like they didn't fear Crooked Snake so much that they stayed home. Long tables groaned with food that was piled on them. It was no wonder the men looked forward to these monthly dances. The quality of the food certainly was better than anything they received in the mess hall.

As soon as Quade entered the room he saw Grace engaged in conversation with Bessie. Unlike Shirl, her dress was modest and flattered her figure well. Any trace of the bruises that she'd sported only two weeks earlier was gone and she literally glowed. He wondered if it was because she was at last free of Miles or if she'd fallen in love with Sam. It wasn't hard to see that Sam was completely taken with her. The smile on his face was broad and he held her hand protectively.

"Quade, it's good to see you again," Red said, as he came to pump Quade's hand. "I see it didn't take you long to find the prettiest girl within a hundred miles of this place. Good evening, Miss Whitfield."

"Good evening, Red," Hannah replied. "I thought we had agreed that we would use first names. These dances are such informal occasions."

"Of course, Hannah."

"Have you had any run-ins with Crooked Snake, Quade?"

"None. The men said he watched while I bathed in the river after I first got here, but there's been no trouble."

"I doubt there will be, at least not from him. From what the men who come to trade tell me, he's changed his ways. Maybe it's old age, or maybe he's just had his fill of killing."

"Whatever it is, I'm not unhappy about it. It's time for peace between the Cheyenne and us. I've had many long conversations with Horace about them and we are in agreement. If we were able to work together, I am certain there is much we can learn from each other. If only the supplies that come from Washington were better, I know we would have a better relationship with them."

"Speaking of supplies, I heard that they came in. Did Simon take them out to the reservation?"

"He took something out there, but it wasn't fresh and it took him four days to do it. I know, for a fact, that Horace can drive out there and back in a day. I'd give anything to know what he does with those supplies."

Red agreed, but the conversation ended when Sam and Harlan Knops began to play and everyone took to the dance floor.

Quade was glad he'd learned to dance while he'd been in Virginia City. Without having to worry about looking awkward, he could enjoy every minute he held Hannah in his arms.

"You're a good dancer, Quade," Hannah said, after the first set. "Did you learn to dance as a child?"

"Hardly, my pa didn't hold with dancing. I think it bothered my ma, but what could she do? I didn't learn how to dance until I was sent to Virginia City. Being in a more civilized setting made dancing almost a skill and I wanted to learn. My Commanding Officer's wife took it upon herself to teach me what I needed to know."

Hannah glanced at Grace Walters. She'd asked him what brought him here and he had told her of Grace's accusations. It had been a foolish thing to do, considering he knew she would be coming to this dance. Unfortunately, telling a lie never set well with him. He was prone to tell the truth no matter what the cost to him personally.

"It wasn't Grace Walters if that's what you're thinking. At the time Major Eaton was my commander. His wife, Julia, was a wonderful woman. I liked both of them. Of course, when her husband died suddenly, she went back East. I miss them both more than I do my own parents. They were very good to me. I wish I could say the same for Grace and her husband."

"The two of you seemed cordial enough to me," Hannah said.

"We've come to a truce of sorts. She knows what she did to me was wrong and I've come to understand her motives. Miles Walters is a very abusive man. I also think he is very self-centered. He has little or no regard for anyone other than himself. When Grace boarded the train, she was terribly bruised. It wasn't hard to realize that he beat her severely before he told her to go back East."

The music began again and Red claimed Hannah as his partner. In glancing around the room, Quade saw Shirl dancing with Simon, leaving Grace standing alone. He could understand the men being reluctant to ask a stranger to dance. "May I have this dance, Grace?" he asked as he approached her.

"I'd be honored. It's a shame that Sam has to play tonight. I would enjoy a dance with him."

"Maybe we could persuade Harlan to do a number without the piano so you can get your wish. I can see that you're much happier than when we first left Virginia City. Is everyone at the railhead treating you well?"

"Very, Shirl is a good friend and Red and Sam make me feel welcome. As soon as I can get to Denver, I'm filing for a divorce from Miles. You'll never know the relief of not having to worry about what kind of a mood he'll be in when he comes home. I've almost forgotten what it was like to be beaten for no reason whatsoever."

"I thought I'd find the two of you together!"

The music stopped at the sound of Miles Walter's voice. "When I found you were gone, I waited to give you time to get to your parents' home, but when I contacted them, they had no idea you'd left Virginia City. I knew then and there that you'd run off with your lover. Of course I couldn't get a train to come anywhere near this godforsaken place, so I had to take one to Denver."

"You told me to leave, Miles. I only did—"

"That was in the heat of an argument. Everyone knows what is said in anger is usually forgotten by the light of day. It's apparent you wanted to be with your lover more than you wanted to be with me. I can't understand how you could give up the luxuries I gave you in Virginia City for this place. From the looks of things, I doubt there's even accommodations for you here. How do you like sleeping with your lover in a single bed?"

"I'm not Grace's lover and you know it," Quade said, before

Grace had a chance to answer her husband. "The only reason she's here tonight is because of the dance. It's a big occasion in these parts. We parted company as soon as I left the railhead for the fort. We wouldn't have even been together that far if we hadn't been on the same train. When will you understand that nothing happened in Virginia City except that Grace was trying to get you to pay her attention in other ways than with your fists?"

"Do you think I'm stupid enough to believe a lying son of a bitch like you? You lied to me in Virginia City and then you enticed my wife to follow you out here. She's nothing but a two bit whore and you're too blind to see it."

Miles' words shocked Quade. Before he could comment, Miles pulled his gun from the holster. "I know what I know and that is the two of you are liars. Don't think for a moment that I didn't see the way every man in Virginia City looked at my wife. You were just unlucky enough to get caught doing what they all wanted to do. The both of you are better off dead."

Quade was close enough to Miles to hear the click of the hammer. If he rushed Miles, he could easily lose his life, or worse yet, a bullet could hit Grace if Miles' gun went off in the struggle. Rather than risk Grace's life, he prayed Miles was a poor shot. Once he discharged the gun, there were others in the room that could disarm him. Since each man was made to leave his side arms at the door, it was the only way he could be assured of Grace's safety.

Without taking his eyes from Miles, he tried to reason with the man. These were the last words he would probably speak so he knew they had to count. "Look, Major, believe it or not, there was never anything between Grace and me. Her attempt to get you to see her as a desirable woman has changed the course of all our lives. If you have a problem with me, let's take it outside. These are innocent people. Don't put them in danger."

"Shut your damn mouth, Lieutenant. That's an order. I outrank everyone in this hellhole. It's time they saw what a son of a bitch you really are."

He raised his gun level with Quade's heart, causing Quade to brace himself for the impact that was certain to come. To his surprise, Mile's face went white with shock and pain. The gun clattered to the floor and Miles pitched forward. When he did, a knife protruded from his back.

Others rushed to lift him from the floor while Grace first leaned against Quade, then swooned from a combination of the tension and the amount of blood oozing from Miles' wound.

"Who threw that knife?" Rollie demanded.

"I did." Everyone turned to face Shirl. "I didn't kill the son of a bitch, if that's what you're getting at. I couldn't just stand by and watch him kill the lieutenant and Grace."

"Of course you couldn't," Rollie said. "This is one time I'm sorry we didn't allow the men to bring guns to the dance."

From across the room Quade could tell Hannah was horrified by what had just happened. He wanted to go to her and assure her that the accusations Miles made were just that accusations without merit.

"I'm dying! I'm dying!" Miles' declaration could be heard as he was carried to the doctor's quarters.

Sam took no time to come to Quade's side and take Grace from his arms. Whether she lost consciousness was a point to be debated later. For now, Sam was comforting her while she cried against his shoulder.

"Can I talk to you, Quade?" Rollie asked, indicating Quade should come to his office.

Quade nodded and prepared to follow his commanding officer. To his surprise, Red, Shirl and Grace joined him. Sam stayed behind to start playing again with Harlan.

"Now, can any of you explain what just happened in there? Major Walters made some strong accusations against both Quade and Grace."

Before Quade could speak, Grace began to tell of her lie to get Miles to pay more attention to her. "After he beat me for the last time, he told me to go back East. I can't begin to tell you what a relief it was to be away from him. I know falsely accusing Quade was wrong. I only wanted my husband to pay attention to me. I never thought he would punish Quade so severely."

"What do you have to say about this, Quade?" Rollie asked.

"If you're asking if I touched Grace inappropriately, the answer is no. Somehow I ended up in the middle of this. You saw how he is. There's no reasoning with the man, even when he's wrong."

Rollie nodded, then turned his attention to Shirl. "What do you have to say for yourself?"

"I learned a long time ago to protect myself. It's easy for a man to think he can rough me up because of what I do. Most of my customers know about my knife and that I can use it. Grace told me about that bastard she's married to. Like Quade said, he's innocent in all this. Major Walters is one man who deserves to be killed, but not by my hand."

"I agree with Shirl," Red added. "That man is trouble with a capital T. I saw the bruises he left on that poor girl. Any man who would treat a woman that way ought to be horsewhipped. Even the Cheyenne treat their women with respect and we call *them* savages."

Quade started to panic. The mention of the Cheyenne brought to mind the fact he'd left Hannah alone at the dance with Simon. Hopefully, some of the men would act as a buffer and not let him near her.

"I'm going to send a wire to Washington tonight and see

how they want this handled," Rollie said, bringing Quade out of his private thoughts. "In the meantime, I know where to find all of you. Before you leave tomorrow, I need each of you to give me a written statement. As for you, Quade, you aren't going anywhere any time soon. You'll be able to speak for yourself, if need be. For now, lets go back to the dance."

Quade waited until Rollie left the office to follow him back to the mess hall. As soon as he entered, he saw Simon standing off to one side, glaring at Bill Edwards as he danced with Hannah. Quade looked around for Elizabeth and found her dancing with Private Zimmer. His concerns for Hannah's safety had been for naught.

"Are you all right, Son?" Horace asked, as he came to Quade's side.

"Shaken, but otherwise I'm fine. I certainly never expected Major Walters to follow me to this post. I was worried about leaving Hannah here alone with Simon."

"That should have been the least of your worries. The soldiers and Bill closed ranks and wouldn't allow him to get anywhere near her. The two of us are blessed to have such good friends."

As much as Quade wanted to question Horace about what the elders had learned when they followed Simon, he held his tongue. This was neither the time nor the place for such questions.

The music stopped and Quade was pleased when Hannah joined her father. "Oh, Quade, I was so worried. I thought that man was going to kill you and Grace. I met her earlier this afternoon and I think she's a delightful person. I don't know how she was able to stand being married to a man like him. Do you think he'll be all right?"

Quade nodded. "I doubt there's any permanent damage done. Shirl knows what she's doing with that knife. I believe her when she says she didn't try to kill him."

"Well, that's a relief."

"Now that you're back to protect my daughter," Horace began. "I'm going over to the doctor's quarters to see if I can give some comfort to Major Walters. If he is as crazy as he sounds, he may find comfort in the words of our Lord. I know the two of you will enjoy yourselves."

Once Horace left the hall, Hannah suggested they get something to eat. In the excitement of the moment, Quade had forgotten about the food that was just a matter of a few feet away from them. As they started over, he realized others were heading in the same direction. A glance toward where Sam and Harlan had been playing told him they, too, had decided to take a break.

"What do you think of your soldier boy now?" Simon slurred. It was apparent to Quade the man had been partaking of the punch meant for the men that was kept in the backroom. "I knew there was a reason he was sent here. I should have guessed it was because he was involved with Grace. It was the reason they both showed up at the same time. I tell you, he's nothing but trouble. You're better off with me. At least I haven't been messin' with a married woman—that is, unless Shirl has a husband she ain't tellin' anyone about."

"Things aren't always the way they seem," Hannah said. "I believe Quade as well as Grace. This was nothing more than a cry for attention that got terribly out of hand. Now, if you'll excuse me, I'm going to get something to eat."

"It ain't right," Simon shouted. "You were supposed to be my girl. As soon as I had enough money saved, I was planning to ask you to marry me and go back East with me where I belong. I certainly don't like being stuck out here mollycoddling a bunch of murderin', thievin' savages. I deserve better, much better. I thought a government job would get me a good post in Washington. Instead, they sent me out here to this stinking hellhole."

Simon's voice was becoming louder and louder and drawing attention toward Quade as well as Hannah.

"I think you've had enough to drink for tonight, Simon," Rollie said as he approached the group. "Why don't you go back to your quarters and sleep it off?"

Instead of complying with or even answering Rollie's request, Simon doubled up his fist and took a swing at Rollie. As though they had been waiting for the confrontation, several of the men were on top of Simon as they pinned him to the floor.

"Take him to the guard house so that he can sober up," Rollie ordered. "I'll deal with him tomorrow. There's no sense in trying to reason with him while he's drunk."

Hannah watched as the soldiers took Simon away. It saddened her, but yet she knew it was what he deserved. He should have been locked up for what he did to her home, but Quade had assured her since no one had seen him do the damage, it would be hard to convict him. She would have to be content to wait until they could prove where he was selling the supplies meant for the Cheyenne. It would mean waiting another month but it would be worth it. Having Simon under arrest for what he was doing to the Cheyenne would be far more gratifying than anything else.

She felt someone touch her shoulder and turned to see Grace standing next to her. "I am so sorry for the way Miles acted. I always knew he wasn't right, but now I'm afraid he's completely crazy."

Hannah pitied Grace. She knew the woman had left a bad situation only to be found once she started a new life. The very thought of anyone beating a woman was horrifying. "We all saw the way he acted here tonight. He couldn't have been in his right mind. Couple that with what you and Shirl told me earlier today and I don't blame you for running away from him."

"That's just the point. I didn't run away. I was in love with him, even when he beat me. At least at those times, he was paying attention to me. I left because he told me to leave. To have him accuse me of running away with Quade wasn't right."

"I don't understand. How could you stay with someone who hurt you?"

"I think I can shed some light on that," Quade said. "My pa was always beating on my ma. When I asked her why she stayed she said he always told her he was sorry and she loved him. I also think there was nowhere else for her to go. As I recall, you didn't want to go back to your folks, did you Grace?"

"Not at all. My father was as bad as Miles. I would have been trading one hell for another. I've been happier in the past two weeks at the railhead than I have ever been in my life. At least there I'm treated with respect."

Even though Hannah didn't completely understand, she had a clearer picture to go by now. Having never been abused it was hard for her to understand how people could live that way.

"I agree with Quade," Horace said. "There is a reason I never speak of my family the way your mother did. Ours was not a loving family. I was but six when I saw my father kill my mother. He died in prison years later, leaving my brother and myself to be raised in an orphanage in Massachusetts. We were well cared for, but even so, my brother turned to violence. Luckily, I turned to the Lord."

Once they finished eating, the music began and Quade took Hannah out onto the dance floor. "I didn't think I'd ever get the chance to be alone with you tonight," he whispered as he pressed his lips against her ear. "I'm looking forward to walking you home."

Hannah couldn't help but smile. "You and most of the people at the dance. The ranchers will be spending the night. The men bunk in with the soldiers, while the women stay with the VanEttes and us. Bill and Elizabeth have their hands full with the people from the railhead. With renegades in the area they fear for their safety when they go home late in the evening."

"Do you think Crooked Snake is as bad as they make out?"

His question shocked her. She certainly didn't like the idea that her father was a murderer and yet the facts were there. "When I went out to the reservation with Papa last week, I talked with Owl Woman. She is the sister of Crooked Snake's wife who was killed by the soldiers. She told me that in the past Crooked Snake had been guilty of everything he's been charged with. She also said that he has changed. He's been hunting for the people, but they don't want Simon to know that is where they get their food. Crooked Snake and his sons have the weapons and are able to bring them game from beyond the reservation. If Simon were to know that, he would report to Washington that the people don't need help and of course we know that they do. She assures me that if there is any mischief going on it is the work of his sons, Growling Bear and Tall Elk, along with the young braves who are discontented with the way they are being treated. Perhaps I shouldn't have told you this, but I thought you should know."

"You can be assured everything you've told me is confidential. I want to see the Cheyenne get what they deserve as much as you do. What Simon is doing is down right wrong."

Hannah relaxed. At least her father was safe from Quade's gun, should the two of them ever meet.

~ * ~

By midnight, the exhausted partiers were ready to call it a night. Quade had learned that two of the ranchers, as well as

Red and Sam, would be sharing his quarters using their bedrolls, leaving more room for the women at the three established homes in the compound.

With the others, Quade walked Hannah to her front door. The men all kissed their wives. It made him want to take Hannah in his arms and do likewise, but he didn't want to embarrass her in front of all these people.

"Aren't you going to kiss me good night?" she asked once they were alone.

"You know I want to. I was thinking you might not be comfortable..."

"Nonsense. If you don't kiss me, these good people will be disappointed."

What did I think? Did I think she wouldn't want me to kiss her good night? "Of course, if you're certain."

Her smile reflected in the moonlight. "Yes, I'm certain. I wouldn't have asked if I weren't. I've wanted you to kiss me ever since our first dance tonight. I enjoyed being in your arms and since you were the perfect gentleman, I decided I would have to be the one to ask."

He wondered if she had ever been kissed before. It didn't matter. More than anything else he wanted to feel her lips responding to his. He just had to go slowly. She wasn't a practiced professional like the girls at the Gilded Lilly in Virginia City.

He pulled her into his arms and covered her lips with his. She leaned into the kiss, her breasts crushed against his chest. The feeling was far beyond any he'd ever experienced in the past. *Could it be because the woman is with me because she wants me and not because she's paid to be?*

"Good night, Quade," she said, once they parted. "It was a wonderful evening."

Wonderful? How could she think having someone try to kill

you was wonderful? He laughed, hoping to drive away the dark thoughts that crowded his mind. "I'll try to get someone to come here with the intention of killing me the next time we have a dance, since you enjoyed it so much."

"That's not what I meant and you know it. I enjoyed being with you."

"I'm sorry. I was trying to make a joke, since I've never been so scared in my entire life as I was scared out of my wits when Miles had that gun pointed at my heart. I enjoyed being with you as well. I just worry about the stories that might start circulating if Miles and Simon end up in the stockade together. If they do, things might not be easy for you."

"Things are rarely easy for me. Even though my parents raised me white, I have Indian blood and most people aren't kind about it. If you don't mind my heritage, I don't mind what might be said."

Quade kissed her again before leaving. As he walked back to his quarters, he thought of how he would be sharing a room with someone else for the first time since transferring to Virginia City. It could prove to be an interesting night to say the least, since he had learned to enjoy his privacy.

Nine

Sunday morning was chaotic. Horace insisted on having an early morning church service before everyone left and he and Hannah went out to the reservation. Even with the lateness of the hour after the dance, everyone, with the exception of Miles and Simon, were in attendance.

The sermon text was *Do Unto Others*, and Quade thought it fit well with what had happened at last night's dance. With the last song sung, everyone prepared to leave.

"It was good to see you again, Quade," Grace said, as she took his hand in hers. "I wrote my statement and gave it to Captain VanEtt this morning. As soon as I'm free from Miles, Sam and I are planning to be married. You'll be coming to the wedding, of course."

"I wouldn't miss it," Quade assured her as he kissed her cheek. "I'm afraid we got off on the wrong foot in Virginia City. It's clear to see that a saloon in the middle of nowhere is the best place you could have landed."

"It certainly was. From what I saw of you and Hannah, this place has been good for you as well. I'll see you next month, unless you get to the railhead before that."

Quade watched as Sam helped Grace get into the carriage. Before Sam got in beside her, he turned to Quade to shake his hand. "I must admit, I thought Grace was exaggerating about her husband. After last night, I can see why she left him. It will be interesting to see what happens to him. I hope the army won't sweep this under the rug, if you know what I mean."

Quade assured Sam it wouldn't happen that way, even thought he had his doubts about the outcome of any investigation. Major Walters was a high-ranking officer and as such would be afforded special treatment when it came time for a trial to be held. He'd seen it before. Officers tended to stick up for each other. It wouldn't surprise him if Miles wasn't given any kind of a sentence at all.

Rather than going directly to Rollie's office, he headed toward the doctor's quarters to check on Miles. "How's Major Walters this morning?" he asked as soon as he entered the outer office.

"Meaner than a two-headed snake. He was dead set on finding you to finish what he started last night, so I had to shackle him to the bed. Didn't like doing that to an officer, but there was no other choice."

Quade laughed. "I meant his wound. How bad is it?"

"Bad enough that he'll have trouble using his right arm for a while. It was deep but not life threatening. I've heard that Shirl was good with a knife, but I'd never seen proof of it before last night. Hell, I didn't even see her pull the damn thing out of the case she straps to her leg. The first I realized that anyone had done anything was when I heard the major squealing like a stuck pig."

The analogy struck Quade as perfectly matched to Miles' personality. "I suppose I should go in and see him."

"I wouldn't suggest it. He's none too fond of you at the moment. He'll be here for a couple more days before he's moved to the stockade. It's best if he's not there at the same time as Simon. Between the two of them, who knows what kind of lies they could start spreading about you. It's best not to fuel the fire, so to speak."

Quade agreed and left the office to search out Rollie. Even though he knew there would be no answer to the wire that had been sent to Washington until next week, he needed confirmation that justice would be done. Even before he got to the office, he had to pass by Rollie's house. He found Rollie and Bessie sitting on the front porch enjoying the day before the heat set in.

"I saw you leave Doc's place. Did you see Major Walters?" Rollie greeted him.

"I thought I should check on him, but Doc didn't think I should see him. Guess it's for the best. Did you get statements from everyone?"

Rollie nodded. "With what I have on him there's certain to be a court marshal and possibly jail time. He threatened your life as well as Grace's life, not to mention endangering everyone at the dance. From what I heard from Doc this morning the man still wants you dead. Should I be worried about you around my wife?"

From the look on Rollie's face, Quade knew he was only joking, but it was still hard for him to understand why Miles wouldn't believe Grace when she told him she had made everything up to make him jealous. At least making him jealous worked, but it didn't give her the end result for which she'd hoped.

~ * ~

Hannah looked forward to going back to the reservation. If she was lucky, she might even catch a glimpse of her father and brothers. She hadn't been there since the day she met Owl Woman. She certainly wanted to talk to her aunt and reinforce the memories of her mother. Before today Hannah had not come out for Sunday services. After services at the fort, she usually spent the day planning her lessons for the coming week or catching up on her reading.

Young and old alike gathered at the center of the village to greet them when they arrived. Off to one side, she saw Crooked Snake with two young men. It was apparent he felt safe with the missionary in the village. Perhaps he had even embraced the Christian God. That could account for his change of heart where the whites were concerned.

Even though she hadn't seen her father in fifteen years, she knew him immediately. She prayed Owl Woman had not betrayed her identity to him. As much as she had loved her birth parents as a child, she could never return to her native way of life. Added to that was the fact she was falling in love with Quade. As Horace and Martha's adopted daughter, she could enter his world. As Crooked Snake's daughter, she could say good-bye to any chance of happiness a life with him could provide.

Owl Woman was the first to greet here. "Come and sit with me. Your father will be busy with his sermon. It would be a shame for you to sit alone."

Hannah agreed and followed her aunt to where the women were seated. To her surprise, she recognized many of the women and even remembered their names.

She listened as those around her began to talk about the men who stood apart. "Growling Bear is so handsome. It surprises me that his wife allows him to come South each summer," Morning Star commented.

Hannah smiled at the piece of information she had inadvertently learned about the older of her two brothers. If he was married, it was more than likely he had children. Even though Growling Bear and Tall Elk were her father's sons by his first wife, she still loved them dearly. The thought of having nieces and nephews warmed her heart.

"Tall Elk has no wife," Winter Flower said. "If he were to ask me to warm his lodge I would be more than happy to do so."

"What would Soaring Eagle say?"

"The men think nothing of taking a second wife. Why should we not be able to do the same thing? I have been with no man but Soaring Eagle. I only want to know what another man is like."

Hannah realized if she had grown up with these people, she would be used to such teasing. Since she wasn't, she tried not to act shocked at what these women were saying.

As her father began the service, everyone grew quiet. It didn't take long for her to realize it was the same text he'd preached on at the fort.

"What makes your God so different from the Great Spirit, Missionary?"

Hanna immediately recognized Crooked Snake's voice. She glanced up to see her natural father standing toe to toe with her white father. She paid closer attention, hoping there would be only a verbal and not a physical confrontation. Horace was no match for Crooked Snake, either in strength or stamina.

"I am told your daughter is of the Eastern tribes," Crooked Snake continued before Horace could answer. "Have you taught her the ways of the people as well as about the Great Spirit?"

"Indeed I have. Your Great Spirit is like our God in the Old Testament. He is all-powerful. What makes the Christian religion different is that our God sent his son to earth to take on our sins. As for teaching my daughter your ways, she speaks many tongues, teaches the children and even has helped your women prepare your wonderful gift to the people for the coming winter."

"What manner of people allow white men to raise a child

away from their teachings?"

Hannah could feel the cold hand of dread tighten around her heart. To perpetuate the myth that she was, indeed, of the Chippewa people, Horace would have to make up a believable lie.

"When we adopted Hannah, we assured her people she would never forget her heritage. Since we were coming West to preach the Gospel to the tribes of the plains and beyond, they knew we would keep our word. Our daughter has learned much from each of the tribes we have ministered to. She is eager to learn the ways of all the people of this great land."

"I have been told you are a fair man. I wanted to see this for myself. I have also heard good things about your daughter. You are, indeed, a lucky man, as the white soldiers murdered my own daughter. She would be a woman now and my wife would have given me many more sons and daughters to love."

Hannah could feel a lump forming in her throat and tears prickling against her eyes. She wanted to acknowledge Crooked Snake as her father, but knew it would only cause more problems that she didn't need. Once such a declaration was made, the soldiers would insist that Horace move on and she would never be able to get to know the man who had fathered her or the brothers she so missed. As though she understood Hannah's confusion, Owl Woman reached over and clasped Hannah's hand.

"It is good that Crooked Snake confronted Horace in front of the people. They spoke of things that others would never ask. It is best that these things are brought out into the open. With Crooked Snake's acceptance of your father, none of the others will question what he says. The distrust is not of his teachings but of the white man as a whole. Everyone knows the wrongs done to the people by the Indian Agent. Those wrongs have made them fearful of anyone with pale skin."

Owl Woman's mention of Simon brought to mind the ugly scene at the dance. Not only was Simon drunk beyond the point of reason, he had also threatened Quade. The next month would be difficult to say the least. Simon would use every opportunity to disgrace Quade and possibly harm both Quade and herself. She wanted him nowhere near her, but had no choice. The close confines of the fort made it impossible for her to avoid the man. They would surely run into each other on a daily basis. She could only hope that he would spend time at the railhead and leave her alone.

Hannah hardly realized the service had ended. "Come with me," Owl Woman said. "We will share the midday meal while your father meets with the elders."

"But what of my father? He is an old man and has had nothing to eat since we shared the morning meal."

Owl Woman laughed. "The elders will not allow him to starve. This confrontation between your fathers was planned so that any who disagreed with the elders helping the soldiers would be satisfied that the whites were trying to help the Cheyenne."

"Did my father know of this?"

Owl Woman nodded. "When he met with the elders to tell them the supplies had arrived, he learned of the opposition to his plan. At the same time, Crooked Snake had joined the elders and questioned Horace about the way he was raising you. It was your father's idea to have the same discussion for all the people to hear. Since you worked with the women there has been much discussion about you. We all knew you were of the people when you were teaching the children, but no one understood why the people would allow a white man to adopt one of their own. For Crooked Snake the hurt is extremely bad, as he has mourned you and your mother since returning to the village to find it destroyed."

"You were with them when they returned. What can you tell me about that day?"

Owl Woman ladled stew into bowls for Hannah and herself, and then made a cup of tea before starting her story. "We had been gone for seven suns when we finally returned to the village. The hunting had been good and we were looking forward to a night of feasting. We were concerned when we saw no smoke and smelled no scent of cooking. The sight of the lodge poles standing naked, stripped of their coverings, was yet another sign that all was not well. The freshly covered graves were the worst to see. It was certainly not something done by the people. We knew immediately it was the work of the whites."

Hannah cried as she remembered how Horace had dug her mother's grave and Martha had grieved for the Indian woman she never knew. "It was my father and mother who buried the people. I had hid in the forest as my natural mother told me to do. When I finally came from my hiding place, I saw she was dead. I was singing her funeral song when Horace and Martha found me. They buried my mother and shed tears of sorrow as they did so. From that moment on, I knew they would love me. If they hadn't taken me, I would have surely starved for the hunters had been gone for only two days. I would have never survived until their return."

"You are right, but remember, your father, Crooked Snake, thinks you are dead. I do not know if the time will ever be right for him to know the truth. It is best if he does not see you too closely. I could arrange for you to meet your brothers, though."

"Isn't it possible they would recognize me as well?"

"It is doubtful. You must remember they were but ten and twelve winters old when all of this happened. Their mother was Sighing Wind. They were but small children when she died and your father married Babbling Brook. They were not as close to her as he was. I doubt they would see a resemblance in the same way as your father and I can."

Hannah contemplated Owl Woman's suggestion. *I've seen my brothers from a distance. Is that enough? If the chance to see them again arises, will I be able to turn it down? I wouldn't if I could be certain they wouldn't equate me with Little Hummingbird. I would be a fool not to meet them. I've always loved them, even when we moved here and I heard the stories of the way they treated the white men in retaliation for the massacre at the village.*

She had little time to think of the proposal her aunt had made as Tall Elk appeared at Owl Woman's fire. "I was hoping you would have some stew left," he said as he ladled the rich mixture into a bowl. "I always prefer eating at your fire."

"You flatter an old woman, Tall Elk. Is it possible that you have come here for more than my stew?"

"It is possible. I would appreciate meeting your lovely guest." Tall Elk's voice was as smooth as silk and his eyes mirrored his desire for her.

Hannah could feel an uneasiness encompass her being when he seated himself beside her. "You are Crooked Snake's son," she said in greeting. "I am Hannah Whitfield, the daughter of the missionary. The people speak well of you as well as your father and brother."

"Do you miss your people? My father tells me you are from the tribes far to the east? Do you miss being among those of your own blood?"

"I know no other life than that given me by my white mother and father. I have traveled with them ever since I can remember and have learned the ways of many of the tribes my father has ministered to in the west."

Tall Elk paid little attention to the bowl of stew he had seemed to desire only moments earlier. "You are far from a young maiden. In all this time has your father not accepted the proposals of the young men who have asked for you to be their wife?"

"No man has asked for such a thing from my father, for everyone I have met knows I am devoted to my father. Since my mother's death, his health has failed. I will never consider marriage as long as he needs me."

"What manner of man demands such a thing of his daughter?"

Hannah saw the lust in Tall Elk's eyes turn to anger. "It is not my father who makes such demands. I am the one who refuses to leave his side. I love him dearly."

"With such loyalty, you will make some man a good wife."

From the look on his face, she knew why the women of this village were willing to sacrifice even the bonds of marriage for this man. "I am told you also have not taken a wife and you are certainly older than me."

"Every summer I come South with my father and brother. It would not be fair to a woman to leave her alone for such long periods of time. My brother's wife is more accepting of this than I would expect, as she waits for his return and loves him without question of what he does during the summer months."

"She sounds like a good woman. Does your brother have children?"

"His wife gave him a son four winters ago and last winter she gave him a daughter. He has named her for our sister, Little Hummingbird, of whom our father spoke when he was debating your father."

Hannah swallowed down the lump that formed in her throat. Not only did she have a nephew and a niece, but also her niece carried her childhood name. "Your brother does your sister a great honor. Her spirit must surely be rejoicing."

Tall Elk leaned closer to her, and then put his hand to her

cheek. "Why do you weep at the mention of my sister? You did not know her."

"I weep for your loss. No one deserves to die as a child. I also weep for myself, for I have no such bond as your sister had with you and your brother. My parents could not have children, so all of their love has been reserved for me. When my father is gone, I will have no one." With all the will power she could muster, she fought the urge to tell Tall Elk that Little Hummingbird had not died, but had been saved by the compassion of two strangers.

"Where is your brother?" Owl Woman asked, taking the burden of further conversation from Hannah.

"He is with the young men while our father meets with the elders."

"I am honored to think you would forgo meeting with either group to come to my lodge."

Hannah knew she needed to verbally acknowledge the fact that Tall Elk had come to visit at the same time as she had come. "I too am honored," she finally said. "I have heard your name mentioned among the people. I was fearful that I would never get the opportunity to meet one of the men who has been so generous that he hunts for people other than those with which he resides."

Tall Elk reached over to touch her hand. "Do not believe all of what you hear either from the people or at the white man's fort. Both stories are undoubtedly exaggerated."

Without waiting for her to comment, Tall Elk got to his feet to walk back to where the young men were gathered.

"Did you arrange this?" Hannah asked as soon as she was certain Tall Elk couldn't hear her.

"I would not have put you in such a position," Owl Woman assured Hannah. "It is obvious Tall Elk is interested in you and with good reason. You are a beautiful woman."

"I am his sister!" she exclaimed, horrified at the very idea that her own brother could be interested in her in any other way.

"But he does not know that. He sees you as a desirable woman. You were wise to let him think you are unattainable. You have set the boundaries. He will tell the others you are not interested in marriage."

~ * ~

Crooked Snake left the council of elders. Even though he'd been one of the men who questioned the missionary when he first proposed the elders follow the Indian Agent, he had accompanied his friend Charging Buffalo. As boys, they had often hunted together. As men, the confines of the reservation separated them. When he returned in the summer, they usually managed to meet. This summer, they had been together often. Since Crooked Snake had stopped the raids on the whites, he could easily enter the village without being detected, especially since the Indian Agent rarely came to the reservation.

When the missionary first proposed his plan, Crooked Snake had questioned it. Once it was explained fully, he approved of it. He'd often wondered why the soldiers didn't do something like this before. It was possible that the new lieutenant he had watched while he bathed in the stream had something to do with it. He did agree with the elders that no one outside the council should know of the missionary's plan. As tempting as it was to put an arrow in the back of the Indian Agent, and take his scalp, he had not acted on his desires. Charging Buffalo had given the missionary his word and Crooked Snake vowed to honor it.

In following the Indian Agent, it had been like when they were young braves and had gone hunting together. The difference was that the prey they were tracking would not bring food to the people until, and if, the white soldiers held up their end of the bargain. It went against everything Crooked Snake believed in to cooperate with the whites, but Charging Buffalo was his friend. He had asked for the help of the best tracker among the people and as such he could not refuse. He only hoped the people were not being lied to as they had been in the past.

He glanced toward Owl Woman's lodge and saw his son leaving. It would be interesting to see what he thought of the Indian daughter of the white missionary. He had studied her intently while the missionary conducted his service. She was a beautiful young woman and older than most girls when they took a husband to their bed. She was the same age as his Little Hummingbird would have been, if the whites hadn't taken her from him.

Even though fifteen winters had passed since he and the other men left the village unprotected, he remembered everything about his tiny daughter. He had only to close his eyes to see her smile or hear her laugh. By the time they returned to Canada for the winter, Growling Bear's daughter would give him the same baby smiles. It would be like having his daughter back in his life, especially since she carried the same name in memory of the life that was lost.

"I have met her, Father."

Tall Elk's greeting brought to mind the fact that Crooked Snake had asked his son to meet with the young woman. "What did you think of her?"

"She is beautiful and any man would be a fool not to want her as his wife. It is a shame no man among us will ever claim her. She is dedicated to the missionary. From the way she speaks, she is more white than she is Indian. And yet, she wept openly when I spoke of my stepmother and sister. She even asked of Growling Bear's wife and children. That was what first prompted her tears. It is hard to understand why a stranger would weep over deaths that took place fifteen winters ago to people she never knew."

"Being raised by the missionary may be the cause of it. They preach compassion for all. It matters not the color of their skin."

Crooked Snake turned from his son. He needed to be alone. Even though Tall Elk didn't realize it, the words he spoke gave credence to Crooked Snake's suspicions. Ever since he'd first seen the missionary's daughter, he had fantasized that somehow Little Hummingbird had survived the attack on the village.

Hannah Whitfield wasn't grieving the deaths of strangers. She was remembering the horror of seeing everyone she loved murdered by the whites. Somehow she had survived and been taken to live with the missionary and his wife. They were the ones who had buried the people, not the white soldiers who had so heartlessly killed women, children and old men. Only the missionary had acted with compassion.

Even though his horse was picketed with the others of the village, he chose not to go to get it. He needed to think and he could only do that by walking. He headed west, away from the village until he finally came to the edge of the forest. Alone, among the trees, he could think and try to come to some conclusion as to how his daughter had survived the massacre. It mattered not how far he walked into the solitude of the forest, the answer was always the same. There was no way Little Hummingbird could have escaped when everyone else was killed.

By the time he returned to the village, the sun had sunk beyond the western horizon and twilight had fallen. Instead of retrieving his horse and riding to the camp he and his sons shared, he went directly to Owl Woman's lodge.

"I thought you left with your sons," Owl Woman greeted him.

"I have been alone, thinking. I know you are the only one who can give me the answers I seek. May I take the evening meal with you?"

"Have I ever turned you away from my fire? Of course you are welcome. What is this question that burns so on your mind?"

Crooked Snake seated himself and accepted a bowl of stew before he began to speak the words that so burned on his mind. "The white missionary's daughter is indeed of the people, but she is not from the east. Is she Little Hummingbird, or are my eyes so old they only see what they want to see?"

Owl Woman reached over to touch his arm. "They do not deceive you. She is your daughter."

"Why did you not tell me this before?"

"Because the time was not right. I prayed you would recognize her and at the same time I prayed you would not. She has lived a life far different from ours. She is no longer of the people."

"How could he take her from us?" Crooked Snake demanded.

"The attack on the village took place two suns after we left to go hunting. Babbling Brook told your daughter to hide in the forest until she told her it was safe. By the time the child returned, everyone was killed. Her mother had been struck down at the edge of the tree line. It was Little Hummingbird who found her. She was singing a funeral song when the Missionary and his wife came. They were the ones who buried the people and even though they buried no young men, they realized they could not leave her there unprotected. If they had not taken her, she could have starved, been attacked by wild animals, or worse yet, the white soldiers could have returned and taken her life."

"She should be with us! I will ride to the fort and—"

"You will do no such thing. For you to ride to the fort would be to ride to your death. What good would it do for her to watch you die? She has already lived through losing both Babbling Brook and her white mother. Would you allow her to see you killed as well? Her life is with the Missionary. If I am not mistaken, there is a young man at the fort who has claimed her heart. She has yet to realize it, but he will become very important to her. The missionary is not well. She says he coughs in the night and she is concerned that he will leave her."

"He does not look sick to me."

"It is because he does not want anyone to think he is sick. It is only when he is alone with Hannah that he admits to his weakness."

"When can I meet her?"

"Probably never. I was pleased that Tall Elk came to her, for I knew she wanted to meet him. I also knew he would not recognize her as easily as you and I."

"How long have you known?"

"The Missionary brought her here to help the women prepare the meat you and your sons brought. That was the first time I saw her and I knew immediately who her parents had been. The Missionary told her that he had promised his wife that she would know her people. That is why he came to this reservation. Even though she taught the children at the school, I had no contact with her. None of the others in the village would have recognized her as easily as I have."

"Are you saying I must be content to know she is alive and not try to see her? I do not know if I can do that."

Owl Woman got to her feet to refill his bowl. When she returned, she looked at him with compassion only the two of them understood. "You have to do just that. When you go back to Canada, do not return. Do not bring your daughter the pain of seeing you killed by the white soldiers. She grieves for what she has lost. Do not let her lose it a second time. It is enough she knows you are her father and you know she is safe and loved. Do not jeopardize her standing with the whites at the fort. Let them believe she has come from the east."

Crooked Snake finished his stew without saying anything further. He knew Owl Woman was right and yet he wanted to hold his daughter in his arms and tell her he never stopped loving her. To go back to Canada without so much as speaking to her broke his heart.

"The hour is late," he said, as he got to his feet. "It is time for me to return to my camp. I will not go to Canada until I am certain this plan the Missionary proposed has worked. Once the people are receiving the supplies that are meant for them, you will no longer need me to come back here to hunt. I will see you again before we leave this place for the last time."

Once Crooked Snake mounted his horse he did not ride in the direction of his camp. Instead, he rode toward the fort. He knew from his hiding place he could watch the comings and goings of everyone who hid behind the gates without being noticed. Perhaps he would be lucky enough to catch a glimpse of his daughter.

Ten

Quade watched as the missionary drove his carriage out the gates. No one would question the old man going to the reservation, since he made the trip almost daily. Considering Hannah rode beside him, everyone would think she had gone with her father to see if everything was in order at the school. Even though it was hotter than hell, it was almost the first of September and school would be starting soon.

"No hard feelings about the other night, Lieutenant?" Simon asked, as he stepped up to Quade's side and held out his hand. "Guess I had a little too much to drink. I know better than to think the self-righteous Miss Whitfield would have anything to do with me. I'm leaving as soon as I can for the railhead. Shirl promised me a good poke but with me being in the stockade, I didn't get it. I surely did miss a night with her."

"As long as you leave Miss Whitfield alone, I don't give a damn where you go."

Simon laughed. "After Saturday night, I've decided that tight old maid ain't worth my time. Shirl knows how to scratch my itch. I don't need some uppity Indian bitch teasing me with her smiles and then holding out at the last minute."

Quade held his tongue. Once they were able to catch Simon selling the supplies meant for the Cheyenne to... he wondered just to whom Charging Buffalo would say Simon was selling the supplies. With Simon preparing to go the railhead, he certainly wouldn't question why Rollie and Quade were riding out in the opposite direction.

"What did Simon have to say for himself this morning?" Rollie asked, when Quade entered his commander's office. "I saw him come up to you."

"He was full of apologies for Saturday night. It was about all I could do to keep from knocking him flat after what he did at the Whitfield place the other night. What time did you say we'd meet with Charging Buffalo?"

"You have a lot to learn Quade. The Cheyenne don't allow clocks to rule their lives. I told Horace we'd ride out about an hour after he and Hannah left for the reservation. That should give Charging Buffalo time to get to the meeting place. I think once you meet the man you will begin to appreciate these people more. He's hardly the savage I thought he would be."

"Then you've met him?"

"Only once, but I was impressed. He's a proud man and the leader of a proud people. He's trying to keep the peace but—"

"But Crooked Snake won't let that happen, right?"

"Horace assures me we won't have a problem with him. It's his sons that are a worry to both Charging Buffalo and me. Of course, Horace assures me they're camped far to the east of the village and the fort."

"I hope you're right. I don't want to run into any of them. I know Horace has been reassuring us that Crooked Snake has changed, but from all the stories I've heard, he's one mean cuss. Guess I'd be too if I'd lost my wife and daughter to an enemy."

By the time they left Rollie's office, Simon was leaving the fort. *At least we won't have to worry about Simon getting curious about where we're going.*

After leaving Sergeant Kelly in charge, Quade prepared to leave. Before he reached the stable, he saw a four-man guard escorting Major Walters to the stockade.

"I'm not the one you should be locking up," Miles shouted. "Why is the bitch who stuck me with her knife running free? For that matter, Lieutenant McPherson should be locked up as well. Not only did that son of a bitch lure my wife to his bed, he helped her run away from me and flaunted it in my face on Saturday night by dancing with her."

Quade decided saddling his horse could wait. He needed to set Major Walters straight before he turned the entire fort against him. He followed at a safe distance and entered the stockade, just as the door closed on Major Walters' cell.

"I'm sorry to see you in a situation like this, Major," Quade said as he stood outside the locked door. "Unfortunately, your problem is of your own making."

"Of my own making?" Major Walters repeated Quade's statement as a question. "I don't see how you can say such a thing. You were the one who took advantage of my wife. In addition to that, you took her from a life of luxury and brought her to this hellhole. You must be damn good in bed for her to leave what she had with me."

"Let's set the record straight, Major. I've never touched Grace, nor do I want to. The story she told you was meant to get you to pay more attention to her. You were the one who ordered her to leave Virginia City. I was surprised to find her on the same train with me and even more surprised when she got off at the railhead. She was only here for the dance. She left yesterday morning and is planning to marry Sam as soon as she's shed of you."

"Sam? Who the hell is Sam?"

"He plays piano at the railhead and treats her a hell of a lot better than you ever did. He doesn't beat the shit out of her.

She's an attractive woman, without the bruises on her face."

"She's lying. I never..."

"I beg to differ," Rollie said from behind Quade. "I just received answers to the wire I sent to Washington. They've had several complaints lodged against you by the marshal in Virginia City for your violent behavior. They also have had one from your post there listing you as a deserter. There will be a military guard sent here from Denver to take you back there for court marshal. At that time I'll be pressing civil charges as well. You not only put Lieutenant McPherson's life in danger but you also posed a threat to everyone at the dance on Saturday night. I doubt you'll live long enough to again be a free man."

"A deserter! Who would have charged me with such a thing? I'm a major. No one has the right to call me a deserter."

Quade could hardly believe his ears. "Did you tell Captain Phelps or your aide, Lieutenant Danks, you were leaving? Did you get permission from Washington?"

"I outrank both Phelps and Danks. I don't need to report my comings and goings to either of them. As for Washington, what the hell do they care where I go? They're too goddamn far away to know or care what goes on in Virginia City."

Quade shook his head. The man had to be mad. As an officer he knew protocol regarding leaving his post without permission.

"Maybe the military guard who comes for you can make you understand," Rollie said. "I can't see even wasting my breath on you. We have matters which require our attention, Lieutenant. There is nothing more to be done here."

"When that guard comes, I'll tell them of your insubordination, Lieutenant. Don't be surprised if you join me in that prison wagon going to Denver. I'd just as soon see you—"

The last of Miles' words was cut short by the closing of the door. None of it made sense. "Could I be taken to Denver with the major?" he asked once they were out of the building.

"On what grounds? Certainly not because of the ranting of a mad man. By the time that guard gets here, your personnel records will have arrived from Virginia City. I doubt we'll find anything to support Walters' claim. For now, we'd best get to that meeting with Charging Buffalo."

Quade agreed and followed Rollie to the stables. His stomach roiled at the prospect of meeting Charging Buffalo. He'd only met chiefs in battle. To meet this man in the hopes of working together for a common good was a bit overwhelming.

~ * ~

To perpetuate the idea that her father was going out to the reservation, Hannah went with him. Since last week, she had vowed to accompany him often. She could see that his health was failing and she didn't want him driving the entire distance alone.

For this trip, she brought along a book to keep her occupied, as she wouldn't be allowed at the meeting. She knew the area well and was pleased that there was a small grove of trees where she could enjoy the summer day, out of the heat of the sun, and read.

As soon as they arrived, she retreated to her sanctuary while here father and Charging Buffalo sat down to wait for Quade and Rollie to come. Owl Woman had told her that Crooked Snake and Charging Buffalo were good friends. Considering he would have known both of her parents, she decided she shouldn't get too close to the man. If Owl Woman could so easily recognize her, Charging Buffalo could do the same. It was best that the people of the village did not know of her connection to them. She especially didn't want Crooked Snake to equate her with the daughter he'd lost. Knowing of his reputation, she was certain there would be trouble and the one to get hurt would be her white father. She loved him far too much to have him emotionally destroyed because of her.

Overhead the birds sang and occasionally a fish jumped in the water of the river. This was what life would have been like if she'd remained with her people. That was one thing the whites lacked in their lives. They were far too busy to enjoy the sights, sounds and smells of nature.

The sound of approaching riders brought her back to the reason they were here beside this peaceful river. Rollie and Quade rode into the meeting area, both dressed in their best uniforms to give the impression that they respected Charging Buffalo. She wondered if they really respected the older man or if it was all a show as most of the people at the reservation thought.

"It is an honor to meet the great chief, Charging Buffalo," Quade said, as he stood in front of the older man. "Horace as well as my commander has told me much about you."

"I, too, have heard much about you. The missionary tells me the plan to discredit the Indian Agent was yours. Why are you so concerned with the welfare of my people, when no one before you has cared?" He shifted his gaze from Quade to Rollie.

"My commander has wanted to put an end to Simon's dishonesty for a long time, but was unable to put any plan into action. Between the two of us we came up with this plan, but the only way it would have worked was with the cooperation of your people. I have Horace to thank for persuading you to help us in this. I must say, I am most anxious to learn where Simon led you and your men."

"There were only two of us who followed him. More than that and it would have been difficult to make certain he did not lose his life. Even the elders of my people are hot tempered where that man is concerned. I took only the best tracker from the people. In this way, only one other person knows where the Indian Agent went. Even then, it was difficult to refrain from putting an arrow in his back and adding his scalp to my scalp pole. The man has taken food from the mouths of our women and children. He does not deserve to live. It was only the fact we gave our word to the missionary that stopped us. Can you guarantee he will be justly punished for his crimes against us?"

Hannah held her breath. Would Quade and Rollie be able to give Charging Buffalo the assurance he needed?

"You have our word," Rollie said. "As soon as we return to the fort with the information we receive from you today, I will wire Washington of the details of our plans for catching Simon in the act of cheating you. Once we do, the ranchers who are foolish enough to deal with him will also be punished."

Hannah watched Charging Buffalo intently. She wondered what the smile that crossed his lips meant.

"This Indian Agent is like a sly fox. When he left the fort, he drove his wagon to the west and north so that none of the soldiers would know where he went. As soon as he was out of view, he again turned his wagon and went south until he was no longer on the reservation. That was when he turned east. We followed him to a box canyon where once our people raided the wild horse herds."

"Why would he go to such a place?" Quade questioned. "Horses certainly don't buy supplies."

The old man laughed. "You are young and there is much for you to learn. When you have more experience, you will be able to better understand the motives of men like Simon. A box canyon is a perfect hiding place for the men the whites call outlaws. They have built their cabin at the far end of the canyon so that they can see their enemies. They can hold off any who come in search of them and not have to worry about attack from behind. Since we know the area so well, we were able to watch from the rim of the canyon without being seen by the outlaws.

"Can you take us to this canyon?" Quade asked.

Charging Buffalo nodded. "It is not far. If you are willing, I will take you there now so you can see where to position your men when you come to catch the Indian Agent."

Quade and Rollie both agreed. Hannah watched as the three men mounted their horses and rode away from the meeting area as though they were oblivious to her presence.

"It is time for us to return to the fort," Horace said, when Hannah reached his side.

Hannah agreed. Hannah could tell that the day had exhausted her father. He had not been well since before they came to this fort, but the mission had been all-important to him. He had especially rallied at the prospect of helping the Cheyenne put an end to Simon's thievery. Now that the plan had been put in place, he needed to rest and regain his strength.

~ * ~

Charging Buffalo's explanation of why he needed to meet with the whites alone satisfied Crooked Snake. It made sense that he didn't want the whites to take his friend into custody, for if that were to happen Crooked Snake would certainly hang for his past violence against the whites. Even so, Crooked Snake didn't trust these white men.

In an attempt to protect his friend, Crooked Snake rode in the direction of the fort. He would follow the white soldiers to the appointed meeting place. If more than two of them came to the meeting, they would have to deal with him. It would give him great pleasure to sink his arrows deep into the hearts of these soldiers.

From the hiding place he used when he and Charging Buffalo tracked the Indian Agent, he saw the missionary's carriage leave the fort. It took only a moment for him to realize his daughter occupied the carriage as well. If he'd had no reason to follow the soldiers before, he did now. This would give him an opportunity to study the young woman to whom he had given life. He couldn't help but wonder what woman's name Little Hummingbird would have chosen when the time came for her to change from child to woman. It pained him to think of her as Hannah and yet that was the name to which she answered.

It took all his restraint not to follow the carriage. Instead, he kept his vigil and waited for the soldiers to leave. As he did, he saw the Indian Agent come out of the gates and head north. It didn't take much thought to realize he was going to the railhead in order to spend the money the government sent him for doing his job and the money he received from the outlaws for the supplies he sold them. If the man weren't brought to justice, he would satisfy his desire to proudly claim his scalp.

Again the gates opened and two men rode out in the direction the missionary had gone. He recognized the young lieutenant as well as the captain. These were the men who had given their word. They were also the ones who would lose their lives if this plan did not go as they had anticipated. If justice was not served, three new scalps would adorn the scalp pole outside his lodge in Canada. It would be worth it, even though he could never return to this area again. Every soldier would curse his name and have a bullet ready to put into his heart.

Ahead of him, the two soldiers rode, unaware of him following them. He couldn't help but wonder how the whites had been able to conquer his people. He could easily kill these men since they had no idea he followed them.

As they neared the meeting place, he saw Charging Buffalo and the missionary. Standing next to Crooked Snake's friend, the missionary looked like a frail old man dressed all in black. Charging Buffalo, on the other hand, wore his finest leggings, breastplate and war bonnet. It was not that he was prepared for war, but it signified his position as the leader of his people. Even the soldiers were dressed in their finest, although he knew the heavy uniforms that denoted their rank must be hot. Even though the sun was not at its zenith, the heat seemed to rise out of the earth.

Off to one side, he saw Hannah, seated under one of the trees in the grove that stood just beyond the river. Since he had not seen her so closely before, he studied her intently. She wore a dress the color of the summer sky and her long black hair was pulled away from he face to cascade down her back. Beneath the material of the dress he could see the swell of her young firm breasts. It took little of his imaginative powers to remember the feel of Babbling Brook's breasts in his hands when they made love. It was not hard to equate her with Babbling Brook. As his second wife, she had been much younger than Hannah when he first took her to his bed.

He shook his head to rid his mind of Babbling Brook's memory. It would do no good to think about what could never be. Instead, he wanted to concentrate on his daughter. He might never have such an opportunity again. It was apparent the other men were not concerned with the young woman who sat just a little apart from them among the trees.

In her lap, Crooked Snake saw she held a white man's book, but it was clear to him that she was not reading it. From the look on her face it was easy to tell she was listening intently to what the men were saying. *Could it be that either the captain or the lieutenant had captured her heart?* From the look on her face it was easy to see that she was ready for a man's love. It broke his heart to think of her in the arms of a white man, but from what Owl Woman told him, she was more white than Cheyenne.

His attention was diverted from Hannah when the men got

to their feet and prepared to leave. He knew there was no need to follow them, since Charging Buffalo would be taking them to the box canyon where the Indian Agent had taken the government supplies. Instead, he remained behind to watch the missionary and Hannah.

Once the men rode away, Hannah got to her feet and hurried to Horace's side. Even though the man appeared to be frail, he had conducted the meeting between Charging Buffalo and the white soldiers as though he was the old shaman Crooked Snake remembered from his youth. The old man had been an ancient in Crooked Snake's eyes, but he had a commanding presence about him. He, like Horace, demanded respect from all those around him.

To Crooked Snake's surprise, once the others left, Horace's demeanor changed. He leaned heavily on his daughter as she helped him to his carriage. It was tempting to leave his hiding place to help the old man. If Hannah had not been there, he would have done just that, but he dared not give away his presence.

Even though the old man drove the carriage, Crooked Snake could see that Hannah was ready to take over the reins if necessary. Crooked Snake decided it was best he follow them back to the fort, in case they should need his assistance.

Once they were safely behind the walls of the fort, Crooked Snake went back to his camp. His sons would soon return from hunting. After they ate the midday meal, he would begin to devise a plan to make certain the whites would uphold their promise to punish the Indian Agent. If nothing else, he would take the young lieutenant hostage until he was certain the supplies meant for the Cheyenne would be delivered. With winter coming, his people needed the white man's help more than ever.

~ * ~

Quade marveled at the beauty of the land he rode across. He could see that the hunting would be good here. This wouldn't be a bad place to settle down and raise a family, but what would he do? Since becoming a soldier, he'd cultivated no useful skills. He certainly didn't want to be a farmer and he knew nothing of ranching. He wanted to do something to help the Cheyenne, but what? He decided to give the matter further thought later and concentrate on where he was going.

Charging Buffalo's English surprised Quade. The man was very articulate. If their situations were different, he knew the man would turn out to be a good friend. Perhaps, when all of this was over, he could make the first step in establishing a friendship with the older man. In doing so, he would, undoubtedly, meet the other men in the village. By doing so, he could come up with a plan to help these people and give him a reason to establish his home here.

At the edge of the canyon, they dismounted and led their horses along the ridge, being careful to stay far enough from the edge to avoid detection. The smell of smoke coming from the cabin that was situated at the end of the canyon brought a smile to the older man's lips. The outlaws were definitely still in the canyon. Leaving the horses in a grove of trees, they belly crawled to the rim to assess the area.

To one side of the shack was a corral with eight horses. That could only mean there were at least eight guns that would be trained on anyone who tried to take the men from their hideout.

"I can see that you are devising a plan, Lieutenant," Charging Buffalo said. "What is it that you are thinking?"

Quade looked up at the chief. "We don't want to alert Simon to our plans. On the morning that the supplies are due to arrive, two groups of four soldiers each will ride out to get to this destination. I will head one group and Captain VanEtt will head the other. Each will ride out in a different direction and meet here. We will surround the mouth of the canyon. It is not the outlaws who interest us, so we will be able to wait until Simon leaves with the rotted supplies to arrest him. He is our responsibility. The outlaws belong to either the sheriff or the marshal who has jurisdiction here. We will also make certain a second shipment of supplies is delivered directly to the reservation. There is no need for your people to spend another month without the provisions the government has promised to provide."

"Your plan is a good one. I will discuss it with the elders."

Quade and Rollie exchanged worried glances.

"I'm sorry, Charging Buffalo," Rollie began. "But I need you to keep our plans secret. No one but the three of us will know what will happen. The men will not be given instructions until they are ready to ride out. In that way, no one will be able to leak the information to Simon."

Charging Buffalo looked disappointed. "I will stand by your decision. No one at the reservation will know of these plans. I must trust you to do what is right for my people. The time for fighting is past. We have signed the treaty. We need to trust each other in this in order to show the people that the whites and the Cheyenne can live together peacefully."

~ * ~

Once back at the fort, Hannah heated up the soup she'd made days earlier and kept cool in the root cellar behind the house, to serve as her father's midday meal. Whoever built the houses at the fort had been wise to dig the root cellars. The men would not have appreciated the convenience nearly as much as the women, so the first people to come here must have been married men.

As soon as they finished eating, Horace went to his room to lie down. With her kitchen cleaned, she picked up her sewing and went out to the porch. The breeze promised rain soon as the clouds were already gathering in the west and the smell of rain assaulted her nostrils.

She couldn't help but think of the last time she'd sat out here sewing. Just the thought of how Simon had broken into her house and cut up her dress brought tears to her eyes. The man frightened her. She prayed whatever plan Quade and Rollie had in mind would rid the fort of Simon for good. Just thinking about it made her wonder if the next Indian Agent would be better or worse than this one.

"It certainly is hot," Elizabeth said, as she came up on the porch. "I do hope those clouds bring us some rain tonight."

"I agree," Hannah replied, setting aside her sewing. "It looks, as well as smells, like rain."

"I saw you leave with your father this morning. Did you go out to the reservation?"

Hannah knew she had to think quickly. "I was checking out the school. It has been vacant all summer. I was surprised to find neither mice nor snakes had taken refuge there." *At least I didn't have to lie. I did check out the school yesterday. In another month I can start teaching. It can't be soon enough to please me. When I'm at the reservation I don't have to worry about running into Simon every time I leave the house.*

She heard a commotion at the front gate and turned to see Rollie and Quade returning from their meeting with Charging Buffalo. She couldn't help but wonder how they thought the meeting went. Of course, she would never be so bold as to ask. She understood the success of the plan depended on secrecy.

"I saw the two of them ride out earlier," Elizabeth commented. "I wonder where they went."

"It's hard telling. I know Quade has been busy here at the fort. Maybe he wanted to get a feel for the lay of the land. I know it's the first thing Papa wants to do when we go to a new post."

"Quade is a very handsome young man. Do you have feelings for him?"

"It wouldn't do me much good if I did. I know how difficult it would be for a white man to be married to an Indian. I'm content to spend the rest of my life serving my father's ministry. I know enough to be able to continue after he is gone."

"What about marrying one of the Cheyenne?"

"I've lived this life far too long to adapt to life on the reservation. If, when something happens to Papa, I am no longer wanted here, I will find another position. I speak enough of the native tongues that I could teach on any reservation in the west."

"I didn't mean..."

"I know you didn't, but I know who and what I am and no matter how much I cared about a man I would never impose such a burden on him."

"Then you do have feelings for Quade. I just knew it. Somehow we're going to have to find a way for the two of you to be together."

Hannah laughed. "You're forgetting one very important thing, Elizabeth. Quade hasn't told me that he has feelings for me. I can't make a man love me."

"Well, if you ask me, it looked like he was taken with you at the dance the other night. He hardly let you out of his sight, with the exception of the one dance he shared with Grace Walters."

"He was being polite and saving me from having to dance with Simon. Even if he does have feelings, we hardly know each other. I certainly don't intend to push myself onto him."

Elizabeth clucked her tongue as though Hannah's fears were unfounded. This was a woman with a mission and Hannah knew that Elizabeth would not stop until she saw Quade and

Hannah happily married.

~ * ~

Crooked Snake could smell the roasting meat before he got to the camp he shared with his sons. Located deep in the woods just outside the bounds of the reservation, he felt completely safe here.

Tall Elk had already begun to eat the meat that was cooked over the open fire, while Growling Bear was nowhere to be seen.

"Where is your brother?" Crooked Snake asked, as he seated himself beside the fire.

"He is with some of the young men from the reservation. I told him you did not want us going there, but he said he didn't care."

"He is a grown man, I cannot tell him what he can and cannot do."

"Did you follow Charging Buffalo this morning?"

Crooked Snake nodded. "He met with the whites as he said he would. I followed to be certain they kept their word. I was surprised when they did as they said they would."

"Were the missionary and his daughter there?"

Crooked Snake again nodded. He knew his son was taken with Hannah, but he could allow nothing to come of it. He also could not tell him that she was the sister he had mourned for the past fifteen winters.

Before he could say anything further, he heard a horse and rider approaching the camp. Both he and Tall Elk grabbed their rifles and prepared to fend off any enemy who might have wandered into their camp. To his relief, the rider was Charging Buffalo.

"I smelled your meat. Do you mind if I join you?"

Crooked Snake smiled broadly. "You know you are always welcome in our camp. Are you not afraid to be off the reservation?"

"I would be if I hadn't met with the soldiers from the fort this morning. I took them to the box canyon. They now know where he takes the supplies."

"I know of your meeting with them," Crooked Snake said. "I watched from the security of the trees."

"Why did you watch?"

"I do not trust these whites. I did not think they would keep their word."

"But they did keep their word. I believe the captain and the lieutenant are honorable men. It is not difficult to see that the lieutenant is taken with the daughter of the missionary. She is a beautiful girl."

"Yes, very beautiful. It is a shame to see a girl of the eastern tribes live her life in the arms of a white man."

"She is more white than Chippewa. Surely you can see that."

I can see much more. I can see that she is the daughter I can never acknowledge. "I can, but I do not want to accept it. There is no use in us speaking of things we cannot change. Sit at our fire and join us for the midday meal."

Charging Buffalo seated himself at the fire and accepted a piece of meat from Tall Elk. "You have been lucky on the hunt, Tall Elk," he said after tasting the meat.

Crooked Snake ate in silence as he listened to his friend and Tall Elk speak of things that held no interest for him. He wanted to know of the plans to catch the Indian Agent, but knew better than to ask.

"Walk with me," Charging Buffalo suggested when they finished eating.

Crooked Snake got to his feet to follow his friend. He knew that Charging Buffalo had something that weighed heavily on his mind. Why else would he risk the repercussions of being caught off the reservation to come to this camp?

As soon as they were far enough from the camp that Tall Elk would not overhear their conversation, Charging Buffalo put his hand on Crooked Snake's arm, causing him to stop and look at his friend.

"Did you follow us to the canyon today?"

"There was no reason. I knew where you were going. I am anxious to know what the white soldiers have in mind."

He listened closely as Charging Buffalo told him of the plan to stop the Indian Agent's thievery.

"Do you trust these men?" Crooked Snake asked when the entire plan was revealed.

"I have no choice but to trust them. Even coming to you is breaking the pact I made with them about this. I promised that I would tell no one on the reservation of this plan."

For the first time, in longer than he could remember, Crooked Snake laughed heartily at his friend's words. "You have broken nothing, my friend. As you can see, we are not on the reservation. If you worry about the soldiers questioning you about why you were here, we will go through the forest where they do not patrol. I will enjoy my time with you now, for once I return to Canada, I will not be coming here again. I am too old to play this hunter and prey game with the white soldiers. I would sooner spend my days playing with my grandchildren than at the white soldiers fort waiting for them to put a rope around my neck or a bullet in my back."

"You're wise, my friend. The path of peace with the whites that I have chosen is not an easy one. It is difficult to see my people starving. It they did not depend on me, I would gladly return to Canada with you. I am tired of life on the reservation, but I have no choice in the matter. My people need me."

As much as Crooked Snake wanted his friend to come back to Canada with him, he said nothing. The reservation had been

Charging Buffalo's life for too many years to give it up now. Crooked Snake had noticed Charging Buffalo's skills at tracking were stale. If he had not been there to guide his friend, the Indian Agent would have noticed their presence and not led them to the box canyon. It was best if when the leaves began to fall, they parted company with only their memories of happier times to sustain them until the Great Spirit again reunited them.

Eleven

Quade stopped at the Whitfield home when he noticed the carriage was still sitting beside the house. There had to be a problem. Horace was usually on his way to the reservation by the time Quade was ready to go to Rollie's office to discuss the men's duties for the day.

Hannah immediately answered his knock at the front door. When he saw her, he was shocked by her appearance. She looked as though she hadn't slept and her eyes were red from crying.

"Is something wrong?" he asked when she stepped back to allow him entry into the kitchen.

"Papa didn't have a good night. With all that has been going on, he's exhausted."

Quade didn't understand. Horace was frail but he had no idea the man was ill. "I didn't know. Is there anything we can do?"

Hannah shook her head no. "He's been failing ever since Mama died. We both knew this would be his last post, but he insisted on making the move. These past few weeks have been very exciting for him, but now that his part in it is over, he has given in to the exhaustion."

"Aren't there medications that he can take? Isn't there anything Doc can do?"

Hannah again shook her head. "It's his heart. Even thought he's a relatively young man, the life he has lead hasn't been easy. We knew he wasn't well when we came here and now he has tried to do too much. He has already petitioned the head of the missions so that I can carry on his work. I only hope he receives an answer before it's too late."

"Are you qualified to take on such a position?"

"More so than anyone they would send here. I speak the language, I have the confidence of the people and I write most of Papa's sermons. There is only one reason they wouldn't approve me and that is because I am a woman."

Quade could see that the decision of the mission was very important to Hannah. He made a mental note to ask Rollie if there was anything they could do to assure Hannah the position she wanted.

"Do you have time for a cup of coffee?" Hannah asked when he made no comment on her previous statement.

The aroma of the coffee on the stove was tempting. "I wish I did, but perhaps another time."

Hannah smiled. "Papa would be pleased if you'd join us for supper."

"I'd be honored. I'll see you around six, if that's not too late."

"Six would be fine."

Quade turned and went back onto the porch. He couldn't help but wonder if it was Horace or Hannah who would be pleased. It certainly was pleasurable for him to think about having dinner at Hannah's table. Even with her background, he found himself attracted to her. His father would have been horrified at the thought of him bringing home an Indian for a wife, but he knew he wouldn't be going home and if he did, it could be to face charges of murdering his father. It was best if he stayed in the west.

He whistled as he crossed the parade grounds and made his way to Rollie's office. The day already promised to be hot and he chafed at the heavy material of his uniform. He certainly envied Charging Buffalo and the clothing he wore. Quade knew that the buckskin leggings the man wore were cool in the summer and warm in the winter, since they were able to breathe. He was also aware that the man wore no shirt under his breastplate. It had to be a lot cooler than his uniform shirt that was already soaked in sweat.

As soon as he entered Rollie's office he saw the telegram Rollie held in his hand. "Did you get an answer from Washington?"

Rollie nodded. "This is one of the few times I am pleased to be able to send and take telegraph messages. I certainly didn't want an enlisted man seeing this one."

Quade read the neatly printed message Rollie handed him.

> *Your concerns are noted—Additional supplies will be sent to the reservation—Wire Denver for military guard when you have Simon Leary in custody.*

"Well, that's a relief. I wondered if Washington would approve our plan."

"I think it was the head of the Department of Indian Affairs who pushed it through. I can't imagine that Simon isn't the only one making a profit at the expense of the Indians. Red commented on it at the dance last week."

"Speaking of the dance," Quade began, "how is our prisoner doing?"

"I'll be glad when that son of a bitch is out of here. He's a royal pain in my ass. Every time I turn around he is demanding that I come to the stockade. He always wants the same thing. He tells me that you should be locked up and he should be free. Hell, you're not the one who came in waving a gun or left his post without permission. He's also demanding I lock up Shirl. I don't know if he wants to use her the way Simon does or if he wants me to punish her for saving your life. Either way, I'm not dragging her back here."

Quade agreed. If it hadn't been for Shirl, he would have been dead before anyone could have stopped Major Walters. Dying over a lie told to get attention was not high on his list of priorities.

"When do you think the prison wagon from Denver will get here?" he asked.

"I expect them by the end of the week. It's a shame we won't have Simon in custody by then. It would make a second trip unnecessary."

Rollie's mention of Simon brought to mind Quade's conversation with Hannah earlier. "Did you know about Horace's health?"

"I'm afraid I do. I doubt he'll live to see Christmas. It's a shame. He's a good man and well respected among the Cheyenne."

"Hannah told me he has petitioned the mission to allow her to take over his duties. Do you think it would help if we sent letters to them as well?"

"I'm way ahead of you, Quade. I wrote to the mission before you arrived. I'm still waiting for an answer. Speaking of answers, I received a letter for you in the mail that came with the supplies. With all that's been going on I just got to open everything this morning."

Quade picked up the letter that had to be from his brother. "Thank you," he said as he prepared to put it inside his shirt to read later.

"Why don't you read your letter now. From the look on your face, I know it's been a long time since you've had word from home. I'll go out and give the men their assignments this morning."

Quade thanked Rollie and waited until he was out of the office to open the envelope.

Dear Quade,

It was good to receive your letter. Things on the farm don't change, but rest assured you didn't kill Pa before you left. He lived until last winter when he contracted pneumonia. In all that time, he never mentioned your name again.

Ma is well, she still asks of you and was pleased to get your letter. She's proud of you. I can't imagine why you were transferred from Virginia City. Was it your temper that got you in trouble or something else?

It doesn't matter. I'm married and Ella is content to continue to live with the folks. I think she was relieved when Pa died. He liked to make her life miserable, but we both know how he was.

In a few more months Ella will give me another child. We have three already. Jenny is three, Matt is two and baby John will be a year old just before the new baby is born. With each one Ella says this will be the last, but the Lord keeps blessing us. At least I will have sons to run the farm once I'm dead and gone.

Please keep writing to us. Your letters mean so much to Ma and I must admit, I enjoyed hearing of your travels and adventures.

Your brother,

Quint

Quade folded the letter and put it back into the envelope. It was good to know that he hadn't killed his father. As for his brother, was he really so ignorant as to think that God was sending them the children? Didn't he know that he had a part in it as well?

Rather than contemplate his brother's family further, he got to his feet. He needed to start his day. He knew he would eventually answer his brother's letter, but that could wait until Major Walters was in Denver and Simon was no longer cheating the Cheyenne.

~ * ~

Hannah set the table with her mother's good china, crystal, silver and linens. They were the only luxuries Martha Whitfield brought West. As she told Hannah, her parents had been quite wealthy and these were wedding gifts. Even though Horace often complained about the extravagance of these things he always enjoyed a well-set table.

"Are we entertaining tonight?" Horace asked, when he got

up from his afternoon nap.

"Didn't I tell you? I invited Quade to take supper with us."

Horace raised his eyebrows in surprise. "Are you interested in this young man?"

"Oh, Papa, you know I am, but nothing will come of it. I'm but a pleasant diversion for him while he's stationed here. Once he moves on, I'll be nothing more than a memory. Besides, my life is among the Cheyenne. I keep praying that the mission will allow me to carry on your work. It would be so important for the children to have me stay on as their teacher and for the adults to have someone they can trust."

"I know of your plans, but I also know the feelings of young men. I hope he hasn't taken liberties with you."

Her father's warning was unnecessary, but she knew he felt the necessity of voicing his concerns. "He kissed me good night after the dance, but only because I asked him to."

"In my day," Horace began, as he winked slyly, "a young lady didn't have to ask to be kissed. As I recall, I kissed your mother for the first time behind the privy of her parents' home."

Horace continued to ramble about people and places Hannah knew nothing about. It happened more and more often, especially after he'd put in a bad night. At times like these, he usually forgot about Hannah's Cheyenne heritage. He would say things like how much she favored her mother and that he could even see his mother's features in her. When he began to ramble, she merely nodded and agreed with him.

A knock at the door gave her a reason to leave her father sitting at the table alone. When she went to answer it, she saw Rollie standing on the front porch. "What a pleasant surprise," she said in greeting.

"I finally got around to sorting the mail and saw this letter for your father," Rollie replied, holding the envelope out to her.

Hannah's hands shook as she took the letter from him. The only people who ever sent them letters were those from the head of the mission. This letter could only be the one accepting or denying their request for her to continue the ministry to the Cheyenne.

"Why don't you ask Rollie to come in for a cup of coffee and a piece of pie?" Horace called, without getting up from the table. Hannah was pleased that his mind had slipped back from the past to the present.

"Don't mind if I do," Rollie said, as he stepped into the kitchen. "I never pass up a chance for a piece of Hannah's pie."

She followed Rollie and placed the letter on the table while she cut three pieces of the pie that was still warm from the over and poured three cups of coffee. When she turned back to the table, her father was tapping the envelope on the table so he could tear off one end without destroying the letter inside.

Hannah hoped Rollie couldn't hear her heart pounding in anticipation of what the letter would say. Once she set the coffee and pie on the table, she seated herself across from her father.

"My eyes aren't what they used to be," her father declared. "Would you read this to us, Hannah?"

Her hand shook as she reached for the letter.

"Maybe this isn't the time for me to stay," Rollie suggested.

"Nonsense," Hannah replied. "It's either good news or bad. Whichever it is, it will affect you and the others here at the fort."

She sat down and took a drink of coffee before she opened the letter.

Dear Pastor Whitfield,

Your years of service to the mission are commendable. It is with a heavy heart that we have read of your failing health. We have been blessed to have you doing the Lord's work.

Rest assured, we have taken your suggestion very seriously. To be honest, we had our doubts about your daughter being qualified to take over your position. It was the letters we received from both Captain VanEtt and Mr. Edwards that made us rethink our decision.

After further discussion and prayer, we have come to agree with you wholeheartedly. When the time comes, Hannah will become the missionary to the Cheyenne in your stead. It is our hope that the time is far in the future.

Yours In Christ—

Ambrose Adams

Hannah looked up at Rollie, with tears in her eyes. "You sent a letter to the mission?"

"Bill and I discussed it and we decided that Horace was right, the only person completely qualified for the position of Christian leader for the Cheyenne is you. I can't imagine anyone else coming here and adapting to the ways of the Cheyenne, to say nothing of being able to speak their language. The people love you and you hold their trust. That, my dear, is worth more than you know."

Hannah smiled at the compliment. "Thank you. This post means a lot to me. I love the children and am just getting to know the adults. I would hate to see someone coming in without any understanding of them and trying to start anew."

"Your mother would be so pleased," Horace said, as he wiped a tear from his eye. "She prayed that you would be able to carry on our work. You have done a wonderful job teaching the children, as she did for so many years. Now you will be able to do my job as well. To be truthful, I am more than ready to join you mother now that I know you will be doing the Lord's work in my stead."

"What kind of nonsense are you talking, Horace?" Rollie asked. "You'll be around longer than any of us. I just know you will."

"You are a good friend, Rollie, and I know you mean well, but the Lord is waiting for me and so is my beloved Martha. The time will come when I am called home. When it does, it will be one of the happiest days of my life, for I will know that my daughter will be able to carry on without my guidance."

Hannah fought the urge to cry bitter tears. She'd heard her father talk like this for several months now. Ever since they'd lost her mother, he'd been declaring that he was ready to go home as well. It would be hard, but it was nothing he hadn't prepared her to accept.

~ * ~

Quade saw Rollie go to the Whitfield home. He couldn't help but wonder what the letter Rollie said he had for them contained. Earlier he'd hinted that it came from the mission. Was it the letter saying that Hannah could carry on after Horace was gone? He hoped so. He certainly didn't relish the thought of someone else living in Hannah's house.

Just the thought of that house, prompted the memory of her asking him to take supper with them this evening. The mere thought of it made the idea of working in the hot sun all day bearable.

Earlier, he'd sent out a patrol to check on the box canyon. He knew full well that he did so only so that the men would be comfortable riding to that area when the time was right for them to arrest Simon. When that happened the Cheyenne could get an Indian Agent who was more sympathetic to them.

As he stood on the catwalk and watched the patrol ride out, he saw the prison wagon along with four soldiers heading toward the fort. From his vantage point he was able to see that one of the outriders was an officer. It seemed strange that an officer would accompany the prison wagon, but he had long ago stopped questioning the military.

"Riders and wagon coming," he called down to the soldiers below. "Open the gate."

He hurried down off the catwalk, to get ready to greet the prison wagon. As they rode into the compound, Quade saluted the Captain who rode with the men. His salute was met with first a surprised stare and then a salute from the mounted officer.

"See to these horses," he ordered, once the men dismounted.

"We're here to see Captain VanEtt, Lieutenant," the captain declared. "Can you direct me to his office?"

"Of course, but wouldn't you and your men like something cool to drink first? I could take you over to the mess hall, while I tell Captain VanEtt of your arrival, Sir."

"Why must you advise him? Isn't he in his office?"

"Not at the moment, Sir. He had business with the missionary and is at his home. I will be glad to get him for you."

"Very well. It was a hot and dusty ride. I just don't want to linger too long. I need to pick up the prisoner and start back to

Denver before it gets too late in the day. It's a long trip and we'd like to get a good start before it gets dark."

"I completely understand. Make yourselves comfortable in the mess hall and I will bring Captain VanEtt over promptly."

Quade again saluted and hurried toward the Whitfield home. He was just about to step onto the porch, when Rollie came out of the house.

"Is something wrong, Quade?" Rollie asked.

"The prison wagon just arrived. They must have rode like the hounds of hell were after them to get here this quickly. They want to leave immediately for Denver."

"That suits me just fine. These sooner Major Walters is out of my hair the better."

Together they hurried toward the mess hall. Quaid pointed out the new arrivals even though it wouldn't have been necessary. They were all covered with trail dust from the trip they had just made.

"I'm Captain VanEtt," Rollie said, extending his hand to the officer seated at one of the long tables.

The man got to his feet. "Captain Donaldson," he said, ignoring the salute Quade gave him when he stood up. "Your man here said you had business with the missionary. I hope it's nothing serious with the Indians. We have a long ride ahead of us and we certainly wouldn't want any trouble."

"You won't have any. I'm just curious about how you got here so quickly. Denver is father away then a two day trip."

"We were picking up two prisoners from Fort Sheridan when we received your wire. Since we were already in the area, my superiors thought it best if we continue on up here rather than go back to Denver."

"I hope you and your men found the food here satisfying.

Can we have our cook prepare something for your prisoners?"

"The prisoners are fed morning and evening and not before or after. We gave them their rations this morning and by evening they will be fed again, but thank you for your offer."

Quade liked neither this man nor the way he treated his prisoners, but held his tongue. It would do no good to question a superior officer about something that was none of his business.

"My men seem to want to linger over their meal," Captain Donaldson said, breaking into Quade's thoughts. "Would you accompany me out to the prison wagon? Then come with me to escort the prisoner from the stockade? When the men finish eating, I want to get started. I want to be out of this god-forsaken territory by nightfall."

Rollie agreed with the captain, making Quade want to retch. As much as he disliked Major Walters, Quade felt sorry for the man. He certainly wouldn't want to spend several days quartered in this particular prison wagon. Donaldson was certainly less than sympathetic to the men he was sent to bring to Denver for prosecution. He had little time to dwell on his dark thoughts as Captain Donaldson got to his feet.

"Are you ready?" he asked.

Quade again let Rollie do the talking since Captain Donaldson made it very clear that he considered Quade inferior in rank. There was no use in riling the man.

Dust devils swirled around the fort in the heat of the late afternoon. The prison wagon stood in the sweltering rays of the sun, making Quade wonder if even one stray breeze could penetrate the small barred windows that were above the heads of the prisoners.

He watched as the captain climbed to the top of the wagon

and returned to them with chains and leg irons. The large cuffs looked like they would chafe the skin in the heat.

Rollie led the way to the stockade. Once inside, he nodded to the guard. The man allowed them entry. Inside it was hotter than hell, making Quade wonder what it would be like to be locked in the prison wagon.

"I see you've come to your senses and brought the right man to the prison," Miles sneered. "I can hardly wait to have that son of a bitching lieutenant in this cell with me. It would give me great satisfaction to have him alone with me for ten minutes."

Quade shook his head at both the man's tone and the words that made him sound even crazier than before. As he stepped closer, he couldn't help wrinkling his nose at the smell of Mile's sweat soaked uniform.

"You will not be given that chance, Major," Captain Donaldson said. "I'm here to transport you to Denver for trial."

"Trial!" Miles shouted. "I'm not the one who should be on trial. What about the son of a bitch who dishonored my wife? He lured her away from my bed. There must be a law. There must be—"

"Even if what you say in true, there's been no law broken," Rollie declared. "You deserted your post and threatened Lieutenant McPherson's life, to say nothing of the lives of everyone at the dance. I have every right to press civil charges against you, but they're nothing in comparison to the charge of desertion."

"Desertion, my ass. Who the hell was I to tell that I was leaving? No one in Virginia City is ranked high enough for me to bother with."

"It's still desertion, Major," Captain Donaldson declared.

"I'm here to take custody of you."

"You're little more than a snot nosed kid. I don't have to..."

"Yes, you do, Major. Now, step back while we open the cell door and hold out your hands."

To Quade's surprise, Miles took a step backwards. He could tell that the man was formulating something within the confines of his mind. He knew Miles was ready to charge as soon as they stepped into the cell. It amazed him at how quickly Captain Donaldson acted. Before Miles could lunge toward them his wrists were manacled and the leg irons were in place.

Miles shouted obscenities as they left the stockade and walked across the parade grounds to the prison wagon flanked by Rollie and Captain Donaldson. Quade followed in deference to the men who out ranked him. It would do no good to anger Captain Donaldson by walking side by side with the man.

Once they stood at the back of the prison wagon, Captain Donaldson unlocked the door. If Quade thought the stench in Miles' enclosed cell was bad, it couldn't hold a candle to what came from the wagon. Inside he saw two men chained to the hard wooden seats.

"I have to be with two others?" Miles questioned.

"I have no need to explain things to you, but due to your rank, I will. Black Father is a renegade who was finally captured and Private Allen killed a man at Fort Sheridan. They're prisoners the same as you are a prisoner. Now get in."

Quade wondered how Major Walters would stand the trip all the way to Denver. The confines of the wagon were bad enough without the stench of unwashed bodies and the bodily functions of those who would be imprisoned with him. The humiliation would be a punishment far beyond any he could comprehend.

He watched as the men with Captain Donaldson mounted

their horses while two of them took their seats atop the wagon in order to guide the team. At Captain Donaldson's command they started toward the gates that had been opened to give them access to the road leading away from the fort.

"I don't envy Major Walters his position," Rollie said, as they watched the wagon leave the compound. "Being kept in the stockade was degrading enough, but can you imagine what that ride into Denver will be like for him?"

"I'm sure it will be far from pleasant. I just hope that the renegades that Black Feather was riding with won't take this opportunity for retaliation. I certainly don't want to think of Miles being killed by Indians. I'd much rather see him face the justice he deserves in Denver. You mentioned Black Feather. Do you think he's one of Crooked Snake's men?"

"I doubt it. From everything I've heard, Crooked Snake has no men other than the young bucks from the reservation who join up with him every summer and his sons. I've also heard that this summer, he's doing little more than hunting for the Cheyenne. I talked to several ranchers at the dance and none of them had any complaints about him. Last year at this time, I heard more complaints."

Quade let out a sigh of relief. He liked Charging Buffalo and knew he would enjoy meeting more of the Cheyenne people. He certainly didn't want to have to think about having to chase down Crooked Snake and losing the respect of these people.

~ * ~

Quade finished shaving for the second time since getting up this morning. He still couldn't shake the memory of Miles climbing into the prison wagon with his hands and feet shackled. The thought of an officer of his rank making a trip of that duration in the company of a murderer and a renegade to say nothing of the stench was troubling. Even though he had no love for the man, it was still upsetting.

As he left his quarters and started toward the Whitfield home, he saw Simon drive into the compound. From the satisfied smile on his lips, it was evident that he and Shirl had enjoyed each other's company.

"Still making those soldier boys keep this place clean I see, Lieutenant," Simon called to Quade.

"There's no sin in having clean living conditions. It pleases me to see that the men actually like having their barracks free of the lice and vermin that shared their quarters for so long. It takes very little prodding to have them keep the area clean."

Simon shook his head. "Things just ain't the same around here. Don't know if I can abide by all of this. I might just have to look for a different position. I'm not completely comfortable here."

I'm sure he isn't. He doesn't like the fact that I watch him constantly. I just hope he sticks around until the next shipment of supplies comes in for the Cheyenne. I can hardly wait to catch him in the act and send him to Denver in one of those prison wagons.

"I guess you'll do what you have to do."

Simon's laughter sounded as he drove his wagon toward his quarters at the far end of the post.

Quade continued on. He dwelled on his thoughts and the idea that within three weeks, Simon would be caught selling the supplies meant for the Cheyenne to the outlaws.

He could still hear Simon's laughter when he stepped onto the porch of Hannah's home. The aroma of a ham roasting in the oven brought back memories of the dinners his mother used to prepare when he lived on the farm in Missouri.

"Come in," Hannah called in response to his knock at the front door. The sound of her voice was like music and he could easily envision sitting across the table from her while they ate.

When he entered the kitchen, Horace got to his feet. "Hannah told me you were joining us tonight. I hope you're hungry. Hannah has outdone herself. I'm sure you'll agree that her sugar glazed ham is the best in all of Montana."

Quade did agree. Just the aroma that filled the kitchen attested to the quality of the food being prepared. He could feel his mouth begin to water in anticipation of the meal he was about to eat.

Throughout supper, the table conversation centered on the hot weather. In speaking of the summer they eventually turned to the anticipation of the hard winter to come.

"What did you think of Charging Buffalo?" Horace asked while Hannah cut pieces of pie for them.

"He seems to be an honorable man, even though I know he fought in the battle against General Custer."

"You will find that many men fight for what they believe, because they are honorable. In our war between the states, brother fought brother, but in the end they all returned to their homes, the battles forgotten. Sometimes I think that if the whites and the Indians would remember they are brothers in the sight of God things would be better."

"What about the renegades, like Crooked Snake and his sons?" As soon as he asked the question, Quade regretted it. He saw Hannah's smile fade and her body tense.

"Crooked Snake has done wrong in the past," Hannah said, joining in the conversation as she set pieces of pie in front of each of them. "The women of the village speak of it freely. For some reason he has turned his energies to hunting for the people this summer. They do not understand this change. If Simon did his job in the way the government expects him to do it, there would be no need for Crooked Snake to return from Canada in the summers."

"No need?" Quade asked. "If I were in his position, I would want to return. These are his people, his friends and his family. I can understand his desire to return to the familiar. The fact that he has not willingly gone to the reservation and has continued to seek revenge has made him a hunted man."

"Enough of this talk of renegades and revenge," Horace declared. "This summer, things have changed for Crooked Snake and his sons. I have had council with him and respect the wisdom he speaks."

To say that Horace shocked Quade by his admission was an understatement. "You've had council with Crooked Snake?"

"I most certainly have. I was not sent here to pick and choose those to whom I minister. He is a wise man who had good reasons for his anger. I have seen villages where the soldiers have killed old men, women and children, and left their bodies for the wild animals to devour their flesh. If this had happened to those you loved, would you be able to forgive and forget?"

Quade shook his head. He'd heard the story of the massacre that had robbed Crooked Snake of his wife and daughter as well as the other members of his band. In no way could he condemn the man for the anger and sorrow that must burn in his heart.

"Hopefully the plan we have come up with will put an end to the need for Crooked Snake to have to hunt for the people. If I had any say in things, the Cheyenne would have the weapons and the opportunity to hunt for themselves."

"But you don't," Hannah said, her voice filled with the

sorrow depicted in her eyes. "Washington has declared that the Indians are a threat to everyone they come in contact with. That is why they have taken away the weapons that they need to provide meat for their tables and put them on reservations that are desolate. They expect the Indians to become farmers on land that is not fit to farm."

"You make a good point. Of course, it's men like Simon who make everything worse. If only they could get someone out here who has the interest of the Cheyenne in mind, things might be different."

Hannah nodded her head. "It would be for the best, but the men who come here come because they cannot find decent work in the east see this as an opportunity to become rich off the misfortune of those they have come to serve."

While Quade and Hannah had engaged in their discussion, Horace had become very quiet. A glance at the old man told Quade that he had fallen asleep. Quade had no doubt that Hannah had seen the same thing, as she put her finger to her lips and motioned for Quade to follow her out to the porch.

"Papa tires easily," she said, as she took a seat in one of the rockers, indicating that Quade should do the same.

"Does he often fall asleep at the table?"

"This is only a recent development. I think his councils with Crooked Snake and Charging Buffalo as well as the plan he formulated with you and Rollie have taken their toll. He was failing prior to that and those things bolstered his spirits for a while. He is not a well man and desires to be with my mother."

"How old is he?"

"He will turn fifty-nine this year. I will miss him, but I know how much he misses Mother. It's time for him to go home. For a while I worried about what would happen with the mission to the Cheyenne, but I have received word from the head of the mission that they will allow me to preach in my father's stead. He has taught me well. It did help that both Rollie and Bill wrote letters requesting that I be allowed to stay on. I received confirmation of my appointment today. It takes a great load from both of our shoulders. Rollie brought the letter and asked if I would be willing to act as chaplain for the fort as well. I said I would be honored. I only hope the men are as receptive to the idea as Rollie seems to be."

Quade smiled. "A woman preacher, well if that ain't one for the books. I think it might be quite interesting to hear God's words from the female point of view. If the men have any problems with these arrangements, they'll have to answer to me. I'm looking forward to listening to your sermons."

~ * ~

Hannah watched as Quade returned to his quarters. His words of acceptance of her new position rang in her ears. She had worried when Rollie first suggested her taking on not only her father's obligations with the Cheyenne but also those at the fort. Winning Quade's support meant a lot to her.

Before he left, Quade kissed her. This time she hadn't asked him to do so. He had wanted her in his arms and his lips had brought promises of the relationship that could possibly blossom between the two of them.

When he finally entered his quarters, she returned to the kitchen. Her father had woken himself up by his snoring and had gone to bed, leaving the job of cleaning up to her. She didn't mind. Doing something as mindless as washing dishes would give her time to contemplate her new role in life.

What if, as spiritual leader to the Cheyenne, she would be required to have council with Crooked Snake? Would she be able to meet with him without blurting out the truth that she was, indeed, his long lost daughter? Could she, in all honesty, minister to the people without telling them that she was of their blood and not of the Chippewa people? These were questions without answers and ones that would only be answered when the time was right. For now, she would clean up her kitchen, read her evening devotions and go to bed to dream of being in Quade's arms in the near future.

Twelve

Quade thought about the statement he'd made regarding Crooked Snake. The idea of family brought to mind the letter he'd received from his brother. Quint had everything Quade wanted, at least what he wanted now. Quint had a wife, kids and a permanent home.

Until Quade met Hannah, he had never desired any of those things, but after spending many evenings with her, as well as her father, he wanted Hannah in his life. Horace was definitely failing. When he was gone, where would that leave Hannah? Of course she had her work, but would that be enough? Would she someday feel the need of a man to protect her? If she did, would she turn to one of the men at the reservation? She wasn't white, at least not by blood. Would she think that she needed to marry someone like herself?

He thought about his future. As a soldier, he was at the mercy of the army. At any time he could be transferred to another post. If that were to happen, he would lose Hannah. The way he saw it, there was no way he could ever ask her to be his wife.

Simon came out of Bill's store, bringing to mind the number of times Quade had followed at a discreet distance when Simon left the fort. He'd made more trips to visit Shirl than he had to the reservation. Just seeing him angered Quade. How could a man sent and paid by the government, put his personal needs before those of the people he came to serve?

Quade mentally calculated the amount of time that had passed since the last supply wagon had arrived. If he wasn't mistaken, the next shipment would be at the fort by the end of the week.

Over the past weeks, he had taken the men he'd hand picked to the box canyon. Four of the men would go with Rollie and the other four would go with him. They would be able to surround the entrance to the box canyon and capture Simon with the money from the outlaws securely in his pocket.

He saw Rollie leave the office and head his way. "It looks like you have good news," Quade greeted him.

"I certainly do," Rollie replied. "I just got this wire from Denver. Major Walter's court marshal not only stripped him of his rank, but he received five years in prison for the charges of desertion and another three for his attempt to take your life. By the time he is released, the threat will be gone. I sent a wire to the railhead, so that Grace could start the necessary steps to get a divorce so that she can marry Sam."

Quade smiled broadly. Major Walters had been the catalyst that sent him from Virginia City to Montana. For that he thanked the man, but his treatment of Grace, as well as the fact he had endangered the lives of the people at the dance, were things that couldn't be excused. He had no doubt that the man was mad.

"I can't say I'm sorry about his situation. It's what he deserves. I hope the men at Virginia City get a better commanding officer this time. They deserve the best."

"The wire said something else. Washington has cleared you of all the charges Major Walters brought against you. They have offered to send you back to Virginia City, if that's what you want. There is even talk of your promotion to the rank of Captain."

Quade thought for a moment before answering. If the offer had been made when he was on the train heading for Montana, he would have jumped at it. He hadn't liked fighting Apaches in the desert of Arizona. He knew he wouldn't want to be stuck in a frontier fort in Montana. He liked the life he'd built for himself in Virginia City. Leaving had been the hardest thing he'd ever done.

He continued to ponder the offer to return to the life he once enjoyed as well as the promotion that went with the offer. Since coming here, he'd changed his mind. He respected the old Cheyenne chief, Charging Buffalo. He liked everyone at the fort as well as the railhead, and he was falling in love with Hannah.

"Going back to Virginia City is not anything I'm interested in doing," he finally said. "My enlistment is up in another year and I'm not even certain that I want to stay in the army. I think I'm much better off where I am. By taking that promotion as well as the transfer, I wouldn't be able to do anything other than reenlist for another four years."

Rollie's smile told Quade his commanding officer had been concerned about his decision in this matter. "I was afraid we might lose you. This place is a good dumping ground for the misfits of the army. Even I came here because of a charge of drinking on duty. I was a major and was demoted to the rank of captain and sent here. I was so depressed, I didn't want to make any changes. Thank God Bessie stayed by my side. She's tried to make the best of the situation. Since you came, I've seen the changes and have decided this is a post I want to lead, but only with you as my second in command."

Rollie's confidence in him made Quade proud. After his treatment in Virginia City, he'd begun to question his ability to lead as well as his right to wear his lieutenant's bars. "I appreciate your faith in me. I'll stay until my enlistment is up. By that time this mess with Simon will be cleared up. Then I'll decide if I'll reenlist. If I don't, I might just stick around here and see what happens to the Cheyenne. I'd like to get to know Charging Buffalo better."

~ * ~

Hannah and her father drove to the reservation. They had taken several days to contemplate how to tell the elders that she was to take over her father's ministry when he was gone. Upon their arrival at the reservation, Hannah sought out Owl Woman. She knew her father would need several hours alone with the elders before she was able to join them.

"It is good to see you," the older woman said in greeting. "I didn't know if you would be returning until it was time to for the children to return to their lessons at the school. I thought perhaps meeting Tall Elk had upset you."

"That wasn't why I've stayed away. There is much I have to tell you. My father, Horace, is not a well man. It is only a matter of time before he will be reunited with my mother. We both knew this when we came here. I've always known that Crooked Snake was my father and that Growling Bear and Tall Elk were my brothers. It was my mother's dying wish that I know my people."

"What will happen when your father walks with the ancestors? Who will minister to the people? They have come to love his gentle teaching and many have accepted his God as their God."

Hannah took a deep breath. She wondered how her aunt would react to what she had to say. "I will be taking my father's place. I have been trained for this all my life. When we arrived here, Papa wrote to the head of the mission and requested that I take his place. The captain at the fort as well as the man who runs the store there also wrote letters. Now Papa is asking the elders for their permission for me to serve them."

"Do you worry about what the elders might say?" Owl Woman asked when she handed Hannah a bowl of tea.

Hannah nodded. "I want to be among the people. If they tell me that I cannot, it would break my heart. I love the children and since I have come to know the women, I have made some good friends. It is hard being at the fort all the time and knowing that my true people are here. The women at the fort are very good to me, but they aren't my people."

"I understand completely. The veiled acceptance of the whites is something that Crooked Snake could not abide. I have talked to him repeatedly about turning himself in but his anger still burned brightly. At least, it did until he returned this summer. He has changed. Perhaps it is his age, but he has declared that the time for killing has ended. I fear that he will not come back to this village once he goes back to Canada in the fall."

Owl Woman's words saddened Hannah. She had wanted to plead her father's case and allow him to spend the rest of his life on the reservation with those he loved. As the schoolteacher, she would have very little say, but as the missionary to these people, her word would carry more weight. Even Quade had listened to her when she outlined her plans to have Crooked Snake and his sons pardoned. Of course, he thought that she was only being merciful to the Cheyenne. In no way did he think that she could possibly be Crooked Snake's daughter.

"If this is what you want," Owl Woman said when Hannah did not respond to her earlier statement, "you will have to tell the people of your connection to them. Are you ready to acknowledge your father and brothers?"

The question caught Hannah completely off guard. "My

white father would be pleased if I would do so before they return to Canada for the winter. I feel if I were to reveal myself to them, I would be dishonoring the man who has raised and loved me since I was but a small child. He is very ill and I have decided to be devoted to him until he can join both of my mothers."

Owl Woman reached over to take Hannah's hand. Tears filled her eyes. "You are such a dear child. Only someone with a gentle heart would be concerned for the peace of the dying. When you do make your connection to the people known, you will find the love your white parents gave you renewed ten times over."

Tears that mimicked the ones of Owl Woman stung Hannah's eyes and ran down her cheeks. "As I told you, it was my white mother's wish that I be reunited with the people. She was a wonderful woman who never let me forget who I was or how God brought me into her life. She also told me stories of how much my people loved me. I once asked her why she didn't return me to them. She said my mother was dead and she didn't know where to find my father. She also said that the people were very angry at the whites and that for her and my father to bring me back could have ended their lives. I loved them so much that I couldn't have that happen. It was my mother who insisted that I repeat the names of my father and brothers every day so that I would never forget them. I remember sitting with her in the kitchen and repeating the story of how the white soldiers had come to kill everyone in the village while Crooked Snake, Tall Elk and Growling Bear were out with the other men hunting for food to sustain them through the long winter."

"Why has the missionary not told Crooked Snake that you are his daughter? I know the two of them met alone in council. It seems like that would have been the perfect time for him to tell Crooked Snake the truth."

"I asked him not to. Until things are better at the fort it would make life difficult for both of us. The soldiers accept me as Chippewa. I don't know how they will react when they know I am Crooked Snake's daughter. If they do not want me, I plan to move to the reservation to be closer to the children as well as my people."

She took a sip of the tea Owl Woman had given her. It relieved her that the older woman didn't press for any more information. She certainly didn't know why she'd said she was prepared to move to the reservation. For that matter, why had she said she wanted the people to know she was Cheyenne? Once she told the truth about her parents, any thought of being with Quade would be just that, thoughts. As a soldier, he would never accept her, knowing that Crooked Snake was her father. He might insist she be imprisoned and sent far away from her people and from him. The thoughts that ran through her mind were terrifying. She wanted to be with the people, but she also wanted Quade in her life. *You can't have both,* the voice of reason sounded within the confines of her mind. *If you have Quade you have to give up your people and if you make your heritage known, you will lose the man you love. Think on this very carefully before you come to any conclusions.*

"The elders want to see you Hannah," Horace said, as he joined her at Owl Woman's fire.

A flock of butterflies took up residence in Hannah's stomach as she got to her feet to accompany Horace to where the elders were meeting.

She wished they would be meeting outside, but said nothing when her father held open the flap of Charging Buffalo's teepee. Inside, the older men sat around a fire that burned brightly in the center of the dwelling and made the air hang heavy with the heat that had to exceed the warmth of the summer day.

The smell of the wood smoke brought back memories of a teepee like this one where she had lived with her parents and older brothers. The memory was one of laughter and love.

"Your father tells us you will take over his position when he dies," Charging Buffalo said as soon as she took a seat within the circle of men. "It saddens me to think of the end of his life. Even though we have known each other for a short time, I feel we have been friends for a lifetime. Do you feel you are able to continue his teachings?"

"My father is a wise man," Hannah said, after taking a moment to search for the proper words. "He has been training me to take over his mission. I never thought I would be called upon to take on this task, but I was thinking as a child who believes her parents will live forever. My father and I both speak your language and are aware of the needs of your people. It would break my heart if they sent someone here with no idea of your language or customs."

Charging Buffalo nodded and allowed another man, Screeching Eagle, to speak. "My grandchildren go to your school. They are learning more than they ever did before. I know you are a good teacher, but what does a woman know about the white man's God?"

Hannah shuddered. This was the question she knew would be asked, and yet she wondered just how she should answer it. "I know that my God loves everyone. He loves them all the same. It doesn't matter if they are men, women or children. It also doesn't matter if their skin is red, white, yellow, brown or black, he loves them all. In the past, you have worshiped the Great Spirit. He is the one God above all Gods, do you not think that the two might be one?"

Screeching Eagle stared at her in disbelief. "I have never heard anyone but the missionary explain the white man's God in such a way. You are indeed the one to take his place when he no longer walks with the living. Our people will be blessed with you teaching not only our children but also preaching about this God of yours who loves all."

Hannah breathed a sigh of relief. Having the respect of the elders would make her ministry to these people easier. After thanking them she got to her feet and left the lodge. It would not be proper for her to remain in their company as they discussed other issues of the village that needed their attention, even though they did allow her father to stay.

Outside, the summer breeze was welcome. The brightness of the sun in comparison to the dark smoky interior of Charging Buffalo's dwelling, made her blink to adjust her eyes. Once she took a moment to compose herself, she crossed the village to tell her aunt all that had transpired. Before she reached her destination, she saw Tall Elk coming toward her.

"It pleases me to see you again," Tall Elk said, when they met. "I was told you were here with your father and that you plan to take over his position after he no longer walks upon the earth."

She smiled, knowing he had been to visit Owl Woman and had received his information from her. "You have heard correctly, but don't you fear being in the village? There are many soldiers at the fort as well as the Indian Agent who would like nothing better than to see you captured and imprisoned."

"I fear neither the white soldiers nor the fool who calls himself an Indian Agent. None of them would even recognize me. It is you who consumes all my thoughts."

Before she could protest, he pulled her into an embrace. "Would you tell them where to find me?" His mouth was so close she could feel the warmth of his breath on her cheek. "I doubt it. Your father and my father have met in council and he has not told the soldiers where to find us. My father says the missionary is one of the few honorable white men he has ever met and we should respect him."

"My father is an honorable man," she replied as she squirmed to free herself from his arms. "There is but one man at the fort who does not have the best interests of your people in his heart. Trust me when I tell you that a plan is in place to have him replaced. There are many people who are trying to help your people. What I ask of you is that you talk to your father and brother and tell them to go back to Canada before they are caught. From what I have learned from the women, you are very generous to the people. I do not want to see you lose your freedom."

Tall Elk released her from his embrace, but continued to grasp her arm. "Would that upset you?"

From the look in his eyes, it was then she realized that he was attracted to her as a woman. How would he feel when he learned she was Little Hummingbird, the sister he had mourned for fifteen years?

"It would upset me more than you know. I understand your desire to be free. I also understand why you return to this area. These people are your family. I would like to see if there is a way you can live on the reservation and in harmony with the whites."

"You would have me live under the thumb of the Indian Agent? If that is what you think, you are wrong. I would not live like these people and be content to watch my family starve."

"Please, don't be angry. I only want..."

"You are more white than Indian. You do not understand us. I am happy to think that I will soon return to Canada and not have to deal with you."

He turned from her and started toward the picket line where she knew his horse must be tethered. She watched as he swung onto the back of a large roan stallion and urged the horse to a gallop as he rode away from the village. Part of her wanted to ride after him and proclaim that she was his sister. She fought her desires. If she wanted amnesty for her father and brothers it was imperative her identity remain a secret for as long as possible.

~ * ~

Crooked Snake returned from hunting and skinned the rabbits in order to cook them for the evening meal. It bothered him that neither of his sons were in camp.

While Growling Bear's anger still burned hot, he wondered if his younger son would come to tell him of the coming of the supply wagon. Considering the position of the sun, Crooked Snake wished he had scouted the wagon himself and not allowed his younger son to do so. At any minute, he expected the boy to bring the wagon into camp and announce that he had ambushed it and killed the driver as well as the guard. It had taken days of arguing to convince his son that attacking the wagon would be bad for the people. He prayed that Growling Bear hadn't gone against his wishes.

Tall Elk's desires took him to the village daily with no regard for the danger of being captured. The attraction his son felt for Hannah was, in itself, dangerous. Not only was she his sister but also she had been brought up in the white world and she was in love with the young lieutenant. Even if Charging Buffalo hadn't told him of his suspicions, he would have known that which was so easily seen at the time of the meeting between Charging Buffalo and the white soldiers.

The sound of an approaching rider put Crooked Snake on the defensive. After picking up his rifle he turned to see Tall Elk riding into camp.

"Is there a problem in the village that sends you here in such a hurry?" Crooked Snake asked.

"Only the daughter of the missionary. She looks like a woman, but I wonder if she is, in reality, a man."

Crooked Snake tried not to laugh at his older son's statement. "Why would you say such a thing?"

"She does not know the place of a woman. Instead of cooking, sewing and having babies, she is planning to take over her father's position with the people when he begins his walk with the ancestors."

"You mentioned babies, where do you think she would get babies? She has no man to give them to her."

"I would give her babies, if she didn't turn away from me when I approach her."

"She is not the woman for you. She is—" Before he could finish, Growling Bear rode into the camp.

"The supply wagon is coming toward the fort. They should be there tomorrow. We should ambush them and take the supplies to the village."

"You will do as I say. I have given my word."

"Who have you given your word to, the blue coats who murdered your wife and our sister? Why would you trust the whites?"

Crooked Snake could see the anger in his son's eyes and hear it in his voice. "Charging Buffalo asked for my help to catch the Indian Agent selling the supplies to the outlaws. I listened to the plans of the young lieutenant as well as the captain from the fort and they make sense. A second wagon of supplies is being sent to the people. When did you say the supply wagon would be at the fort?"

The exasperation in Growling Bear's eyes burned brightly. "They are far enough away from the fort that they will not arrive there until morning."

Crooked Snake nodded. "It is just as well, for in that way we can get a good night's sleep. In the morning we will ride toward the fort. When we see the young lieutenant's group leave the fort, we will follow until we can surround them. When they are at our mercy, we will bring him back here."

"And kill the others?" Tall Elk questioned.

"There will be no killing!" Crooked Snake shouted. "These men are not the ones who attacked the village and took Babbling Brook and Little Hummingbird from us. I only plan to hold the lieutenant hostage until I know the Indian Agent has been caught and is in custody. He will be my assurance that they keep their word."

He knew his sons were not happy with his directive, but they would abide by his decision. He wanted the lieutenant as a hostage, but he wanted his daughter to come to him more. *If what Charging Buffalo says is true, Hannah has feelings for the man. If she is anything like her mother, she will do everything in her power to keep him safe.*

~ * ~

Hannah rode in silence back to the fort. "Is something bothering you, Daughter?" her father finally asked.

She understood his concern. Usually she talked non-stop as they returned from the village. "It is Tall Elk."

"Your brother? Was he at the village today or did you merely hear talk concerning him?"

"He was there and when we met, he took me in his arms as though I was a young maiden in search of a husband. I asked him if he wasn't frightened about the prospect of being captured and he said no. Then he asked me if I would tell the soldiers that I had seen him in the village. I also said no. When I suggested that I would like to see him living on the reservation in harmony with the whites, he became very angry and left the village. It was all I could do not to steal a horse and ride after him to tell him I am his sister. Instead, I allowed him to ride away from me in anger."

"Your feelings are natural ones. I completely understand them. I know you do not want your true identity known until after my death, but perhaps now is the time to tell the people that you are, indeed, Crooked Snake's daughter."

"No, Father, this is not the time. Our position with the people as well as the whites is too precious to jeopardize it. I will say nothing until you are gone. In that way if the whites no longer want me as their chaplain, I will be able to move out to the reservation and live among my own people. For now it is best if no one other than Owl Woman knows my identity."

Horace agreed and urged the horse into a fast trot. With the sun sinking in the west, she knew he did not want to be away from the fort when night fell. She realized they had stayed too long in the village.

Ahead of them the gates to the fort were open, adding credence to the fact that the soldiers were comfortable that Crooked Snake had not led any raids in the area all summer. It made them believe that her father was not in the area. She knew differently. Just this afternoon, she had seen Tall Elk. If he was in the village, her father was not far away. The three of them stayed together, hidden from the whites but close enough to provide for the people.

"I was getting worried about you," Quade said, when they drove the carriage up to the house and prepared to get out.

He was immediately at her side of the carriage to assist her in getting down. The feel of his large hands on her slender waist made her wish she were free to profess the love she felt building for him.

"Our business at the village took longer than expected," Horace said, in reply to Quade's statement. "The elders were skeptical about Hannah's abilities to take over my ministry, but we eventually persuaded them that she was the best choice for the position."

Quade broke into a wide smile. "Then that means you'll be around here for a good long time."

"It looks that way. Since I have the respect of the elders as well as the children, I think the people will accept me as well. Would you like to join us for supper? I made stew before we left this morning as well as fresh bread. It shouldn't take long for me to get the stove going and reheat it."

"I'd like that. Your cooking beats the swill they serve in the mess hall. While you get started, I'll unhitch your horse and give him a rubdown."

"Thank you, Quade," Horace said. "I have no appetite. I was given refreshments at the village. I think I will go to bed and leave you two alone. It's hard to court a young woman with her father looking over your shoulder." He winked, making Hannah smile. She knew he was tired, but she also appreciated the time alone with Quade.

It didn't take long for the fire in the stove to come to life. When it did, she put the stew on to heat. While she waited for it to come to a boil, she set the table for two and sliced the bread she'd made earlier in the day. After putting out the jelly pot, she turned back to the stove to stir the stew so that it wouldn't scorch the bottom on the pan.

"It certainly smells good in here," Quade said as he entered her kitchen.

She turned in time to see him take off his hat and run his fingers through his unruly hair. "Have a seat at the table and help yourself to bread and jelly. I'll have your stew dished up in a minute."

She turned back to the stove but could feel him watching her every move. "I figured you were out at the reservation. I stopped over earlier to tell you that the scouts saw the supply wagon heading this way. They should be here by tomorrow."

A shiver of dread ran down her spine. "I'm worried about

this mission. Simon can be a dangerous man. I know he carries a rifle in his wagon. If he's cornered, he might just use it."

She put the bowls of stew on the table and took her seat across from Quade. Instead of beginning to eat, he placed his hand over hers. "I wouldn't worry about that. Simon isn't stupid. He knows if he shoots one of us there would still be nine left to either kill him or take him into custody."

Tears welled up in her eyes. "What if you're the one he shoots? How could I go on knowing that you were lost to me forever?" As soon as the words passed her lips she knew she had made a terrible mistake.

"Do you really care?" Quade asked. He tightened his grip on her hand.

Unable to lie she nodded. "I know it's wrong. I have no right—"

"What are you talking about? I'm the one who has no right to love you, but I do. I know you have your work and you love these people. I have nothing to offer you except the life of a soldier. I could never ask you to leave here and as you know I am at the mercy of the army. Just this morning I was offered a promotion and the chance to return to Virginia City."

Her tears flowed harder. She wished she'd never said anything, but it was too late. Words couldn't be taken back as though they were candy given to greedy children. "When will you be leaving?"

"I won't. I turned it down. Had the offer come while I was on the train, I would have jumped at it. Now it means nothing. I couldn't think of leaving this fort and you behind. I also like and respect Charging Buffalo and I want to do everything in my power to help the Cheyenne. That's why tomorrow's mission is so important to me."

She watched as he got to his feet and came around the table to pull her into his arms. "I love you, Hannah Whitfield. My enlistment is up in less than a year. I'm not going to join the army again. Instead, I'm going to find something to do around here. I might even try my hand at ranching but only if you'll consent to be my wife."

"Your wife? Are you certain? I'm not white. I'm—" He silenced the last of her words with a passionate kiss.

"I don't care if you're red, white, yellow or even green. It doesn't matter. What does matter is that I love you and if you'll have me, I'll make our lives ones of happiness and love."

"Oh, Quade, I love you as well. I don't want to wait for another year. I want Papa to marry us and for that to happen, we cannot wait. His time is quickly coming to an end."

Quade leaned back and looked her directly in the eyes. "That suits me just fine. My quarters are a bit cramped, but..."

She put her finger to his lips. "This house is big enough for the three of us. I know Papa would agree. Why do you think he wanted us to be alone tonight?"

"I thought the trip to the reservation had tired him."

"It did, but he's like a sly old fox. If he hadn't told us he was tired, I would have insisted he have something to eat. I'm afraid he knows me too well. He understands that I want to be alone with you."

Their supper sat on the table, getting cold but Hannah didn't care. At this moment her heart needed the nourishment of Quade's love more than her belly needed food. His kisses were something that she knew Tall Elk had wanted to give her earlier and she rejected. There would be no rejection of Quade. It wasn't necessary. This was the man who had dominated her dreams ever since she first saw him. This was the man she wanted in her life.

A knock at the door interrupted them. As much as she wanted to ignore it, she knew that since the inside door was open in order to catch the evening breeze it was impossible.

To her surprise, she found Simon standing on her doorstep. "Good evening, Hannah. I thought I'd stop by and visit, since I heard the supply wagon will be arriving tomorrow. I thought—"

Hannah sensed Quade standing behind her. "What did you think, Simon?" Quade asked.

"It doesn't matter. It looks like you beat me to it. I wonder how Washington would feel about you courting the enemy."

"I see no enemy here. The time of war with the Cheyenne is over. Neither Hannah nor the people at the reservation are any different from us."

"Have it your way, but when I get back I'll be heading up to the railhead to see Shirl. Maybe then I'll be able to send a wire to Washington. It would be a shame to see you stripped of your rank over a squaw." Simon turned and walked toward his quarters.

"Could you lose your rank because of me?" Hannah asked as she turned to face Quade.

"I doubt it. You must know by now that Simon is full of idle threats."

His warm embrace was all the reassurance she needed. They would be happy together. Even the thought of telling him of her connection to Crooked Snake didn't bother her. He loved her because of who she was, not what she was. The fact she carried Indian blood didn't seem to bother him, so she would not let it bother her either.

Thirteen

Quade left the mess hall unable to hide his annoyance with Simon any longer. In his book, Simon had no business taking meals with the men. Just because the government employed him he had no right to think he was entitled to the rations sent for the troops.

"Aren't you man enough to be in the same room with me, or are you turning into a squaw man?"

Quade turned at Simon's question. "You're accusations sound about as phony as you are. I left, not because you came in, but because I was finished eating. There's no use sitting around when I have things to do." Quade glanced toward the gate and saw the supply wagon arrive. "By the looks of things you'd best eat your breakfast. You have a wagon to load and supplies to take to the reservation."

Simon followed Quade's gaze, a sly smile on his lips. "Guess I do. We'll have this discussion again once the supplies are delivered. Maybe by that time that squaw of yours will have spread her legs for you and you'll have gotten her out of your system."

It took all the will power Quade could muster in order to not punch Simon. Instead, he watched the man return to the mess hall. Simon certainly knew how to get to him. Instead of following and causing a scene, he merely clinched and unclenched his fists in anger. *You'll get yours, Leary. I'll be the one with a smile on my face when we catch you with the money from the outlaws.*

Rather than dwelling on his anger, Quade made his way to Rollie's office. It was time to put their plan into action. He had chosen his men well. Privates Matthews, Kanter, Zimmer and Kane would accompany him while Rollie had chosen higher-ranking men to go with him. It was by mutual agreement that Corporal Collins had been told about the plan and would be left at the fort in charge of the men. After his first run-in with Collins, they had formed a friendship of sorts and Quade deemed him trustworthy. The success of this mission depended on secrecy. Even the men who would accompany them didn't know why they were going to the box canyon.

"Good morning, Quade," Rollie greeted him when he entered the office. "I saw the supply wagon pull in. Are you ready for this?"

"More than ready. That bastard has been bothering Hannah again and this morning he slandered her name and accused me of not wanting to be in the same room with him."

"Do you want to be in the same room with him?"

"Of course I don't, but that wasn't the reason I left the mess hall. I'd finished eating and nothing more. As for him, he came to Hannah's last night and—"

"And found the two of you together. He was at the office earlier and wanted me to wire Washington and tell them that you were giving comfort to the enemy. I told him to mind his own business. Of course that did raise some questions. Why were you with Hannah last night?"

"I saw her and Horace come back from the reservation and I went to help them with the horse. Hannah invited me to supper and one thing led to another and before I knew it, I asked her to marry me."

"*You what?*"

"I asked her to marry me. I know I don't have a lot to offer her, but I love her."

"Well, it's about time. Bessie has been after me to push you into asking Hannah since that first dinner party. It's been clear to everyone there that the two of you were attracted to each other. When we get back from this mission, the women will have to start planning the wedding. You two aren't going to wait too long, are you?"

"I wanted to wait until my enlistment was up, but Hannah wants to be married soon so that Horace can perform the ceremony. I can understand. He seems to fail more every day. I doubt that he'll see Christmas to say nothing of lasting another year."

"Hopefully, Hannah will spread the good news to the ladies while we're gone. For now, we'd better get going. I'll get my men together first. Give us about half an hour and follow us but go in a different direction."

Quade understood. Ever since they devised the plan they had gone over and over the way they would execute it.

Rollie went to assemble his men while Quade tried to look busy. He certainly didn't want to draw attention to the fact that he was nervous as hell about all of this. Even though no one but Rollie knew of the plan, the men had to know that something was going on. At a fort this size secrets were hard to keep. If their plan didn't work, he'd have to face Charging Buffalo and tell him they'd failed.

Waiting didn't sit well with Quade. Once the proper amount of time passed, he nodded toward the men he'd chosen to accompany him. After mounting up, he glanced at the wagon Simon was filling with supplies. There would be enough time for them to get into position before Simon would be finished and ready to leave the fort. The game of cat and mouse had begun.

Ahead of him he saw Hannah step out onto the porch to shake rugs. As much as he wanted to take her in his arms, he merely smiled at her and touched the brim of his hat in greeting. Her anxious smile and shy wave would sustain him throughout the entire mission. Once he got back they would begin to make plans in earnest. Before school started at the reservation, she would be his wife.

He thought about sending a wire to his brother when he returned. He knew it wouldn't do any good. Being a Missouri farmer, there was no way that he could leave the farm when the harvest was so close. At least he would be able to let his mother know that Hannah was going to be her daughter-in-law.

They rode far enough to the west so that they could turn and ride south before heading east toward the box canyon. Quade knew it was a round about way, but he had scouted the area many times and decided this was the best route in order to avoid running into Simon. He wanted nothing to stand in the way of his capture of Simon. This had to work. He'd given his word to Charging Buffalo as well as to the Cheyenne who populated the reservation.

"It's time that I tell you about this mission," he said, once his men were gathered together. "We're going to that box canyon we've been to before in order to catch Simon selling the supplies he gets for the Cheyenne to the outlaws that have a camp there."

"Won't we be outnumbered?" Private Matthews asked.

"We would be if we were going into the canyon, but we're going to be waiting at the mouth of the canyon in order to catch him after he has gotten the money from the outlaws. At that point it will be us against him."

"That son of a bitch," Private Zimmer spat. "I've always

wondered how he had so much money at the poker games. He keeps saying that the government doesn't pay him worth shit."

"How do we know he'll go there?" Private Kanter questioned.

"We asked the chief of the Cheyenne to follow him. We met with Charging Buffalo after the last time and he led us to the canyon. The outlaws have a cabin at the backside of the canyon, but it's not them we're interested in. Once we capture Simon, we'll alert the local marshal as to the hideout and turn their capture over to him and his men."

Quade no more than finished speaking than he heard the sound of approaching riders. At the same time he caught the glint of sunlight off the barrel of a rifle. He turned in his saddle to see three Indians approaching them, their faces painted and their rifles trained on his men.

Private Kane reached for his gun, but Quade stopped him. "Do you want to get all of us killed? If you do, draw your gun. It will never clear the holster. Now, this goes for all of you, stay calm."

"You are a wise man, Lieutenant," the oldest man of the trio said, his English surprisingly good. "I know of your mission. You will come with us. The others will continue on to complete that which you have come to do. If it is successful, you will be returned to the fort unharmed."

Quade could feel his heart pound against the walls of his chest. He was being taken hostage. These men could only be Crooked Snake and his sons. Quade swallowed hard before commanding his men.

"Do as he says," he managed to say, hoping his voice sounded composed. "This mission is too important to fail it because of one man."

"Three of you do as he says," Crooked Snake instructed. "One of you return to the fort and tell them what has happened.

Be sure you tell them that it was Crooked Snake, Tall Elk and Growling Bear who captured the lieutenant."

Quade certainly couldn't understand the man's reasoning. If he knew of the mission, he must also know that there would be no ranking officers left at the fort. Instead of questioning his captor, he nodded to his men to do as they'd been told.

He watched as Private Kane returned to the fort while the other three headed south to where they would cut to the east. Once they were out of sight, one of the younger men bound Quade's hands and took the reins of his horse. With his hands bound in front, he was able to grasp the pommel of the saddle to keep him from falling to the ground as the horses ran across the countryside.

He felt as though he had been jostled for at least a half an hour before the horses slowed to a walk and they entered a grove of trees. They carefully picked their way through the trees until they came to a clearing next to a fast running stream.

Three teepees dominated the area making Quade realize they had reached their destination, the camp of Crooked Snake. It was no wonder the patrols were never able to find where the man and his sons disappeared to when they were being chased.

One of the young men pulled him roughly from his saddle and held a large knife close to his face. *This is it. This is how I will die. In all the battles I've fought, I never expected to be killed while I was bound and unable to protect myself.*

The man smiled, making him almost handsome in appearance, as one by one he cut off the buttons on Quade's shirt exposing his chest. He closed his eyes, expecting the bite of the knife to rip open his chest at any moment. Instead, the bindings were cut from his wrists. Before he could react, the two young men grabbed his arms and pulled him away from the horses. Once he was forced to the ground, they took off his shirt and boots before making him lay on the ground while they tied his hands and feet to posts in a spread eagle position.

He watched, helplessly, as the younger men joined their father. He spoke to them in a language Quade didn't understand. Once the older man finished speaking, the other two mounted their horses and rode away from the camp.

"Where are you sending them?" Quade asked.

"That is none of your business," Crooked Snake replied.

"Why did you take me prisoner and not Captain VanEtt? I'm certainly not a very important person at the fort."

"You are important to me. We will have a long while to wait, so why don't you tell me about the daughter of the missionary?"

"Hannah? Why would you want to know about her?"

"That is my business. I have been told that you have feelings for her. Is that true?"

"Yes it's true, but what is it to you?"

Crooked Snake leaned close to Quade's face and delivered an open handed blow to his cheek. "You will learn, Lieutenant, that you are to only answer my questions, not ask ones of your own. Do you want her only to grace your bed?"

Crooked Snake's question seemed to come out of nowhere. "You're a bigger fool that I took you for." His words brought another blow to his face.

"Answer me!" Crooked Snake demanded.

"I love her," Quade managed to say, once he recovered from the pain in his cheek. "When this mission is over we plan to be married."

"She is Indian and you are white."

"She is a woman and I am a man. The color of her skin makes no difference to me. I want her for the person she is. I would never condemn her for the people who gave her life."

"In time you might see things differently."

"When I say the words to make her mine, it is not something

I would take lightly. Marriage is forever. When a man takes a wife, it should be because he loves her and plans to cherish her all through their marriage."

"Fancy words," Crooked Snake said. The way he spoke the words, made Quade cringe in anticipation of the next blow. "Would you change your mind if you knew she was Cheyenne?"

So that's what this is all about. My suspicions were right. She isn't Chippewa. Is it possible that she's the daughter that Crooked Snake has avenged for all these years?

"Not at all. I never believed she was from the east. I suspected that she was an orphaned child of one of the plains tribes. Is she your daughter?"

Again the pain of Crooked Snake's hand connecting with Quade's cheek knocked him senseless for a moment.

"I told you that you are not to ask questions. Any woman of the people who looks for love with one other than her own kind brings questions to my mind."

Quade watched as Crooked Snake got to his feet and walked back to one of the teepees. He didn't have to be a genius to realize that their conversation was finished. From the position of the sun, Quade decided it must be just past noon. Without the interchange with Crooked Snake, Quade realized the reason his shirt and boots had been removed was to expose his tender white skin to the burning rays of the sun. Instead of staring directly into it, he turned his head to one side and concentrated on his captor.

As though oblivious to Quade's discomfort, Crooked Snake built up the fire and put a rabbit on the spit to cook. The aroma of it made Quade's mouth water while the sun seemed to cook him as Crooked Snake cooked the meat on the spit.

He wanted a drink of water, but knew that the if he were to ask for it, Crooked Snake would use his request as an excuse to again hit him. Rather than suffer the pain of another blow to his already swollen face, he remained silent and tried to think of things other than the cool water that was only a few feet away in the stream.

~ * ~

Hannah watched as Quade and his men prepared to ride away from the fort. He looked so handsome on his horse that her heart pounded with the memory of his proposal last night. She'd told no one of it, but knew it was too good a secret to keep for long.

She stood on the porch, shaking her rugs and doing chores that didn't need doing until Quade and his men rode out. As he passed her house, he touched his fingers to the brim of his hat and smiled. She couldn't help the smile that tugged at her lips as she waved to him, trying to make it look like she was waving to all of the men in his group.

"Looks like the soldier boys are heading out to play," Simon said, once Quade and his men were finally away from the fort.

"They've been going out on patrol a lot lately," Hannah replied.

"If that supply wagon hadn't come, I'd stay here and protect you and your pa. It's too bad I have to take them supplies to those savages."

"They aren't savages," Hannah retorted. "If you went out to the reservation more often you would see that. They're a proud people. The whites have stolen their land and given them a worthless reservation in return."

"You really are an Indian bitch. I guess you can fool most of these morons, but you can't fool me. It doesn't matter none that you came from one to them fancy tribes in the east or that you were raised by some Bible thumper, underneath you're nothing but an Indian bitch. I wouldn't waste my time on you if I were that lieutenant. You're not worth—"

"Is this man bothering you, Miss Hannah?" Corporal Collins asked, interrupting the horrible things Simon was saying.

"We were only talking," Simon said, much too quickly.

"It sounded as though you were insulting her to me."

"You don't know these god damned savages like I do. You just don't get it. If you were with them for any length of time you'd know that you can't insult an animal. The sooner those jackasses in Washington realize that they should have eliminated the vermin years ago the better."

Before Hannah could respond, Simon stalked away. "Well, I never," she said as she watched him climb onto the seat of his wagon and slap the reins against the backs of his horses.

"Lieutenant McPherson told me to watch over you until Simon left to take the supplies to the reservation. Did he harm you?"

Hannah took a deep breath in order to regain her composure. "Words can't harm people unless they let them. I know exactly who and what Simon Leary is. It won't be long before he'll be singing a different tune. God knows what he has been doing to the Cheyenne. If he doesn't get his punishment on earth, he will surely get it in heaven."

"Well, as long as you're not harmed, I'll be on about my duties. If you need me, I'll be close by."

"Thank you, Corporal. Now that Simon is gone, I doubt that there will be any reason that I would need your assistance."

"What's all the commotion out there?" Horace called from within the house.

Hannah picked up her rugs and went into the house. When she entered the kitchen, she saw her father sitting at the table. "It was just the men going out on patrol. The supply wagon came in this morning. Rollie left with his men first and then Quade followed. By nightfall they should have Simon in custody."

Horace grinned broadly. "I certainly hope so. Speaking of Simon, didn't I just hear his voice? Was he here?"

"He was here and intent on being very insulting to me. Thank goodness Corporal Collins came by before he could get physical. I had the feeling Simon wanted to strike me."

"I will be certain to commend Corporal Collins to Rollie when he returns. If he hadn't come along there is no telling what might have happened to you."

"Please don't, Papa. There is enough bad blood between Quade and Simon without adding fuel to the fire."

"Did you and Quade have a chance to talk last night?"

Hannah beamed at her father's question. "We certainly did. He asked me to marry him."

"I wondered what took him so long. I can easily see that he's as much in love with you as you are with him. Did you consider your answer well? He could be transferred from here as quickly as he came. Would you be willing to leave the Cheyenne if that were to happen?"

"Quade said he has less than a year of his enlistment left. He was offered the chance to return to Virginia City with the rank of Captain, but he turned it down. When his enlistment is up, he plans to settle here so that we can be close to the reservation. He wanted to wait to get married, but I insisted that I wanted no one but you to perform the ceremony. We will be married as soon as we can make the arrangements."

Horace got up from his chair to embrace his daughter. "Before you even start to make them, please tell Quade who your real parents are. He has a right to know that you are Cheyenne before he commits himself to marriage and before you tell the people at the reservation that you are, indeed, one of their own."

Hannah agreed. Even so, she couldn't help but wonder what Quade's reaction would be when she told him that Crooked

Snake was her father and Tall Elk and Growling Bear her brothers. If her plan worked, she would try to get them a pardon from the government so that they could return to the reservation and be close to her.

Throughout the morning, Hannah busied herself making bread and pies for this evening's meal. She planned to invite Rollie and Betsy as well as Bill and Elizabeth. Hannah wanted the announcement of the plans she and Quade were making to be a special event.

She'd just taken the last pie from the oven and put the stew on to heat for her father's dinner, when loud voices filtered through her window. She knew it was too early for the men to be back from their mission. Something must have gone wrong. Out of curiosity, she hurried to the porch to see what had happened.

"Just like that they was on us," Private Kane said, snapping his fingers for emphasis. "It was Crooked Snake and his men. There had to be twenty of them with their rifles all trained on us. They insisted the others go on their way and that I come back here to tell everyone what happened. They took Lieutenant McPherson prisoner. I think they plan to kill him."

The thought that Crooked Snake held the man she loved prisoner sent a shiver of dread through Hannah's body. If Quade's life was to be saved, she was the only one to do it. It didn't matter if she put her own life in danger. Without Quade she didn't want to go on.

While the men were huddled around Private Kane, she would seize the opportunity to steal his horse and bolt for the still open gate. Knowing that Quade had gone west helped. She, too, would ride to the west and pray that she would find where her father and brothers had taken Quade. Although she doubted Private Kane's description of the war party that had taken Quade away, she knew she had to be prepared to face more than her father and brothers if she did find their camp.

She waited until she was certain no one was paying any attention to her. When the time was right she ran from the porch and swung onto the saddle of the horse that waited patiently to be stabled. She regretted running the horse further, but she had no choice. There were no other horses that were saddled and ready to ride.

Her skirt bunched up over her knees, but it couldn't be helped. She needed to ride as fast as possible and there wasn't time for her to change into a pair of her father's britches.

"Stop her!" someone yelled as she cleared the gate and urged the horse to a gallop.

Of the men who were left at the fort, she knew none of them would have the courage to follow her. The best men had left with Quade and Rollie. With no one in pursuit, she knew that she could prolong the explanation of why she was riding to Crooked Snake's camp for as long as possible.

She followed the trail of bent grass left by Quade and his men until she came to a spot where there was evidence of many horses crowded together in a circle. She didn't know how she was able to recognize the signs. She certainly hadn't been taught such things as a child. Nevertheless, she was able to tell that Crooked Snake didn't have twenty men with him. She could also tell that Quade's men had turned south in order to continue on to the box canyon, while another trail went further west.

It took no time for her to decide which trail to follow. Turning the horse to the west she continued following the bent grass until she came to the wooded area. As though they were waiting for her, she saw Growling Bear and Tall Elk emerge from the trees.

"You!" Tall Elk spat. "I never expected the men at the fort were such cowards that they would send a woman to look for the lieutenant."

"No one sent me. I demand to be taken to where you father holds Quade prisoner."

The words hardly passed her lips when Tall Elk dismounted and pulled her from the back of the horse. "Is he the reason you turned from me yesterday when we were in the village?"

His mouth was so close to her ear that his shouted question reverberated within her mind.

"Do you reserve your woman's soul for a white man? Is that why you did not want me? I will show you what a real man is like in the marriage bed. You will be my wife."

Before she could protest, he lifted her in his arms and threw her face down over the back of his horse. "Don't do this to me," she protested, as he swung up on the horse behind her.

"As a woman, you must learn your place," he said as he swatted her hard across the bottom. "You are mine. I lay claim to you as the spoils of battle. Before your lover dies, he will see me take you and make you my own."

"You can't! It would be wrong!"

"How would it be wrong, woman?" Growling Bear asked. "My brother is right, you are little more than the spoils of battle. It is our right to take that which belongs to our enemy. It has been so for generations."

"It is wrong, because I am your sister."

"My sister is dead," Tall Elk said as he ran his hand up her leg. He seemed disappointed to find that she was wearing drawers under her dress. "What do you know of her?"

"I know that Little Hummingbird hid in the forest when the white soldiers came and killed her mother along with all the others that were in the village. I also know that the missionary and his wife found her crying over her mother's body and singing her own death song."

"She lies!" Growling Bear declared. "No one survived. They

were all buried by the time we returned and the village was nothing more than charred ruins. If it were not so, our father would have told us. We will take her to our father and he will decide if what she says is true. If her words are lies, she will die along with the lieutenant who says he wants to help our people. I told our father that we should have ambushed the supply wagon and taken the food to the people, just as you told him that he should kill the soldiers once he took the lieutenant prisoner. He gets soft in his old age."

Tears stung Hannah's eyes. At least she knew that Quade was still alive. She'd planned to tell him about her connection to Crooked Snake and his sons privately, but she now knew that he would learn her secret while being held prisoner by her own father.

Tall Elk urged his horse forward, leaving Hannah no choice but to watch the forest floor beneath her, while her body was bounced and bruised with every step the horse took. It took all her strength to keep from crying out from the pain being inflicted on her body. She would have given anything in the world to ride astride, no matter how unladylike it looked. It would certainly be more comfortable than being bent in half and suffering as she was.

The ground beneath her turned from the brown of dried leaves from past seasons to lush green. She could smell water and wondered if they were close to their destination.

Tall Elk reined his horse to a halt and jumped down before pulling her from the back of the horse and throwing her to the ground at Crooked Snake's feet.

"What is the meaning of this?" Crooked Snake demanded as he helped Hannah get up.

She was surprised that his touch was gentle while his voice belied his anger. Afraid to look around she stared at her father praying that he would recognize her.

"This is the woman I told you about. She reserves her love for the white soldier we hold prisoner, when she should be my wife. I will take her and make her mine in front of him so that he will know that she is not what she says she is."

~ * ~

Quade opened his eyes at the sound of arguing. Even though he couldn't understand their language, he knew that Crooked Snake and his sons were fighting. It was possible that the younger men wanted him dead.

As soon as he glanced in their direction, he saw Hannah standing in front of Crooked Snake. Her dress was ripped, her hair was no longer pulled away from her face and she looked dirty. He wondered if the sun had addled his brain and was playing tricks on him. Hannah couldn't be here, she just couldn't. She was safe back at the fort and Corporal Collins was keeping watch over her as he had promised.

"No!" he heard her say. The rest of her words were spoken in the language of the Cheyenne and were lost to him.

"Believe what you want," she shouted in English. "I am your sister and—"

"And the prisoner has served his purpose," Crooked Snake said, also speaking in English. Quade decided the words were for his benefit. Otherwise they would have continued the conversation in Cheyenne. "My daughter has been returned to me. She who was dead lives."

"How do you know that she is Little Hummingbird? Perhaps she is but playing a cruel trick on you."

"I recognized her mother in her as soon as I saw her. I asked Owl Woman and she confirmed my suspicions. She told me that Hannah is devoted to the man who saved her life and raised her as his own daughter. That is the devotion of a true Cheyenne maiden. I only took the lieutenant prisoner in order to bring her to me so that she could tell me herself that she is my daughter."

"Yes, I am your daughter, but I am also the daughter of Horace and Martha Whitfield. Had they not taken me from the sight and smell of death, I would have died as well. I never forgot your names, nor would my parents allow me to forget. When my white mother died it was her wish that I return to you."

Quade quit listening. Hannah had come in order to save his life. He prayed she wouldn't lose hers in the bargain.

He knew he couldn't continue on in this vein. He had to change his thoughts and perhaps even turn them inward. The skin on his chest and arms burned like someone had poured hot bacon grease on him. His face throbbed, not only from the sun but also from the beating he had taken at the hands of his captor.

He had given up trying to strain against his bindings hours ago. It did no good. No matter how hard he struggled, he did nothing but allow the bindings to cut into his wrists until he was certain they were raw and bleeding. He was no luckier with the ones around his ankles, for although he'd been allowed to keep on his trousers, his boots and socks had been removed. The leather bindings seemed to cut into his ankles and the heat from the sun touching the tender skin that was rarely uncovered made him even more uncomfortable.

The hunger and thirst that plagued his body drove him into delirium. In such a state, he slipped into the blessedness of unconsciousness. The black void that produced pleasant dreams was a welcome relief from the pain of his burned and bruised skin.

Fourteen

As much as Hannah wanted to run to Quade's side, she did as her father and brothers expected her to do and sat down at the fire. It was apparent that her father had cooked meat earlier and she couldn't help but wonder if he'd given any of it to Quade.

She watched as Growling Bear expertly put the carcass of a young rabbit onto a spit and place it over the fire. Hannah knew she had much to learn about the people of her birth. She wouldn't be able to so deftly handle the raw meat. She was used to frying meat on top of the stove or roasting it in the oven. Her training had not been in how to cook over an open fire. If she'd been raised Cheyenne, things would have been different.

"Tell me what you remember of the attack," Crooked Snake instructed, once he handed her a piece of the cooked meat.

"Mother and I were heading toward the woods to go berry picking. It was very early in the morning and she wanted to finish before the sun grew too hot." She paused looking over at Quade. He'd been out in the sun too long, but she knew it was not her place to say anything until her family allowed it. "When we heard the sounds of rifle fire and hoof beats mingled with the screams of the dying, she told me to run deeply into the forest and hide. I did what she told me and ran until I found a hollow tree. The opening was just large enough for me to squeeze inside and be hidden completely from view. I must have fallen asleep for when I awoke it was just prior to dawn. I thought I had hidden so well that Mother could not find me. As I walked out of the forest, I tripped over a log only to realize that it was a body. It was Mother's body. I didn't know what to do, so I tried to sing a funeral song for her. When I saw a wagon coming toward me, I changed the song to my own funeral song. Of course, I had no reason to fear for the wagon carried Horace and Martha. They gave me food and water and took me away from the newly dug graves of Mother as well as the other people I knew and loved."

"Why did you go with them?" Growling Bear accused. "You should have known we would return to look for you."

"I was a child of only five winters. I had no concept of time. I had been hiding in the forest for almost an entire day. I was hungry and thirsty. I did not know how long it would be before your return nor did I know if you would ever return. If the white soldiers had found the village and killed everyone I knew, had they also found the hunting party and done the same to them? Would you have had me stay there and starve to death?"

"Your sister is right," Crooked Snake said. "The missionary and his wife had compassion for her as well as for the people. It had to have been the two of them who buried the people so that the wild animals could not feed upon their flesh. It was better that they were buried with honor, even if it was by a white man who prayed to the white man's God for their safe journey to the afterlife. Can you tell us of your life in the household of the missionary?"

Hannah again glanced at Quade. He no longer looked at her and she wondered if he was unconscious or if he was so disgusted by the thought that she was the daughter of the man who held him prisoner that he couldn't stand to see her face.

"I was very frightened when they took me away from the village, but I knew they meant me no harm. They were very patient in teaching me to speak their language and at the same time they learned Cheyenne. We taught each other. From there we continued on until we came to the village of the Crow. There they began their ministry. It amazed me that they were able to speak the language and insisted I learn it as well since my playmates were the children from the village. We never stayed with one tribe for any length of time. I learned many languages and I also learned to read and write English and to believe in the God who sent his only son to die for our sins."

"What of the Great Spirit?" Tall Elk inquired. His tone told her he was still skeptical of her declaration that she was his sister.

"We learned of the Great Spirit, the one great God who ruled all of the people, no matter which tribe they belonged to. After many hours of prayer, Father decided that although each people had a different name for this God, they were all the same. Each was the God that we loved and preached. He has never changed his mind about that and neither have I. When I met with the elders at the reservation they asked the same question and I gave them the same answer."

"Why would you choose to preach like a man rather than do the things that all women do?" Tall Elk asked. "I would have willingly given you babies and taken care of all your needs."

"So you have said, but we both know that is impossible, not

only am I your sister and such a union would be an abomination to the people, but I do not love you."

"What does love have to do with anything?" Growling Bear questioned. "I did not love my wife until after we were joined together for life."

"For me, love is very important. I remembered that our father loved my mother and was loving to me. Added to that was the love that Martha and Horace shared. They had been together for over twenty years before I came into their lives. In all that time, even though they couldn't have children, they loved each other. Marriage is more than what occurs in the wedding bed. It is a bond between two people that must be strong enough to last a lifetime."

She stifled a yawn with her hand when she finished speaking. She couldn't believe that the sun had already begun to sink behind the hills and that she was so tired she could hardly keep her eyes open. Was it the stress of the day catching up with her or had they put something in the food and drink she had consumed while they talked of her life in the white world? Whichever, she knew she needed to sleep, but she wanted to know that Quade would be safe as well.

"What of Quade?" she finally asked.

"No harm will come to him," Crooked Snake assured her. "You need to rest. Close your eyes and sleep."

~ * ~

Crooked Snake watched as his daughter's eyes became heavy. He had laced the bowl of tea he had given her with an herb that he knew would induce sleep. He needed to make some decisions and they couldn't be made with her awake. Her loyalty to the whites was far too strong for her to listen to what he had to say.

"How can you believe that this woman is our sister?" Tall Elk asked.

"The two of you were young when all of this happened and you spent your time in the bachelor's quarters. You did not know Babbling Brook as I did. If you had, you would have recognized this woman immediately. I saw her in the village when I was with the missionary. I went to Owl Woman and asked her if my suspicions were correct. She confirmed that Hannah is indeed the child I loved so dearly and mourned so deeply. Owl Woman told me she could see me in Hannah's eyes and Babbling Brook in her smile. I can see my wife in many more ways than just in this woman's smile. I knew that if we took the lieutenant prisoner she would come to his rescue."

"How could you know such a thing?" Growling Bear questioned.

"Because that is what Babbling Brook would have done if I were the one held prisoner. She is her mother's daughter in every sense of the word. It was Charging Buffalo who told me of the love she has for this man. A woman in love is worse than a she bear who is guarding her young where her man is concerned."

"Then why did she not ask about him? Why did she sit in council with us and not beg for his release?" Tall Elk asked.

"In her place would you have put the life of someone you loved in danger? With all of the stories she must have heard about us over the years, I would imagine she is confused. Add to that the way you brought her to this camp and the suggestions you made did little to put her at ease."

Crooked Snake tore off a piece of the cooked meat from the carcass of the rabbit that was on the spit. He said nothing as he chewed thoughtfully. There were things that must be done before it was far too late to rectify any of his past transgressions. He hoped his sons would understand the conclusion he had come to concerning not only his future but also theirs.

"I want the two of you to help me make the lieutenant comfortable. Once that is done, you must leave immediately for Canada. It is no longer safe for you here."

"What of you?" Growling Bear inquired.

"I will make certain Hannah and the lieutenant get back to the fort safely. Once I get there I will turn myself in."

"But that is wrong," Tall Elk protested. "You cannot give up your freedom."

"I can and I will. I am an old man who has mourned the loss of his only daughter for far too long. I want to get to know her and I cannot do that if I am in Canada. I will ask the soldiers for mercy, and if I am allowed, I will be willing to go to the reservation and live in peace. I will also beg for you to be able to return to be with the people."

"But the soldiers will kill you," Growling Bear declared. "How can you trust them to show you mercy?"

"I can't, but I must. I have cheated death many times in the past. If it catches me now, it is no loss. I do not have much time left to me. I feel the tug of the ancestors more with each passing winter. That is the reason I am insisting that you return to Canada. You have your lives ahead of you."

"And you, Father? Will you be content to remain behind and perhaps end your life in the white man's stockade?"

Crooked Snake contemplated Growling Bear's question. He certainly didn't relish imprisonment, but the thought of returning to Canada and never seeing Hannah again was worse. He had mourned her death for fifteen years; he could no longer mourn since she had returned to him. That being so, he knew he wanted to spend the rest of his life close to her. If what she said was true, it was possible that before too long his sons along with his daughter-in-law and grandchildren, would be joining him, if not in prison, then on the reservation.

"I am resigned to my fate. I want to be close to my daughter for no matter how long it might be. I have spent these past years with you avenging her death. I plan to spend whatever time remains for me rejoicing in her life."

Darkness had fallen completely and he could only see his sons' expressions in the flicker of the firelight. Even so, he knew they understood. They had all regained that which was lost to them for so long. Parting would be difficult, but not impossible. As he had been able to return summer after summer, his sons would be able to return if he was not confined to the stockade.

~ * ~

Quade awoke shivering and burning up all at the same time. He pulled the blanket up around his neck and prayed that healing sleep would return to him. The only answer he could formulate was that he was sick. He had to get better because the supply wagon was due soon and he didn't want to miss the opportunity to catch Simon in the act of selling the supplies to the outlaws.

"I think he's waking up, Father," Hannah said.

He wondered why he was in Horace's home and not his own quarters. As conscious thought returned, he realized he slept on the ground and his pain was not from being sick, but because of the beating he'd received at the hands of Crooked Snake to say nothing of the sunburn on his chest, arms, face and feet.

Slowly he opened his eyes, to see Hannah kneeling next to

where he slept with a wooden bowl of water in her hands.

"You've returned to us," she declared, her smile one of genuine happiness. "We were worried when you slept for so long. Take a drink of this water and I will get you something to eat."

He was surprised when someone helped him to a sitting position. "Take the water slowly." The voice of Crooked Snake was one he would have recognized anywhere.

"Why are you helping me?" he managed to ask.

"My daughter has taught me that my anger over your love for her is wrong. As soon as you are able to travel, I will go back to the fort with you and turn myself in."

"You must know what that could mean. Why would you do something like that?"

"My anger has been fueled by my sorrow over what was done to my wife, daughter and everyone else in the village. I now realize that it was wrong. The people I took my anger out on were innocent of the crime. I will ask for mercy to be able to spend the remainder of my life in the company of the one I lost as a child and regained as a woman."

Hannah forced the bowl to his lips and encouraged him to drink.

"Are you really his daughter?" Quade knew he didn't have to ask the question. He had only to look at the two of them side by side to know the answer.

"Yes, I am. I had planned to tell you when you returned from your mission, but when you were captured I knew I had to make my true identity known sooner. I am sorry if I deceived you and will understand if you do not want me."

Quade was confused. How could he not want her? She was the woman he had fallen in love with and needed in his life.

The pain in his face made even drinking water threaten a slip back into unconsciousness. With all his might he tried to remain awake. He thought of the pain in his wrists, chest and feet from not only the cuts from the leather bindings, but also the sunburn. To his surprise, the only pain he felt was in his face from the beating he'd taken at Crooked Snake's hands.

With that realization, he knew he had to remain awake to get the answers he needed. While regaining his strength, Quade weighed his words well. The memories of the blows he'd received coupled with the pain in his face. He remembered that every question he asked was met with Crooked Snake's cruel blows. Even though none had been forthcoming now, he cautiously asked the next question. "Why beat me when I was unable to defend myself?"

The sadness in the older man's eyes somehow touched Quade.

"I had heard of her feelings for you but doubted yours for her," Crooked Snake began. "She is a beautiful woman, but for a white man to desire her for more than someone to warm his bed was unthinkable. The whites have done terrible things to our people. I know of women, both here and in Canada, who professed their love for white men only to end up in places where they must sell their bodies to other white men. I did not want that kind of a life for my daughter."

Quade understood what Crooked Snake was saying. No matter where he'd been stationed, he'd heard the stories of young Indian girls being tricked into leaving their people only to end up in the whorehouses that seemed to pop up in every backwater town west of the Mississippi.

"I tried to tell you of my love for her yesterday, but you wouldn't listen. What has made the difference now?" To his surprise, the more words he spoke, the stronger he became.

"Because my daughter has touched my heart. By morning, you will be ready to travel, but only on a travois. Even though the ointment that I used on the flesh that was rubbed raw by the bindings and that which was burned by the sun has lessened the pain in your body, you are weak. We will fashion a travois for you, and Hannah will ride your horse, as hers was left behind when my sons took her. Once we get to the fort, I will become your prisoner, rather than the other way around. I can only ask for mercy from your captain."

"What of your sons?"

"I encouraged them to leave here and return to Canada under the cover of darkness. Growling Bear has a wife and children there and it is best if he is with his family and not taking the chance of losing his life. They followed me because they became men feeding off my anger. I have told them that the time for killing has stopped. At first they didn't understand, but once they realized that Hannah was their sister and she had survived only by the goodness of the white missionary, they agreed with me. They will not return to seek revenge from the whites again."

Crooked Snake got up from Quade's side and returned with a bowl of stew that smelled good to Quade. He realized it had been a long time since he'd had breakfast at the fort before starting out on his mission. After allowing the older man to feed him, Quade slipped back into the sleep that he knew his body craved.

~ * ~

"Will he be all right?" Hannah asked.

"Yes, Daughter, he will. Once we go back to the fort, I do not know if I will be allowed to live. The one thing I will do is plead with them not to take my life before I see you and the lieutenant joined in marriage. That will make my life complete. I have lived a long time and I know that death is a certainty, whether it is at the hands of the white soldiers or because the Great Spirit calls me to come to him. Just knowing you survived the attack that took so many is enough for me."

"But I can't lose both my fathers so close together."

"What are you saying?"

"Horace is very ill. He will not live much longer. We knew this when we came here, but he was carrying out my mother's wishes that I be reunited with my people. I am concerned that my absence from the fort has been hard on him."

"Tomorrow, my daughter, we will return. Throughout this night I will pray to the Great Spirit to keep your white father under his protection."

Hannah couldn't help the tears that ran down her cheeks. She had been praying for Horace for so long and he didn't seem to be getting any better. Now her prayers were that he would survive long enough for her to return to his side.

Fifteen

The wait at the box canyon was longer than Rollie had anticipated. It was apparent that Simon spent two nights with the outlaws, since they had seen him drive the wagon into the canyon, but so far he hadn't come out. With guards posted around the clock there was no way Simon could have slipped through their trap.

Added to his concern for the mission was the fact that Crooked Snake had taken Quade prisoner. *Why Quade? Why not all the men who rode with him? Why had Crooked Snake insisted that three of the men continue with the mission and one return to the fort?* He prayed that the men left at the fort wouldn't try to go after Crooked Snake. If they did, they might be putting Quade's life in danger. After all, Crooked Snake had told the men that Quade was to be his hostage to insure that the mission was a success.

"He's coming," Private Matthews whispered when he came to where Rollie was sitting.

Rollie got to his feet and followed the younger man to the vantage point where he could see down the canyon. Even from this distance he could see the smile on Simon's face. He knew how much there usually was in his wagon when the supplies came. Now he could see only one or two barrels and something covered up with a tarp that could possibly be rotten meat.

His men knew that they were to allow Simon to clear the mouth of the canyon before they surrounded him. The minutes that ticked by seemed like hours. He wondered what was taking the man so long to drive the short distance from where he'd been spotted to the mouth of the canyon.

As he got closer, Rollie mounted his horse and motioned to his men. As soon as Simon cleared the mouth of the canyon, the soldiers surrounded him.

"What the hell is going on?" Simon asked.

"You know very well what's going on, Simon. We've finally caught you selling the supplies that were meant for the Cheyenne to the outlaws in this canyon. You're under arrest."

"What are you talking about?"

"Playing dumb doesn't become you, Simon. You know damn good and well what's going on. I can smell that rotten meat you're taking to the reservation. I'm sure if I search your pockets we'll find the money you got for selling the good meat and flour to the outlaws that are camped at the end of this canyon."

Two men dismounted and climbed up onto the wagon in order to search and bind Simon.

"Here's the money, Captain," Private Zimmer said, waving the pouch he retrieved from Simon's pocket, like an Indian brandishing a freshly taken scalp.

"McPherson's behind this. Where is that son of a bitch? Why isn't he here gloating over his victory?"

Rollie's anger came to a fast boil. "I don't know if you're a praying man, Simon, but if you aren't you'd better start. Crooked Snake took Quade hostage to insure that we caught you. If he isn't an honorable man, he might just kill Quade even if we do get you back to the fort in one piece. As soon as we do I'm sending to Denver for the prison wagon to come and get you. If Quade doesn't get back, I might be tempted not to send that wire and turn you over to the Cheyenne."

"You—you wouldn't do that, would you?"

"I can, and I would. You deserve everything that those people would do to you. It's them you've cheated. They should have the satisfaction of seeing you pay for your dishonesty. Of course, you've cheated the United States government as well so I do suppose they have first chance at you. I will suggest turning you over to the Cheyenne when I send the wire to Denver, though."

To Rollie's amazement, tears formed in Simon's eyes at the thought of being at the mercy of the Cheyenne. Even though Rollie knew it would never happened, he rather enjoyed holding the threat over Simon's head.

He watched as two of his men lifted Simon from the wagon's seat and put him in the back along with the buggy flour and rotten meat. Once he was secured, they began the trip back to the fort. With any luck, Quade would be waiting for them when they returned. It was still early enough that they could easily arrive by mid-afternoon.

They rode for several hours, all the time listening to Simon's complaints. The constant chatter the man insisted upon keeping up made Rollie wish he had gagged him when he had him bound.

It was well past noon when they finally arrived at the fort. Even though they had missed their dinner, no one said a word. Rollie decided it was because of the stench that came from the wagon and drove all thoughts of hunger from their minds.

As they got closer, he noticed that the gates were closed and sent one of the men on ahead to announce their arrival. At the top of the catwalk he noticed more sentries than usual with their rifles trained on anyone who might approach the fort.

"What's the meaning of this?" Rollie asked when they were

finally inside the gates.

"Didn't Lieutenant McPherson's men tell you?" Corporal Collins questioned. "Lieutenant McPherson was taken prisoner by Crooked Snake and twenty of his men. When Private Kane returned to the fort to tell us about it, Hannah Whitfield stole his horse and rode out. We took Horace into custody when he told us that his daughter is, in reality, Crooked Snake's daughter."

"*You what?* How could you take that old man into custody? Didn't anyone go after her?"

"And get killed in the bargain? We thought she was behind this and returning to her people to watch as they killed Lieutenant McPherson."

"Riders coming," a sentry called before Rollie could vent his anger. "It's Miss Hannah and one of them Injun friends of hers."

Rollie hurried to the gate. When it opened, he saw Hannah and an older Indian approaching the fort, a travois trailing behind the Indian's horse.

"Hannah are you—"

"I'm fine," she interrupted. "Quade needs some medical attention."

"Who is—"

"I am Crooked Snake," the Indian replied. "As the father of Hannah, I have come to turn myself over to you and to ask for your mercy."

Before Rollie could comment, Crooked Snake swung down from his horse. As soon as his feet touched the ground he went to the travois and checked on Quade.

"Treat him with respect," Hannah cautioned when the men surrounded Crooked Snake. "He is my natural father and has come to you willingly, rather than return to Canada where he would be safe from the imprisonment he knows he will face."

"How badly is Quade injured?" Rollie asked, when he got to Hannah's side.

"He is terribly sunburned and his face is bruised. He is weak and that is why my father insisted he be brought back to the fort on the travois."

"What happened?'

"Not now," Hannah said. "I want to get Quade to my house and put my white father's mind at ease. He must be worried sick with me gone for two days."

Rollie put his hand on Hannah's arm to stop her before she went to the house she and Horace shared. "Horace isn't there," he said.

"What do you mean he isn't there? Has he gone out to the reservation?"

"I don't know what's been going on here. I just arrived, but it seems that Horace is in the stockade. The men arrested him after you stole Private Kane's horse."

"The stockade! How could they? He's a sick man. I have to go to him. I—"

"You have to explain what's going on and why you stole a horse and rode out of here alone. Were you and Crooked Snake in on this together? Are there men planning to attack the fort? Are we in danger?"

"What are you talking about? No one is planning to attack the fort. No one but my father is in danger."

Rollie hated the sound of distress he heard in Hannah's voice, but everything he'd said to her so far was what he deemed to be the truth. "You stole a horse, Hannah. You ran to the enemy. I'm afraid I have to arrest you and confine you to your house."

"No!"

Rollie turned at the sound of Quade's voice. "Hannah didn't run to the enemy, she came to plead for my life. There was no one else at the fort who could have done it."

Rollie could tell Quade's strength was fading. "We'll take you over to the infirmary. Until this is settled, Hannah and Horace will be confined to their house and Crooked Snake, as well as Simon, will be housed in the stockade."

"You got him?" Quade asked, his voice hardly more than a whisper.

"Yes Quade, the mission was a success. We caught Simon with the money from the outlaws. Now I just have to hope the government kept their word and sent a second wagon to the Cheyenne."

Rollie watched as one of the men took the reins of the horse pulling the travois and led it toward the infirmary.

"Where are all your men, Crooked Snake?" Corporal Collins asked.

"My sons should be with the people in Canada by now, the old man replied, as he held out his hands to be bound.

"I'm not talking about your sons, old man," Corporal Collins shouted. "Private Kane said you had twenty braves with you when you took Lieutenant McPherson away. Were they from the reservation? Where can we find them so that we can have them arrested?"

Rollie watched Crooked Snake's expression closely. Rather than replying, the old man shook his head. "The man who came back to the fort did so because I told him to. He also lied. I had no one with me but my sons."

"What are you talking about?" Rollie finally asked. If nothing else he wanted to get to the bottom of the accusations being made and refuted. He saw Private Kane move to the back of the crowd that had gathered to watch Crooked Snake taken into custody. "Three of the men who rode with Quade came to the box canyon. They said nothing about twenty braves. Just who is telling the truth here?"

"We are," Private Zimmer said. "There was only Crooked Snake and his sons. Only a coward like Kane would make up such a story. We weren't observant enough and found ourselves surrounded. As embarrassing as it was, Crooked Snake allowed all of us but Lieutenant McPherson to leave. He said the lieutenant would be his hostage to be sure that Simon was caught."

Rollie had never been more confused. After having Private Kane arrested and taken to the stockade with Crooked Snake and Simon, he escorted Hannah to her house. "I'm sorry about this, Hannah. Really I am, but—"

"Don't try to explain, Rollie. It's been a long and tiring day. I need to be alone so I can wash up and prepare a proper meal for my father."

Before Rollie could respond, Hannah pushed him toward the door.

"You said that I am to be secluded in this house. Since seclusion means alone with my father I can see no need for you to be here. I need time to pray on what has happened and I cannot do that with you here. For now, I want nothing to do with the men of this fort and that includes you."

~ * ~

Hannah watched as Rollie backed out of her front door. Once he was gone, she shut it tightly and leaned against it. *How could everything have gone so wrong?*

Tears filled her eyes and spilled over to run down her cheeks. She slid to the floor and cried until there were no more tears left. Spent, she got to her feet. No matter how terrible her personal life had become in the past three days, she had her white father to consider.

With great effort she crossed the kitchen to the stove. In her absence, the fire had gone out. The pan with the stew was where she'd left it when she ran to Quade's rescue. The contents were dried out and burned to the bottom of the pan. She knew it would never come clean. She'd have to throw the whole mess away.

From the porch, she heard footsteps. As much as she wanted to bar her door against the men of the fort, curiosity got the better of her. When she opened the door, she saw Horace standing on the porch. The men, who had brought him from the stockade, now stood guard on the porch.

"We aren't going to bolt and run," Hannah shouted toward their turned backs.

Private Zimmer turned to face her. "Captain's orders, Miss Hannah."

"Pay them no mind, Hannah," Horace said, his voice as soft and loving as it had always been when he addressed her. "The Lord has returned you to me. You've come home and are unharmed. Come into the house where we can be alone."

"Yes, Papa, I've come home, but what have I come home to?" she asked when they were finally alone in the kitchen. "Because of my actions, you were taken prisoner. As many times as I asked Quade if he loved me, he never gave me an answer. I'm no more than the enemy to these people. If we are ever free again, I must leave."

"Leave? I don't understand your meaning. This is your home. How could you leave here?"

"This has been my home, but these are not my people. To them I am Cheyenne, a savage."

"You are Cheyenne, that is true. You are not a savage and neither are the Cheyenne. Will you move to the reservation?"

Hannah nodded as she fought back the tears that threatened to fall. "I don't want to leave this house and you behind, but I can't stay."

"Then I will go with you. There is a house for the missionary. Under the circumstances here, I am certain they will want a new chaplain as well."

"Oh, Papa, I didn't mean you should leave. You must stay close to the doctor."

"Not if it means not being close to you. I'd go to the ends of the earth to remain at your side. I'm only sorry I couldn't have saved you from that ugly scene this afternoon."

"I'm the one who should have said those words to you. If I hadn't stolen that horse, you wouldn't have been taken prisoner. I can't imagine the humiliation you suffered in that place."

Horace pulled Hannah into his warm embrace. "Are you thinking of me or Crooked Snake? If it's me, I can tell you I've lived in far worse conditions and eaten worse food. The humiliation came when they shackled my hands and led me away. After that I was treated with respect. I fear that for Crooked Snake it will be far different."

Hannah could make no response. Over the past two days, she had pleaded with Crooked Snake not to give up his freedom, but he had been firm in his decision. Quade had said little and she could understand. He had suffered at the hands of Crooked Snake. She prayed he would understand her need to have her father and brothers pardoned and allowed to return to the reservation.

~ * ~

"The sunburn is bad, Quade," Doctor Anders said, once he finished his exam. "I'm more concerned about the cuts on your wrists and ankles, though. What went on out there?"

What did go on out there? Quade asked himself. *Crooked Snake went from wanting me dead to treating my wounds.* "Doesn't make any difference. What happened here? How could you let them arrest Horace?"

"You have no idea what it was like here. Private Kane came riding in like the hounds of hell were chasing him. He told us that Crooked Snake and twenty braves had taken you prisoner. When Hannah stole his horse and took off, everyone went crazy. It got worse when Horace told us Hannah was Crooked Snake's daughter. The men seized him and took him to the stockade."

"How could you let that happen? You know his condition better than anyone here."

"I kept a close watch on him. He held up much better than I would have ever expected. The man was actually forgiving everyone who got within shouting distance of him. Since he's been released, my priority is you. I want you to drink this. It will make you sleep."

"I don't want to sleep. I have to talk to Hannah."

"You've had two days to do your talking. Sleep is more important."

Quade did as Dr. Anders said, all the time thinking that he needed to see Hannah. It was true that they'd been together for the previous two days, but they hadn't had the chance to talk. Even if Crooked Snake hadn't been there, he had been less than coherent most of the time. He didn't even know if he'd told Hannah he loved her.

~ * ~

Hannah opened the back door to throw out the pan of burned stew. As she did, an armed guard met her.

"I'm sorry, Miss Hannah, but I can't allow you to go outside."

"I wasn't planning to leave the house. I only wanted to throw out this pan that was smelling up my kitchen."

"I'm just doing my duty, Ma'am."

Hannah nodded and hurried to get back in the house and slammed the door. Knowing that she was being guarded and seeing the guards for herself were two different things. She had never felt so discouraged in her life.

Once she peeled the potatoes and put them on the stove to boil, she put meat into the pan so it could fry while she started putting her belongings into a bag. As soon as she could, she would be moving to the house that waited for her at the reservation.

"Are you certain about this?" her father asked.

"I'm not certain about anything. What I do know is that I can't stay here. I'll take only what I need. In time I'll be able to return for the rest of it. You should be comfortable here."

"As I told you before, I will go with you."

"You must know that is not necessary."

"Necessity has nothing to do with it. I want to be by your side for as long as God allows me to live. I could not stand the thought of being separated from you until I am reunited with your mother."

Hannah worried about moving her father to the reservation, but she couldn't leave him behind. She knew the house at the reservation was completely furnished, but she would miss her treasures. There was no way she could take her mother's precious china, crystal and silver with her. She would have to pray that no one would break into the house during her absence and steal it.

They were just finishing supper when someone knocked at the front door. Even though Hannah didn't want to see anyone, she got up and answered it. It came as a surprise to see Rollie and Bessie standing on the porch.

"May we come in?" Rollie asked.

Hannah was on the verge of saying no, but it went against her nature to be rude to her friends, at least to the people she called friends less than three days ago. "Of course you can, that is, unless you're afraid to be seen associating with a horse thief who is also Crooked Snake's daughter."

"Hannah!" her father's tone was one of admonishment.

"What has happened to your manners?"

"I'm sorry, Papa. It's been a trying day. Please come in and sit down. Can I get you some pie and coffee? The pie isn't fresh, but it hasn't been cut."

"Thank you Hannah," Rollie said. "You know I never pass up the opportunity to have a piece of one of your pies."

"I'll help you, Hannah," Bessie suggested.

Hannah nodded before turning to the counter. When she picked up a table knife to cut the pie she thought she saw Bessie cringe, but the older woman said nothing. Rather than commenting on Bessie's reaction, she slid the knife into the crust of one of the pies she'd made for the dinner party she'd been planning when her entire world turned upside down.

"I'm so sorry all of this has happened to you," Bessie said. "I told Rollie that I was horrified by the way your father was treated in your absence. Of course, as a woman, no one listened to me. I imagine you must have been frightened as well."

Hannah sighed deeply. "I had no reason to be frightened. I was in no danger and didn't know that my father was being imprisoned because of me."

She picked up the plates and forks while Bessie brought cups and the coffee pot.

"I've been asking questions about what happened here," Rollie began once they were all seated at the table. Considering you and Quade got Crooked Snake to give himself up to us and the horse returned on its own, there is no reason for the two of you to remain under house arrest. I've already dismissed the guards and hope you will be able to forgive us."

Hannah put down her fork. "The forgiveness will come, but for now, I cannot remain here. When we came here we were prepared to stay on the reservation, but as you may recall, you asked my father to act as chaplain here. It is best if we relocate to the reservation at first light."

"But you can't," Bessie protested. "This is your home. Your friends are here."

Hannah could be civil no longer. "My so-called friends allowed my father to be imprisoned for something that was of my doing. I don't feel comfortable here any longer. When everyone thought I was Chippewa, I was accepted. As Cheyenne, I need to be with my own people to gain the same acceptance. I know a lot of people around here have been hurt by Crooked Snake. I only hope you will remember what the soldiers did to my mother, as well as the other women and children in the village. I thank you for being my friends, but that time is ended. You'll have to excuse me, I have packing to do."

Hannah pushed her chair away from the table and left the kitchen. Her father could deal with Rollie and Bessie without her. If she wanted to leave by first light, she'd have to work for most of the night to have her possessions packed and ready to go.

"Please let me help you, Hannah," Bessie said from behind her. "You're my friend, no matter who your true parents were. I don't like the fact that you're moving out to the reservation, but I refuse to allow you to move out of my life. I'll be coming out to visit, so get used to it."

Hannah began to cry and turned to hug Bessie tightly. "I thought everyone hated me. Even though I can't stay here, you will always be welcome in my home."

The clock struck midnight when Bessie and Hannah finished the packing. Rollie had long since gone home and as soon as the summer sun set, Horace retired for the night. Hannah watched as Bessie crossed the compound. She knew it might be the last time she saw her friend. No matter what words had been said, now that everyone knew she was Cheyenne, she realized she would no longer be welcomed as she once was.

Rather than going to bed for the rest she so badly needed, she worked through the hours of darkness until the carriage's rear seat was packed with as many of her possessions as she could fit in.

As the first rays of the morning sun crested the horizon, Hannah went to the stockade. Standing on tiptoe, in the early morning shadows, she looked through the barred windows until she found the cell where Crooked Snake was being held.

"Father," she said, just loud enough to get Crooked Snake's attention, yet softly enough so as not to alert the guards.

Within the semi-dark cell, she could tell that her father got to his feet and crossed to the barred window where she stood.

"What are you doing here, Daughter?" he asked in Cheyenne.

"I have come to tell you I am leaving the fort. After what these people have done to my white father, I cannot stay any longer. I'm going to the reservation, to the house that is there for my father and me. I will tell the people that when I left, you were in good health and had willingly turned yourself in. I will pray that you will receive the mercy you deserve."

Crooked Snake reached through the bars to take her hand in his. "Do not judge these people too harshly. It saddens me to see you leave not only this fort, but also the young man who loves you. I do understand your feelings. You have been hurt. Perhaps it is best that you get to know the people of your birth, but do not forget those you have called friends."

"These friends, as you call them, turned on us. It is possible that time will heal the wounds of hurt, but for now I must leave. As for Quade, I'm not certain of his love for me. In all the while we were together in your camp, he never once professed his love for me. What my father perceived as love was probably little more than infatuation with someone who was different. When he learned of my true identity, I am certain he changed his mind about me."

"I hope you will find that your conclusions are incorrect. He is a brave man. I would be proud to call him son as the husband of my daughter."

He pressed her hand to his lips and held it there for a long moment before releasing it. "May the Great Spirit protect you no matter where you go or what you do. If we are not reunited in life, may the Great Spirit reunite us after death."

Hannah turned from the stockade so that Crooked Snake could not see the tears running down her cheeks. As she left, she was careful to remain in the shadows as much as possible. Before going back into the house to make breakfast for her father, she hitched the horse to the loaded carriage. As soon as they finished their meal, they would leave the fort never to return, not even for her most cherished dinnerware and crystal.

~ * ~

Quade opened his eyes to see Rollie sitting next to his bed. "Welcome back to the land of the living," Rollie greeted him.

"How—how long did I sleep?"

"Let's put it this way, we didn't keep your breakfast warm for you. It's about two in the afternoon. You've slept through all the excitement."

"What excitement?' Quade asked, as he shifted into a sitting position. As he did, he could feel a wave of dizziness and nausea sweep over him.

"It looks like you need something to eat. Doc said that you'd be waking up soon, so he went over to the mess hall to get you a plate of food. He also said you'd be weak until you were able to get some food into your stomach."

"I don't give a damn about that," Quade replied, trying to fight the weakness that threatened to keep him flat on his back. "What's this excitement you were talking about?"

"All in due time, Lieutenant," Dr. Anders said as he entered the room. "The first thing you need to do is eat. I doubt that savage gave you anything. From the beating you took—"

"Don't call him that!" Quade shouted. "In his place I'd probably do the same things. Now, are you going to tell me what is going on?"

"As soon as you eat, you'll get your answers," Rollie declared.

Quade resigned himself to doing as he was told. He'd had to admit the food helped, but it was swill compared to the rabbit stew Crooked Snake had made for him.

"All right, I ate this shit, now tell me what's been going on around here?" He watched as Rollie clenched and unclenched his fists. He knew the feeling. Whatever it was that Rollie had to say, had provoked anger not unlike that which Quade had felt for Simon only days earlier.

"I hardly know where to start. It's taken a lot of investigation, but I've finally come up with what I think is the truth. Before I did, I had to put Hannah and Horace under house arrest. It only lasted for a few hours, but it was something that had to be done, considering the circumstances. Crooked Snake didn't have the twenty braves that Private Kane said he did, so that makes Kane out to be a liar. I've already put him in the stockade with Crooked Snake and Simon."

The thought of Hannah being under house arrest for even a few hours made Quade sick to his stomach. "What about Hannah? Is she all right? How could you even think of arresting her? This is Hannah, not some common criminal."

"She wasn't harmed, if that's what you mean. As for how I could arrest her, it was my job. She did break the law. She stole a horse, but it came back to the fort before she did."

Quade could feel his head spinning. He had to see Hannah for himself to be certain no harm had come to her. "Can I see her? Has she been here while I was asleep?"

"She's gone, Quade."

"What do you mean she's gone?"

Quade watched as Rollie's brows knotted as though he was trying to decide what to say. "After all that happened, Hannah said she couldn't stay here. She went out to the reservation. They have a house for the missionary out there. If we hadn't needed a chaplain they would have already been staying there. I don't like the idea of Horace being so far away from the doc, but Hannah says it's where she belongs. Of course, Horace wouldn't allow her to go there alone. Hannah also says she needs to be with *her* own people, whatever that means. Just what the hell went on when you were with Crooked Snake?"

Rollie's question confused Quade. "I was out of it most of the time. As I recall, Crooked Snake did most of the talking as well as the hitting. I don't remember much after Hannah got there. I don't know what he planned to do with me if she hadn't come."

"What are you talking about?"

"From what I could gather, he sent Kane back to the fort so that Hannah would come out to find me. He knew, I swear he knew, that she was his daughter even before she told him. I think he wanted to see her and have a chance to talk to her."

"What makes you say that?"

"Just the way he acted when I asked him if she was his daughter." Quade closed his eyes and turned his head so he didn't have to look at Rollie. He let his mind wander to the beating Crooked Snake gave him. There had been little time for them to say anything to each other. Crooked Snake had released him and nursed him with the expertise of any white doctor, but Hannah had kept her distance.

"Talk to me, Quade. Help me make sense out of all this," Rollie demanded. "Hannah left here mad as a wet hen. Crooked Snake won't say why he took you hostage and you're talking in riddles."

"What do you want me to say? I don't remember much of what went on out there after Tall Elk brought Hannah into camp. I do know that Crooked Snake sent his sons to Canada and brought me back here. If I'd been him, I don't know if I would have done the same."

Rollie shook his head and turned to leave, but Quade wasn't ready to end the conversation. He needed to see Crooked Snake, needed to get to the bottom of everything that had happened to him while he'd been in the old man's camp. "Can I see Crooked Snake?"

"I don't know why you'd want to, but the doc says that tomorrow you can get out of bed. Tomorrow will be soon enough."

Quade watched as Rollie left the room. Their conversation had exhausted him. He drifted off to sleep with the promise that tomorrow he would be out of this bed and able to get the answers he needed.

Sixteen

Hannah swept the dust of summer from the building she'd soon be using for classes. Every time she brushed the head of the broom across the rough-hewn boards of the floor, she thought of the life she'd thrown away. Her heart ached at the thought of never seeing Quade again, but she knew anything she felt for the man had been wrong. If only he'd told her he loved her, things would have been different.

"We didn't think we'd ever find you."

Hannah turned to see Bessie and Elizabeth standing in the doorway. "I didn't expect to see the two of you out here," she said, before she had time to think about the words that passed her lips. Rather than continue to regret the harshness of her tone, she hurried to embrace her friends.

"Didn't Bessie tell you we'd come out to see you?" Elizabeth asked.

Hannah nodded.

"Then why didn't you believe me?" Bessie pressed.

"So much happened so quickly. I was certain that when people realized who my true father was they would hate me. Crooked Snake has hurt so many people and—"

"And nothing," Elizabeth said. "Bill has told me that Crooked Snake and his sons have been hunting for the

Cheyenne this summer. He also said that as far as he knew, the raids on the whites had stopped. Everyone deserves a second chance, or at least that's what Bill says."

Hannah nodded. Since her arrival at the reservation two days earlier she'd heard the same thing echoed over and over again.

"Did the two of you come all the way out here alone?" she finally asked.

"Of course we didn't," Elizabeth replied. "Rollie asked Bill if he would come out and check to see if the second supply wagon had arrived at the reservation. If it hadn't, Rollie wanted to buy some supplies from Bill so that the people wouldn't go hungry."

Hannah smiled. "It was already here when Papa and I arrived. The people were so grateful not to be given food that wasn't fit to eat that they had a celebration. They were especially thankful that my father wasn't injured when the whites captured him. Do you have any word of his condition?"

"Bill checked on him before we left," Bessie said. "He is just fine, even though he won't talk to anyone about why he took Quade or what happened when he had him prisoner. Rollie says that as soon as Quade is well enough he wants to talk to Crooked Snake. Rollie doesn't like the idea, but I doubt that he can stop him from doing what he wants."

The mention of Quade made Hannah's heart pound and tears form in her eyes. She willed them not to fall. Quade was her past. The Cheyenne were her future. She couldn't allow herself to dwell on what could never be.

"You haven't asked about Quade," Elizabeth commented. "Don't you want to know how he's doing?"

"There's really no need. He'll do just fine. His enlistment is up in a year and he will be going back to wherever it was that he came from. Maybe he'll even reconsider and take the position they offered him in Virginia City. I have no claim on him."

"Now if that isn't the most ridiculous thing I've ever heard," Bessie scolded. "Quade asked you to marry him and, from what I heard, you said yes. I'd say that's plenty of claim."

Bessie's words shocked Hannah. "How—how did you know? The only person I told was Papa."

"Men talk, too, my dear," Bessie assured her. "Quade told Rollie about it the morning they left on the mission to capture Simon. Of course, Rollie told me about it as soon as he got back. I was so thrilled, and then you told us you wanted to leave. I decided you'd been under a lot of strain and that you'd come to your senses. I see that you haven't."

"Quade doesn't need me. I'm little more than a savage to him. He needs a white wife. I'd be nothing more than a hindrance to him."

"Well, if that isn't a bunch of nonsense," Elizabeth declared. "For your information, Quade has been at the infirmary ever since he got back. Dr. Anders kept him sedated for the first couple of days. I think he is planning on letting him get up today. Don't you want to be there when he does?"

Hannah shook her head no. It would be too hard to watch as the man she loved with all her heart turned from her. Things were better the way they were. If he wanted her he would have to come to her. She wasn't about to make a fool out of herself over someone who didn't want her.

~ * ~

Quade shoved his feet into his boots. No matter how tender his skin was from where the sunburn had peeled, he wouldn't have complained. More than anything else he wanted to get out of this bed and back to his life. He also wanted to talk to Crooked Snake and he certainly couldn't do that confined to the infirmary.

"Rollie told me that he wants you to see him before you go to see Crooked Snake," Dr. Anders said.

"Don't see why, but I guess I can't go against orders."

As soon as he got to his feet, he realized just how much strength it took to get vertical. He reached for the back of the chair to steady himself as the dizziness washed over him.

"I don't think you're up to this. Are you sure you want to leave here?"

Quade looked at Dr. Anders making no attempt to mask his anger. "I'm positive. Nothing against your hospitality, Doc, but this is the last place I ever want to be again."

"Guess I can't blame you none. If you need me, you know where to find me."

Quade thanked Dr. Anders and left the infirmary.

Once outside, he reveled in the scent of the August air. Even though it was hot, he enjoyed being outside and away from the smell of bleach and alcohol he associated with the infirmary. No one seemed to take notice of him crossing the parade grounds and for that he sent up a silent prayer of thanks. It wasn't that he didn't want to see his men. It was more like he didn't want to have to be sociable to anyone of them.

The door to Rollie's office was open, leading Quade to believe that it was done in an attempt to catch any stray breeze that might be blowing.

"You wanted to see me?" Quade asked, once he sat across the desk from Rollie.

"That was the general idea behind having Doc send you over here," sarcasm dripped from his words. "There are some things I think you should know before you go over to the stockade. To begin with, I got a wire today saying that the prison wagon should be arriving next week, and along with it they're sending not only a military escort but also a judge."

"A judge? Why?"

"With both Simon and Crooked Snake on trial, they want to hear from not only the people here at the fort, but also the ranchers and the leaders of the Cheyenne. It looks like the government is bending over backwards to be fair in this matter."

"I don't like it at all," Quade replied. "If the verdict goes against Crooked Snake we could have problems with the Cheyenne, and if it is in his favor we'll have the ranchers to contend with. The same goes for Simon. I don't see this as a positive thing at all."

"Do you have any doubts about the verdict in either matter?"

Quade weighed his words well. "I plan to act in Crooked Snake's defense."

"You what!"

"Hear me out. How many soldiers have killed entire villages of innocent women and children and not been tried for it? They saw it as an act of war and were called heroes. Isn't that what Crooked Snake did? His people were massacred and they were old men, women and children. It was an act of war, as was his revenge. I'd hate to be put on trial for the Apaches I killed in the Arizona Territory. How about you?"

Rollie sat as though contemplating his answer. "You have a point, but that doesn't change the fact that he took you hostage and damn near killed you. Are you doing this because you feel sorry for the old man, or are you doing this because you want Hannah back? The first reason sounds a bit asinine to me and the second is downright selfish. How could we ever be certain that letting someone like him go wouldn't be signing our own death warrants?"

"We can't, but when I was in his camp, I learned that he had been the one who helped Charging Buffalo with the tracking of Simon. If he was intent on murdering us, why help us? Besides, at that time he had every opportunity to kill Simon, but he didn't."

Rollie nodded. "You should have been a lawyer. I just hope what you say is convincing to the court and that the end result is one you can live with."

Quade left Rollie's office with his emotions in turmoil. Would he be considered a traitor for defending the man everyone in the area hated? He hoped not. He could see the old man's side of things. If it had been his family who had been massacred he didn't know if he would have stood by and done nothing. Wasn't that the reason so many raids were held against the innocents of not only the Cheyenne but also every other tribe West of the Mississippi?

The stench of the stockade was worse than when he had gone there to get Miles ready to be taken to Denver in the prison wagon. Not only was it due to heat, but now there were three men living within these walls without the possibility of bathing.

"It's about time you showed your face around here," Simon shouted as Quade entered the cell area. "You're behind this, I know you are. Before you got here I could do my business and no one ever cared. You're one sick son of a bitch and an Indian lover to boot. I should have guessed at what you were when I first met you at the station. That bitch Shirl told me that she was planning to do you, but I got priority. You'll be sorry when she comes to you crying because she's lost my business. I doubt that you're man enough to satisfy her."

"Shut your mouth, Simon. I didn't come here to listen to you rant and rave. I've never met a bigger bastard, to say nothing of a blowhard, than you."

"What about me, Lieutenant?" Private Kane asked. "Are you going to let them keep me here? I was the one who came back to the fort and told them what happened. I did you a favor!"

"A favor? You did what Crooked Snake wanted you to do and nothing more. The fact that you blew the entire thing out of proportion and got Horace arrested is unforgivable. Lying is a capitol offense. If that's the way you've acted throughout your enlistment, it's no wonder you ended up here. You'll be lucky if all you get is a dishonorable discharge. If you do, and I ever hear of you telling lies about what went on here, I'll come to wherever you are and personally wring your scrawny neck."

"Don't listen to him, Kane," Simon shouted. "He ain't nothing more than a squaw man. The army had to be out of their minds to send an Indian loving bastard to a place like this. He ain't a true soldier, not with his attitude."

Quade ignored Simon's last words and went to the cell where Crooked Snake was being held. Once the guard let him inside, he assessed the older man.

"It looks like I am now the prisoner and you are my captor," Crooked Snake greeted him.

"I want to help you."

"Why? Is it because you love my daughter and she has deserted you?"

"Partially, but I've had a lot of time to think about everything. You're being punished for acts of war. I think that's unfair. I'd hate to be imprisoned for something I did while fighting the Apache."

Crooked Snake looked at Quade as though he was having a hard time believing what he just said.

"I'm prepared to act as your defense counsel," Quade continued when the older man said nothing. "I want to see you be able to be with your people, be it here or in Canada. I believe it's wrong to punish a man for an act of war. Will you let me speak for you at the trial?"

"The words you speak are kind, but would you go all the

way to Denver in order to do this thing you suggest?"

"I won't have to. The trial will be held here. There have been wrongs done to both the Cheyenne and the white ranchers. The government feels that both sides deserve to be heard. If the trial were held in Denver, it would only be the word of the government against both you and Simon. In your case, I fear that the verdict would go against you, and in Simon's, it is entirely possible that he could go free and never have to account for the food he stole from the Cheyenne or the money he took from the government for a job he never did."

"You make good sense, Lieutenant."

"I wish you'd call me Quade."

Crooked Snake smiled and then laughed heartily. "The day is coming, Quade, when I will be able to call you Son. Even if I walk with the ancestors I will proudly give you that name. I can see that you love my daughter. It is she who is blind to it. Promise me that when this is over you will go to her and give her comfort."

"That will be one promise I'll be able to keep without any problems. I love her. I wanted to make her my wife before we left on the mission to catch Simon and that hasn't changed. I was a fool not to tell her of my love while I was in your camp."

Quade spent the remainder of the morning in Crooked Snake's cell, asking questions and getting answers. When he finally left, he went directly to his quarters to write down things he was certain he wouldn't remember when the time came for the trial. It would take several days for the prison wagon to arrive and he planned to spend them with Crooked Snake so that he could give the old man the best defense possible.

Seventeen

Quade was just finishing his noon meal when he heard the prison wagon arrive. This was what he had been waiting for. Tomorrow morning the trial would begin. He prayed he was ready to give Crooked Snake a good defense.

Over the past few days, Rollie had visited the ranchers as well as the Cheyenne. Quade had no doubts about the ranchers coming to the fort, but would the Cheyenne be as trusting of the soldiers? Rollie told him that Charging Buffalo had said the elders would be coming, but that Horace had taken ill and would be unable to attend. When Quade had asked about Hannah, Rollie merely shook his head and said that Hannah refused to ever return to the fort again.

With the preparations for the trial, Quade hadn't had the time to ride out to the reservation and talk to her. There would be time for that after this was over. If things went the way he wanted them to go, Crooked Snake promised to talk to Hannah about what her future would hold and about the man who loved her. If he didn't, Quade was certain she'd never want to see him again.

Before Quade could leave the mess hall, the trail dusty men who had come with the prison wagon entered. The man in charge was not the same one as had come before. This time several high-ranking officers were among the men who were sent to guard the wagon on its return to Denver.

As soon as they came into the room, Quade got to his feet and saluted sharply.

"It's good to see a soldier who knows military procedure in this hell hole," the major who returned his salute said. "It seems to me that we will be working together for a few days and if we continue to salute each other every time we meet, we might never get this trial over with. I'm Major Atkinson and you must be Lieutenant McPherson. Your name came up several times during the trial of Major Walters."

Quade extended his hand. "I'm certain it did. There was no love lost between the two of us. He's the reason I was sent here in the first place. How is he doing as a prisoner who has been stripped of his rank?"

Major Atkinson's expression changed drastically. "Just before we left Denver, we had word that he hung himself in his cell. It's a shame to see a fine man like Miles change so. We served together when we were captains and there was none better than him. He certainly wasn't the same man when he stood before us during the trial. It was one of the reasons I wanted to come here. I'm told his widow is at the railhead. I'd like to offer her my condolences."

"I'll send someone up there to get her. Now, if you'll excuse me, I have work to do, if I intend to be ready for the trial to begin tomorrow."

"Are you defending Simon Leary?"

Quade laughed at Major Atkinson's question. "Hardly, I'm defending Crooked Snake."

The expression on the major's face was one of complete disbelief. "Why would you, a military man, defend a savage?"

"I'm not. I'm defending a man who has fought a war against the whites for fifteen years because they murdered his wife, daughter and everyone else in his village that he knew and loved. Wouldn't you want to fight against the invading forces that did such an unthinkable thing to your people?"

Major Atkinson stared at Quade as if at a loss for words. He finally nodded his head, as though giving Quade permission to leave the mess hall.

Before going back to his quarters, he went in search of Private Matthews. Quade found him caring for the horses. "I want you and Private Zimmer to ride out and meet up with the people from the railhead. The trial will be tomorrow and I'd like the two of you to act as escort for them. It's hard telling what the Cheyenne will do when they hear that the trial is about to start. I don't want any trouble."

"I'm not supposed to question a direct order, but two against so many, don't you think the odds are a bit unfair?"

"There will be other men. I don't expect any trouble. I'm just trying to be on the safe side."

Private Matthews agreed and went in search of Private Zimmer. With his mind at ease about the safety of the people from the railhead, Quade headed toward Rollie's office.

"I see the prison wagon got here," Rollie greeted him.

"I met up with Major Atkinson in the mess hall. He wants to start the trial tomorrow. I think the people from the railhead should be here to see this one."

"I couldn't agree more. I've already sent a wire and gotten a reply. They're heading out as soon as they can."

"Good. I sent two of the men to meet up with them and give them an escort. There's something else you should know before they get here."

"What's that?"

"Major Walters hung himself in his cell. It's a shame, but I doubt he could stand the humiliation of being a prisoner. At least Grace is free of him now. If Horace wasn't so sick, we could ask him to do the honors and marry her and Sam while they're here."

"I think that can wait. I don't want to put too much of a burden on Horace. There will be time enough for a proper wedding once Hannah takes over Horace's duties. I don't think she'd object to riding up to the railhead for something as special as Grace and Sam's wedding. Speaking of weddings, when are you and Hannah going to tie the knot?"

Rollie's question brought to mind the pain of not seeing Hannah since Quade returned from Crooked Snake's camp. "Probably never if I can't get her to talk to me."

"It will happen. Both Bessie and Elizabeth have been out to the reservation to see her and they assure me that she'll come around."

"I certainly hope so, but I don't have a lot of faith about it happening that easily. With all the meetings I've had with Crooked Snake about the trial, I haven't had a chance to ride out to the reservation. Crooked Snake tells me that it's best if I don't go out there until the trial is over. I tend to agree with him. She sees me as the enemy, especially since I never told her that I still loved her when I was her father's prisoner."

"Well, that's a hell of a reason if you ask me. If I was afraid that I'd be killed at any moment I certainly wouldn't be thinking about telling a girl I loved her. I'd be praying for my own hide."

"Ah, there's the difference between men and women. You and I would be praying for our lives, but a woman would be thinking that the man's silence meant that he didn't love her enough to accept her for who she is. Crooked Snake and I have talked about it a lot. He doesn't understand women any better than we do."

Rollie laughed out loud. "I guess you're right. We may be white and he may be red but women are the same the world over. Men have been trying to figure them out for years."

~ * ~

Dusk was just falling when the people from the railhead arrived. Quade made certain he was the first one to meet them when they entered the gates.

"It's good to see you, Quade," Red said, jumping down from the wagon in order to assist Shirl and Grace.

"It's good to see you as well. I told the cook to keep supper warm for you. You're all welcome to go over to the mess hall and get something to eat. The women are welcome to stay with Rollie and Bessie and there's plenty of room for the men at Horace and Hannah's place."

"Won't that put a burden on Hannah?" Grace asked.

"I doubt it. They moved out to the reservation when Crooked Snake gave himself up. It's been standing empty ever since."

"What does that do to your relationship with Hannah?" Grace asked.

"I think you can figure that one out on your own. I haven't been able to get out there with all the preparations for the trial. You might as well know now, I'm planning to defend Crooked Snake."

"You're kidding," Sam said, surprise sounding in his voice.

"Someone has to do it. I thought it best if it was someone sympathetic to him."

"How in the hell can you be sympathetic to that old fox?" Red inquired. "From what we heard he held you prisoner for three days."

"It's too long a story to go into now. After the trial you might understand things from my perspective."

They all agreed and started to make their way over to the mess hall when Quade stopped Grace. "There's something else you should know."

"Just me?" she questioned.

"Just you, for now at least. Miles hung himself in his cell. You won't have to worry about getting a divorce in order to marry Sam. You're officially a widow now. I thought I should be the one to tell you."

Grace nodded. "He was a vile man, but I am sorry that his life had to end like that. He was so proud of his rank in the army. I can only imagine what having it taken from him must have done to what remained of his mind."

Quade didn't think that Grace would have shed tears over the man who had caused her so much pain. On the other hand, he hadn't expected her to be without emotion. It was as though he had told her that a casual friend had died. He watched as she hurried to catch up with Sam and couldn't help but wonder if she would do her crying in private.

~ * ~

The trial had been scheduled to be held in the mess hall, but throughout the morning it was due to begin, more and more people began to arrive. With the amount of people and the heat that seemed to be rising with each passing minute, Rollie and Quade agreed it was best if it was moved outside. The bright blue sky told them that rain wasn't an option, so on Rollie's orders, the long benches that accommodated the men for meals were moved out to the parade ground.

Around the compound, the people from the railhead mingled with the ranchers, while the elders from the reservation stood off to one side, as though almost afraid to mix with the whites who were accusing one of their own.

After careful deliberation, it had been decided that Simon would be tried first. That being the case, Quade requested that Crooked Snake be allowed to be present. It wasn't until this morning when Quade and Rollie met with the officers who had come to form the panel of judges, that his request was approved.

"Why is he here?" Simon sneered when Quade brought Crooked Snake to the area where the trial would be held.

Quade looked intently at Simon. While Crooked Snake was shackled, Simon was neither shackled nor guarded. Did this military court think him less a criminal because of the color of his skin? "Because he was one of the men who followed you and told Captain VanEtt where you went with the supplies that were meant for the Cheyenne," Quade replied, not raising his voice above that of a normal speaking level.

"Have you turned into an Indian lover? Now that was a dumb question. You're in love with Hannah, aren't you? Now we all know exactly who and what she is. When this is all over someone should shut your mouth permanently. Any white man who turns squaw man doesn't deserve to live."

The tone of Simon's voice was a definite threat. If this court didn't find him guilty, Quade knew he would have to watch his back for the rest of his life.

"You're the one who should shut your mouth, Leary. I doubt there's much you can say to save your sorry ass, so why don't you just sit down and pray these judges don't send you to the Cheyenne as your punishment. It's what I would have suggested, but I wasn't given a say in the matter."

With those few words, Quade dismissed Simon and turned to say something to Crooked Snake. Without warning, Simon attacked him from behind. The feel of Simon's hands around his throat shocked Quade. His military training kicked in and he tried to fight back, but the attack came too quickly and his attempt to save his life was to no avail. He could feel his wind being cut off. His last conscious thought was of Hannah.

~ * ~

Crooked Snake allowed the lieutenant to shackle his hands. The white soldiers had every right to fear him. He'd killed enough of them since the massacre. This summer when he returned to the area from Canada, he'd been troubled by the fact that the Indian Agent wasn't bringing the needed supplies to the reservation.

For the first time in fifteen years, he turned his anger at the soldiers toward the Indian Agent. Even if Charging Buffalo hadn't asked him to follow Simon when he left with the supplies, he would have done it. His plan had been to follow Simon until he was certain the man was alone and then kill him. With his best friend riding with him, there was no way he could have carried out his plan.

Having recognized Hannah as his daughter, Charging Buffalo's casual comment about Hannah being in love with Quade had made Crooked Snake's blood boil. How could she love a man who could have been one of the soldiers who took her mother's life? The desire for revenge had prompted him to take Quade prisoner. He decided such an act would serve two purposes. He wanted to see and talk to the man who had stolen his daughter's heart, but he never expected his anger to get the better of him. The second and most important reason was to get Hannah to come to him. He knew if she really loved the man, she would come and plead for his life.

His regret was the punishment he'd given to Quade had left him too weak to confirm his love for Hannah. When he asked Quade why he didn't go out to the reservation to talk to Hannah, the young man had replied he thought it his duty to stay at the fort and plan for today.

Why this young man would even want to represent him was beyond Crooked Snake's understanding. What he did know was that Quade and Hannah belonged together.

Crooked Snake didn't question Quade as they walked to the area where the trial would be held. The actual area was deserted with the exception of Simon, who stood next to the table Quade had explained was where the defendants would be seated. As Crooked Snake studied the Indian Agent, he realized the man was neither shackled nor guarded. He merely stood as though this proceeding had nothing to do with him and he was but a spectator. Although there were several groups of people in the area, they were all engaged in their own conversations and paying no attention to Simon.

A commotion near the main gate pulled Crooked Snake's focus away from Simon. He smiled to see Charging Buffalo and the elders enter the compound. He prayed he would be able to convince them that no matter what the outcome of today's trial, he wanted the peace kept. His daughter had returned from the dead and he wanted nothing to jeopardize her life or standing among the Cheyenne. If things had been different, she would have been the daughter of a chief. Instead, the very people who had stolen so many people he loved from him had brought her up. He was pleased that the missionary had spared her life and kept alive the knowledge of her heritage.

The sound of someone gasping for breath from behind him diverted his attention from the elders. When he turned, he saw Simon with his hands around Quade's throat, chocking the life from his body.

With his shackles, he didn't know if he would be able to move fast enough to counteract the attack. Before he could form any more thoughts within his mind, a shot rang out and Simon loosened his grip, allowing Quade to slump to the ground, unconscious. As soon as Crooked Snake looked up to see who had fired the shot, he recognized one of the men who had ridden with Quade when he had become Crooked Snake's prisoner.

Simon moaned in pain while soldiers rushed to where the two men lay. "What happened?" Captain VanEtt demanded of anyone who could give him an answer.

The soldier who had fired the shot came to the area. "Lieutenant McPherson and Simon were talking, Sir. I saw the lieutenant turn away. When he did, Simon attacked him from behind. It all happened so quickly I doubt that anyone else even saw it. I was afraid Simon was going to kill him. That's why I shot Simon in the leg."

"You should have shot to kill the bastard," another soldier said, as he joined the group of people beginning to form around the two men.

Crooked Snake quit listening to the chatter of the soldiers and focused his attention on Quade. Already the doctor and several others were tending to Quade and Simon. As much as Crooked Snake wanted to come to Quade's side, he didn't. He knew the white men would take care of their own and consider his offer of help as interference.

He heard Quade choke and then gasp to bring life saving air back into his lungs. Earlier he'd questioned his right to help Quade, now he decided that it was his duty. Squatting behind the younger man, he helped him into a sitting position. As he did, he glanced toward the elders. He had hoped to see Hannah among them, but she wasn't there. Unless his friends told her of Quade's attempt to help her father, she would never know.

~ * ~

Conscious thought returned and with it Quade felt an overpowering need to gasp for breath. He opened his eyes to see Dr. Anders and Rollie kneeling beside him.

"What?" The one-word question sounded more like a croak than a word.

"What about me?" Simon demanded, his tone a mixture of anger and pain.

"You're in no danger of dying," Dr. Anders replied before returning his attention to Quade. "Don't try to talk, Quade," he advised. "Just take some deep breaths."

"You can thank Private Zimmer for saving your life," Rollie said. "Simon attacked and tried to kill you."

The memory of the attack began to creep into the fringes of Quade's befuddled mind. Simon had actually wanted him dead.

"He deserved to be killed," Simon shouted. "If it hadn't been for that son of a bitch, I wouldn't be in this situation."

"No, you wouldn't," Rollie spat, "Because you'd be dead. From what I've learned from Charging Buffalo, if Quade hadn't come up with the plan to stop you from cheating the Cheyenne, they would have killed you. I don't know which option I favor the most. It would have saved us a lot of trouble if I'd turned you over to them to begin with."

Someone helped Quade into a sitting position, while Rollie held a cup of water to his lips. "Take it slowly, Quade," he suggested.

Quade sipped the water, never taking his eyes from Simon. He could see blood staining the leg of his britches and realized that Private Zimmer hadn't shot to kill. He'd seen the man practicing and knew that he was a crack shot. He had hit exactly what he shot at every time. He didn't want the life of another man on his conscience. He wanted to see Simon pay for his crimes, not die before justice could be done.

"The bullet went straight through," Dr. Anders said, as he examined Simon's injured leg. "There's nothing to dig out. We'll take you back to the infirmary and dress the wound. There's no reason why the trial can't continue. Unless you're not up to it, Quade."

Quade allowed the water to trickle down his throat before answering. "I'm up to it," he replied, his voice still sounding hoarse.

"Do not do this because of me," Crooked Snake said.

He turned to see it was Crooked Snake who sat behind him supporting his body in the sitting position.

"Other than coming closer to death than I ever wanted to come, I can continue. What I don't understand is why Simon wasn't shackled and guarded like Crooked Snake? Who is responsible for representing him?"

"I am his counsel," a well-dressed man said. "I've known Simon for many years and happened to hear about this case. It was I who suggested having the trial here. I could see no reason for my friend to have to suffer the humiliation of being transported to Denver like a common criminal. He didn't kill anyone, for God's sake."

"After what went on this morning, how can you say that?" Quade asked. "He should have been shackled and guarded. As for not killing anyone, what about the women and children who depended on the supplies he sold to the outlaws? There's no telling how many of the Cheyenne died, since there was no one out at the reservation who could account for the deaths. The Cheyenne are a proud people. They would never report such a thing on their own. If it weren't for Crooked Snake and his sons, more of them would have starved over the summer. This isn't Denver. These people can't go to the store and buy what they need. They can't even go out to hunt, since our government, in its infinite wisdom, put them on land that isn't worth the powder and shot to blow it to hell and took away their weapons. This so-called friend of yours is their only way of getting food."

The sound of applause came as a surprise. Quade turned to see several high-ranking officers standing behind him.

"Well said, Lieutenant," one of them said. "I'm Major George Roberts. When we heard of this trial, I wanted to meet you for myself. I heard good things about you from Cass Eaton. It came as a surprise when Major Walters sent the wire requesting your transfer. I was at his court marshal and heard your name mentioned again. I also heard that you turned down a promotion, as well as a transfer back to Virginia City. It all prompted me to review your service record. Why would you turn down a transfer to a post you requested four years ago?"

Quade swallowed hard. How could he explain the admiration he was beginning to feel toward the Cheyenne? Would it have been as strong if he hadn't met and fallen in love with Hannah?

"I fought coming here, but I was given no choice in the matter. With less than a year of my enlistment left, I'm certain I would fight leaving here just as hard. I've come to know and respect these people. God knows I didn't want to fight Indians, but I don't want to see them mistreated either."

"Interesting," Major Roberts replied, before melting back into the sea of people milling around the area.

Crooked Snake's trial began with ranchers and soldiers testifying to what they had suffered at the hands of Crooked Snake and his sons.

"Have you ever heard of Crooked Snake killing any civilians?" Quade asked one of the ranchers.

"Come to think of it, I haven't. He stole horses and cattle, but I'm beginning to think it was to help the people at the reservation."

The other ranchers all said the same thing to Quade. It was finally being told that Crooked Snake's aggression was against the military and not innocents like the ranchers and their families.

At last it was his turn to plead Crooked Snake's case. "As a soldier, I wonder if there will come a day when I will be tried for the deaths of the Apache I fought in the Arizona territory. What we're doing here is trying a man for his personal acts of war. Fifteen years ago, he returned to his village from hunting to find his home destroyed. Everyone he knew and loved was dead. No one was spared. Innocent women, children and elders were killed, their homes burned. There had been no aggression against the soldiers to prompt such an atrocity. In his place, I would have wanted revenge as well."

He paused for a moment to allow his words to sink in. "Since I have been at this post, I have heard all the stories and have lived in fear of this man," he pointed toward Crooked Snake. "I did become his prisoner and although at first I suffered at his hands, I was also shown compassion. He had just learned that the daughter who he thought was dead had returned to the people. Hannah Whitfield is that daughter and by capturing me, he felt she would come to him."

He again paused as excited whispers rippled through the people assembled to watch the proceedings.

"What I am asking is that you show him mercy. If it had not been for him, there would be unrest among the Cheyenne. The meat he and his sons brought to the reservation has kept the people from starving and supplied them with food for the coming winter. He is also responsible for the capture of Simon Leary. It was Crooked Snake, along with Chief Charging Buffalo, who followed Simon and told us where to go in order to capture him. He also told us of the outlaws who had their hideout in that canyon. By now, they are probably in the custody of the U.S. Marshall in Deadwood."

"Where are your sons, Crooked Snake?" one of the officers that comprised the judges hearing the evidence asked.

Crooked Snake got to his feet to address the judges. "Before I came to the fort to turn myself in, I advised them to return to their homes in Canada. My son, Growling Bear, has a wife and children there. I could have gone with them, but I have been with them for all of their lives. My daughter is here. If the Great Spirit is willing, I want to be close to her and any children she may have."

"Your daughter has been raised by a man and woman who

do not believe in your Great Spirit or have the same heritage as your people. Can you accept the woman she has become?"

"The missionary is a good man. He and his wife have kept the heritage of her people alive for her. She speaks the language of the Cheyenne and teaches the children to read and write the language of the whites and to respect the white man's God. While Lieutenant McPherson was in my camp, she came and we spoke of all these things. She is now living on the reservation in the house that has been provided for the missionary."

The judges talked among themselves. "If this court were to have mercy on you, would you be able to sign a treaty of peace and lay down your weapons?"

Quade watched Crooked Snake closely. He could only guess what thoughts were going through the old man's mind. Agreeing to the terms these men were offering would mean he could no longer hunt for his people.

"My freedom is important to me. If gaining it and remaining close to my daughter means I am no longer able to hunt for my people, it will be but a small sacrifice to make."

"Why would you not be able to hunt on the reservation?" Major Roberts asked.

"It would be best if this question were asked of my brothers, the elders of the Cheyenne. They are the ones who live on the reservation where there is no game to hunt. They are also the ones who gave up their weapons when they were told to farm the land. My people know nothing of farming and have been told the land they have been given is poor."

Quade concentrated on the expressions on the faces of the judges. Unable to read anything from them, he returned his attention to Crooked Snake.

"You spoke well for me," Crooked Snake said. "I can only pray that these men will heed what you have told them. If they do not, go to my daughter and love her as I know you are capable of loving her. That will take away the hurt of not being with her father and brothers."

"I appreciate your words, but if this goes against us, not only will you lose your freedom, but I will lose the woman I love." Quade walked away from Crooked Snake, too absorbed in his own thoughts to even speak of them to the man who had become his friend.

While the judges were debating, Simon returned to the area, using a set of crutches that Quade had seen at the infirmary. The attention that had been focused on Crooked Snake now turned to Simon. It wasn't hard to see that the man was making the most of his injury.

"Did they find the animal guilty?" Simon asked, once he sat down in the chair he'd shunned earlier.

"Shut your mouth, Simon," the man who'd said he was representing him ordered. "Even if you had a chance before you tried to kill the lieutenant, it's gone now."

Quade glanced at the panel of judges. There was no way they missed the exchange between Simon and his counsel.

"Mr. Leary," Major Roberts said. "I have heard none of the testimony in this case, and yet I'm positive I know what will be said. From what I've gathered, if it weren't for Crooked Snake and his sons, even more of the Cheyenne would have starved. The government signed a treaty and hired you to take care of the needs of these people. The charges against you have told me that you have been selling the supplies meant for the Indians for your own profits."

"But... but..."

"At this point, I want to hear from the elders of the Cheyenne."

"You would take the word of animals over mine? They don't even speak a language that can be understood."

Quade could stand to listen to the slander Simon was spewing no longer. "If you will allow Chief Charging Buffalo to address the court, Major Roberts, you will see for yourself that he is a highly intelligent man. He also speaks English better than most of the soldiers on this post and is fluent in French."

"I agree," Major Roberts said. "Chief Charging Buffalo, would you please come forward and tell this court what has been happening at the reservation?"

Quade watched as Charging Buffalo got to his feet and came to where Major Roberts sat. There was no doubt that this man was a chief of high standing. His buckskin shirt and leggings beaded in reds and blues with matching beaded moccasins made an impression on everyone gathered in the parade grounds.

"It pleases me to be able to speak in this white man's court. Many years ago, when I was but a boy, the white man first came to this area. They were trappers and mountain men and even though I was but a small child, they taught me to speak English and French. In return, my people taught them the tongue of the Cheyenne. These men brought with them rifles and taught us to use them. How could we have known that they would also bring others who did not respect the land?

"I am not ashamed to say I fought those who came after and not only took our land but also killed our women and children. I fought them until I realized we were outnumbered and would never win. It was then I signed the treaty with the Great White Father in Washington. My people gave up their weapons and agreed to live in peace. With that agreement, came the promise of supplies for the people.

"The Great White Father sent a man named John to be the Indian Agent. He was a good man. He lived among the people and learned our language. The people respected him. He stayed until he received word that his parents were very ill. He went back east to be with them, but only after several meetings with the elders. Returning to his home was not his idea but ours. We told him he needed to do so out of respect for his father and mother.

"That was when the Great White Father sent Simon here. He looked at the house and met with the elders. When he did, he told us that he could not live with animals and came to live at the fort. The first time the supplies came, he brought them to the people, but the next time they did not arrive. We waited for two full moons before he finally returned to the reservation with buggy flour and spoiled meat.

"When our brother, Crooked Snake returned to us, it was not with war in his heart. He had finally begun to soften toward the whites. Instead of making war, as he had done before, he and his sons hunted for our people so we would not starve when the cold winds of winter again blew."

"Were you not given seeds to plant?" Major Roberts asked.

"For two seasons, John helped us to plant the seeds and to tend the plants, but he said the ground was bad and the yield was poor. Our women also gathered berries, roots and nuts, but it was still not enough for the winter. Three of our women died because they fed their husbands and children first and had nothing left for themselves. Seven children also died from lack of food and there were many babies who were born but never drew breath."

Quade watched the faces of the judges. It surprised him to see tears in the eyes of these officers.

"Enough!" Major Roberts declared, holding up his hand for silence. "I have heard enough. There is nothing you can say in your defense of this evidence, Mr. Leary. Your greed has sealed your fate."

"Would you believe the word of this animal?" Simon

shouted as he got to his feet.

"Yes, Mr. Leary, I would. Especially in light of the word received in Denver about your capture just outside the box canyon with the buggy flour and the spoiled meat. You, sir, are a thief and a murderer. To say nothing of the fact you tried to kill Lieutenant McPherson before these proceedings began. You will be returned to Denver and sent to the Colorado State penitentiary for the rest of your life."

"But you can't do that," Simon's counselor objected. "We have not given our defense yet."

Major Roberts shook his head. "Just what defense can there be?"

"You allowed Crooked Snake to plead to acts of war. Why not give Simon the same right?"

"Because, Mr. Adkins, your client was not at war with these people. He was not acting in vengeance because of the murder of his loved ones. Instead, he was lining his pockets at the expense of the people he was sent to help. If you think you can find a defense in that, you are a bigger fool than Mr. Leary."

Quade couldn't help but smile when Simon was led to the stockade under heavy guard. As soon as Simon was gone, he looked at Crooked Snake. The old man's trial had been first and yet he didn't know his fate.

"Major Roberts, what about Crooked Snake? What judgment do you impose upon him?"

Major Roberts motioned for Crooked Snake and Quade to approach the table where the judges sat. As they did, the four men talked quietly among themselves.

"It is our decision, that since Crooked Snake turned himself in willingly and has readily admitted to his acts of war that..."

The major paused and Quade could feel Crooked Snake stiffen in anticipation of being sent to prison for the rest of his life.

"That," Major Roberts continued, "he be allowed to spend the remainder of his life on the reservation, but only if he signs the peace treaty and you, Lieutenant, are accountable for his conduct. If his sons are also willing to turn themselves in and sign the treaty, they will be afforded the same offer."

Quade felt his heart sink. "But how can I do that?" he finally asked. "My enlistment is up in a few months.

"That, too, has been discussed. If you would be willing to take on the job of Indian Agent, your enlistment would be up today. It is evident you hold these people in high regard. I have no doubt that you would do your best by them."

Quade thought for a moment before answering. He had already decided he wanted to remain in this part of the country, but that had been before Hannah went to the reservation without so much as a parting word to him. Could he live on the reservation and among the Cheyenne without Hannah's love? A glance at Crooked Snake and the elders gave him his answer. In the short while he'd been in Montana, he'd come to respect these people and wanted to call them his friends.

"You wouldn't be that far away, Quade," Rollie said, as he came to his side. "You know I don't want to lose you, but the men have learned a lot from you. I think they can continue to carry out your orders."

"What about Private Kane?"

"I can't punish him much longer for his exaggeration. He knows what he did was wrong. I doubt there will be any more trouble from him. The Cheyenne need you. They deserve to be treated with respect and you're the man to do it."

Quade nodded. "Would the Cheyenne be given weapons in order to hunt for the food to supplement that which the government sends? Would the government agree to allow them to go into the forest to gather roots, berries and nuts as they have in the past?"

"I—" Major Roberts began.

"It would be under the supervision of myself and the elders," Quade said interrupting the man who was his superior officer.

Major Roberts motioned for Charging Buffalo and the elders to come forward. Once they stood shoulder to shoulder with Crooked Snake and Quade, Major Roberts told them what they had been discussing. "Would you be willing to abide by our decision if we agree to this plan?"

Without hesitation or discussion, they all agreed.

"Our people have lived for generations from the land," Charging Buffalo said. "It wasn't until the white men came that we became dependent upon the supply wagon to survive. Lieutenant McPherson is a wise man. By allowing us to hunt and gather, the supplies would not be so essential. They could be used to supplement our people but not be our main source of food. In time, we could require less from the Great White Father and regain our pride."

"Then, I think we are all in agreement. Effective immediately, Lieutenant McPherson will be a civilian in the employ of the government. I have been told that a second supply wagon was sent to the reservation and the people have food. In your new position, Quade, you will be expected to live in the house provided for you. I will also expect a wire detailing the needs of the people."

Quade broke into a wide grin. Instead of saluting, he extended his hand. "I think we have a deal. As long as the Cheyenne want me, I'll gladly accept the position. There is only one condition."

Major Roberts raised his eyebrows in question. "And what is that condition?"

"I would ask that Crooked Snake and I be allowed to go to Canada to bring his sons back to the reservation. As an old man, he deserves to have his entire family near him."

Major Roberts looked at the other men seated at the table. "Would you allow me to ride with you as a military escort?"

"You are a wise man," Crooked Snake said before Quade could speak. "I would be honored to have you with us."

Eighteen

Quade was up early and dressed in civilian clothes for the first time since leaving home. It felt strange not to put on his uniform.

After going to Bill's store last night for the clothes for his new lifestyle, he had spent the evening discussing the future with Crooked Snake and the elders. Having Crooked Snake talk about reuniting his family made Quade ache for his brother and mother. Even though he couldn't see himself returning to Missouri, he wanted to keep in close contact with them. He finally decided to send Quint a wire, no matter what the cost, to let him know what changes were being made in his life.

> *Quint and Ma—Many changes in my life— Have left the military and taken the job of Indian Agent for the Cheyenne—Leaving for Canada on business—With luck, Hannah will agree to marry me when I return—*
>
> *Quade*

He'd added the part about Hannah at the last minute. He knew it was foolish after all that had happened. In his last letter home he'd mentioned her. With his family so far away, what difference did it make if the wedding never happened? Would it matter? Wouldn't it be better to put his mother's mind at ease over his future? She would never meet Hannah, but at least she would think her son was happy.

"Good morning, Rollie," Quade said when he came into the office.

"I hoped you'd stop by," Rollie replied. "It seems strange to see you out of uniform."

"Believe me, it feels strange. I was wondering how much it would cost me to send a wire to my brother?"

Rollie began to smile broadly. "For you, nothing. If it hadn't been for you, Crooked Snake would not be allowed to return to his people and Simon would still be cheating the Cheyenne. What do you want sent?"

Quade handed the carefully printed message to Rollie and watched while he read the words.

"Are you sure you want to put in the part about Hannah?"

Quade nodded. "I questioned that part myself, but I know Ma wants me to be happy. What harm is there in telling her that I've found a girl to share my life?"

"None, unless the two of you don't get together once you get back from Canada."

Quade thought about what Rollie said. From the way Hannah hightailed it out to the reservation, she'd made quite clear she wanted nothing to do with him. He prayed he would be able to change her mind once he was living in such close proximity to her. She was the only girl he'd ever wanted in his life. He certainly didn't want to lose her because of something beyond his control.

After saying good-bye to Rollie, Quade walked across the parade grounds to where the elders and Crooked Snake had made their camp the night before. It had surprised him when Charging Buffalo and the elders didn't return to the village. Of course, it shouldn't have. The proceedings had lasted much longer than anyone had expected

"Are you ready to leave, Crooked Snake?" Quade asked when he joined the group of older men.

"Almost," Crooked Snake replied. "There is something we must speak of."

"Something?" Quade questioned.

"We will be returning to our village," Charging Buffalo began. "We will be telling Hannah about her father's trial and how the white major showed him mercy. We will also tell her about Simon. What do you want us to say about your position as Indian Agent?"

Quade pondered his answer. Hannah had left without speaking to him. What if she wanted no part of the love he had professed? He'd allowed himself to be captured and degraded by her father. Would she see that as weakness on his part?

"Tell her nothing," he finally said. "It's best if she doesn't know I'm coming to the village. What I have to say to her will be best said in private. I doubt if she will be pleased to see me, but that's something I'll have to deal with later."

"Are you certain?" Crooked Snake asked.

Quade nodded. "Once you and I return with her brothers, it's possible she will see me in a different light. As much as I admire the Cheyenne, I want to prove to her that I'm sincere. Just saying so isn't enough. Actions will speak louder than words where she is concerned. There is also a chance that she isn't comfortable with me now that her heritage is known among the people."

"I do not agree," Charging Buffalo declared. "She deserves to know that you still care for her. Even so, I will not go against your wishes. It is true that she is Cheyenne and if things had been different Crooked Snake would have been our chief and she would be the daughter of a chief. Things are not different, though. I have learned that all things happen for a reason.

Perhaps the reason for this was for my friend to learn that not all whites are the evil men who killed our women, children and elders. Because of this, Hannah has been returned to us and she has found a good man to love. You are, indeed, a good man, Quade McPherson."

~ * ~

The journey to the Cheyenne village in Canada took three days of hard riding. If Major Roberts was uncomfortable, he said nothing about it.

At last they arrived at the village and were met by Tall Elk and Growling Bear. It certainly wasn't the welcome that Quade had expected, as the two men pointed their rifles at them.

"Why do you bring the white soldiers to this village?" Tall Elk demanded.

"Put down your weapons and listen to what we have to say," Crooked Snake replied.

"Why does this one not wear the blue uniform of a soldier?" Growling Bear questioned, pointing at Quade.

"I am no longer a soldier," Quade said. He tried to keep his voice calm even though he was afraid of being killed at any moment. "The Indian Agent was convicted of stealing from the Cheyenne and sent to Denver to prison. I've been appointed to take his place and treat the Cheyenne with the respect they deserve."

"Why?" both young men asked at the same time.

"Because I like and respect the Cheyenne and am determined to see that they are treated fairly. I have already gotten the military to agree to return the weapons to the people so that they can hunt for the food they need, rather than be dependent upon the handouts from the government. I have many plans to make the Cheyenne a proud people again."

"But you fought and killed our brothers the Apache, or so we have been told," Tall Elk said.

"Yes, but it wasn't because it was what I wanted to do. I was a soldier and as one I was told what to do and when to do it. As soon as I could, I transferred to Virginia City. It was a misunderstanding that brought me to Montana. For the first time, I saw the people I once fought as proud and brave warriors. I respect Chief Charging Buffalo and look forward to serving and speaking for his people."

"Then why do you come here?" Growling Bear asked. "We are not of Charging Buffalo's people. Have you brought our father back to us as his punishment? Would you deprive an old man of the daughter he has mourned and sought revenge for over the past fifteen summers?"

"If my sons would listen, they would understand why we have come to this village," Crooked Snake said. "I turned myself in to the blue coats. I admitted to my acts of war. It was Quade who explained my rage and sorrow to those sent to judge me. I have agreed to live in peace on the reservation, close to my daughter."

"And what of us?" Tall Elk questioned. "Growling Bear has a wife who has given you two grandchildren. Would you leave us for a woman you hardly know?"

"I have come to bring you back to the people of your birth. The mercy extended to me is for you and your families as well. These people are Cheyenne, but they are not your family. You show that by returning to Charging Buffalo's village each summer."

"I care for the mother of my wife as well," Growling Bear said.

"Your mother-in-law is the wife of my friend, Running Horse. She was also a friend of Owl Woman. She was with us when we went hunting. You must remember her being with us, even though you were hardly more than a child yourself."

Quade watched as Growling Bear hung his head. It was

apparent that his mother-in-law had married Crooked Snake's friend and lived her life in exile away from her people. It would be his pleasure to reunite her with the friends she had been separated from for so long.

"What about the other blue coat who rides with you?" Tall Elk asked.

"I'm Major George Roberts," he replied. "I was sent from Denver to judge both your father and Simon. Your people made such an impression on me; I asked to come to this village with Quade and Crooked Snake to act as escort for you and your brother as well as your families. Your father is a good man who got caught up in a war he couldn't win. The time for war is past. He wants to live in peace and he wants his children and grandchildren with him. The sister you mourned and sought revenge for lives. She deserves to be close to her brothers. Can you agree to live in peace in order to be reunited with her?"

Quade held his breath. Would these belligerent young men agree to a peace they had not known for the past fifteen years? Could the sister who had been dead to them reconcile them with the people of their birth?

~ * ~

Quade rode next to George as they made their way South toward the reservation and Hannah. The trip that had taken three days now stretched into a week. Added to the time they had taken in preparation for the journey, it would soon be a month since he'd last seen Hannah.

He turned in the saddle and surveyed the line of people behind him. Crooked Snake and Wind Dancer led the group. The old woman had actually cried when Crooked Snake told her she would be going with him.

Behind them, rode Tall Elk with Growling Bear's daughter sitting in front of him. Growling Bear and his wife and son followed him. Each of the horses trailed a travois with the lodges and belongings of those who were making the trip to the south. Even though it was a long trip, the atmosphere was one of a long anticipated journey.

Throughout the trip, Quade had marveled at how quickly the lodges could be raised for the night and dismantled in the morning for the continuation of that journey.

What have we done to these people? We've taken their land, killed their women and children and stolen their dignity. Can someone like me even hope to do right by them? Dear God, I pray you will give me the strength to do this job. For some reason you sent me here. If I'm not mistaken it was to help the Cheyenne.

"We are on the reservation," Crooked Snake declared as he rode up next to Quade. "We will spend the night here while you and George go to the railhead. We will not return to the village without you."

"I will miss you, Crooked Snake," George said. "I consider you my friend. I hope you feel the same way about me."

"You gave me back my family. You will always be welcome in my lodge."

It amazed Quade at how quickly the bond had grown between George and Crooked Snake. They had to be close to the same age. Had they fought on opposite sides of the same battles? Were they each mellowing in their old age or had they just put aside the differences that had set white against red for far too many years?

With camp made, Quade and George rode to the railhead "Did you mean what you said to Crooked Snake?" he asked as they neared their destination.

"Yes, I did. We are both old soldiers. When I was younger, I was more like you than you would think. I joined the army to get away from my parents. With the Civil War over, I didn't think I'd have to kill anyone, but I followed orders. I fought many men like Crooked Snake. I was pleased when I was sent to Denver. These past few weeks have been my way of making amends for the things I have done."

Quade pondered George's answer. It was a shame that more people didn't see the Cheyenne and the other tribes as human beings who were only interested in saving the land that had been theirs since the beginning of time.

They rode in silence until they came to the railhead. The dusty street was as deserted in the clear fall evening as it had been on the hot summer afternoon when he first arrived in Montana.

"It's not much, is it?" George observed.

"That's what I thought when I first came here," Quade replied. "I thought I'd been sent to hell."

"Then you met Hannah and the Cheyenne. It's not hard to see that you respect these people, but you love Hannah. I wish you well. I loved my wife in that way. I still miss her. She died five years ago. Don't let Hannah get away from you."

"I don't plan to. For now, let's get you settled with Red. It's hard telling how long it will be before a train to Denver comes through. At least you won't starve. With Grace doing the cooking I've heard business has picked up. Red told me that more of the ranch hands show up on Saturday nights and the ranchers bring their wives over on Sunday."

"I'm looking forward to it. Nothing against Wind Dancer or Morning Sun's cooking, but I certainly would like a good steak and some potatoes and gravy. No matter how long it takes for the train to get here, I'm certain I'll enjoy sleeping in a real bed. Of course, I'm also looking forward to the trip to Denver by train. It will certainly be much better than by horseback. It's been a long time since I've spent so much time riding and sleeping outdoors. I don't know how Crooked Snake does it. At my age, I like the comfort of my office, bed and carriage."

Quade thought on George's declaration. Just a matter of weeks ago he would have described his life in much the same way. His quarters in Virginia City were luxurious compared to the crude ones he'd found at the fort. Although he rode daily, he was much more comfortable in his carriage and his duties as aide to Major Eaton were much different from the things he'd carried out here and expected to do for the Cheyenne.

"It's good to finally have you back, Quade."

Red's comment set Quade's stomach churning. Had something gone wrong at the fort, or worse yet, at the reservation? Had Horace died, leaving Hannah alone with no one to love her?

"What's wrong?" he asked, hardly able to get the words past the lump in his throat.

"It's nothing bad, Quade," Red assured him. "You have a visitor. When she arrived, I sent Sam down to the fort and learned that you'd gone to Canada with Crooked Snake to bring his boys back. We've made her very comfortable."

"She?" Quade questioned, his mind whirling as he tried to decide who would have come to the railhead in search of him.

"I had to come, Son," the woman who stepped into his line of vision said.

"Ma?" he asked as he recognized the woman who gave him life. "How... why..." Without further words, he rushed to embrace her.

"I always worried about what happened to you. Your father swore if you ever returned he'd kill you. I prayed every day for God to keep you safe. When we didn't hear from you, I was afraid you'd been killed. Then your letter came and it was as though God had answered my prayers. Quint wanted to come with me after we got your wire, but with the harvest he's too busy to leave the farm."

"I can't believe you came alone."

"I wanted to come. I decided that there was no reason that I couldn't make the trip. I'm not exactly helpless you know. I lived with your father long enough to learn how to defend myself. As a matter-of-fact, I rather enjoyed traveling alone. I met some of the nicest people. I think the fact that I couldn't stand the thought of knowing where you were and not seeing you gave me the courage I needed. Of course, I do have to admit, your wedding to Hannah gave me another reason to come. You haven't married her yet, have you?"

"Ah, no."

"Good. I can hardly wait to meet her. It's not that Red, Shirl, Grace and Sam haven't been good to me, but I'm anxious to see where you'll be living."

"Just how long have you been here?"

"I arrived two weeks ago. When will you be returning to the reservation and your wedding?"

Quade took his mother's arm and directed her to one of the tables. "I think we need to talk about this, Ma."

Once they were seated, Grace served them plates filled with steak and potatoes.

"What's wrong?" his mother asked. "I can see that there is something troubling you, by the look in your eyes."

"It's a long story. Let's just say I haven't seen Hannah in over a month. I'm not sure if she still wants me."

"But why wouldn't she want you?"

"She's Cheyenne and has just returned to her people. It could be that she has found a man among her own people."

"But *you* will be at the reservation. How could she not want you in her life?"

Quade sighed deeply. As much as it pained him, he told his mother about the treatment he'd received when he'd been Crooked Snake's hostage.

"After that, how can you even consider serving these

people, to say nothing of marrying Hannah?"

"You don't understand. I respect these people. What the former Indian Agent did to them was an atrocity. I was the one who formulated the plan to have him arrested. If I had been in Crooked Snake's position, I would have done the same thing. He has fought his own private war against the people he knew killed his wife and thought killed his daughter. To find her again and realize that she was in love with one of the very people who took her from him had to be terrible. We've become friends. I even acted as his counsel when he was finally granted mercy by the men sent to judge him."

"If this is what will make you happy, I would never stand in your way."

Quade breathed a sigh of relief. He knew it was hard for his mother to understand his position, but at least she was willing to try.

"Do you mind if I join you and this lovely lady?" George asked.

"Of course not. George Roberts, this is my mother, Josephine McPherson."

George took her hand and held it to his lips. "Josephine is a beautiful name to match a beautiful woman."

Quade watched as his mother blushed.

"I'm much more used to being called Jo. May I call you George?"

"I would be pleased if you would. You've been holding out on me, Quade. You never told me that your mother was such a fine figure of a woman."

"I honestly didn't expect that the two of you would meet. It's been a long time since I've seen my ma. To be truthful, I didn't expect to find her waiting for me. I'm glad that she decided to come out here and find me."

"Now the two of you are making me blush even more than I

did before. I will be getting a big head."

Quade hadn't felt this good in a long time. Not only had he gained his mother's approval of his lifestyle but also that George had taken quite an interest in her. It was obvious that the two of them would enjoy each other's company in the days that she waited to join him at the reservation. From the look on George's face, it was apparent that he would not mind whatever wait he had for the train to Denver.

~ * ~

Hannah stood in front of her class, her mind more on Quade than the arithmetic problems she was writing on the board.

It had been almost a month ago when the elders had returned to the village with word that the whites sent to judge Crooked Snake and Simon had sent Simon to prison. They also told her that Crooked Snake had been shown mercy and was going to Canada with a military escort to bring back her brothers. She couldn't help but wonder why it was taking so long for them to return.

The other thing they had told her was a new Indian Agent would be arriving soon and he would be living in the house that Simon had shunned. She couldn't help but wonder if he would be better or worse than Simon.

More than her father and brothers or even the Indian Agent, she worried about Quade. It was true that she'd left the fort without seeing him, but she had been certain he no longer loved her. Now she knew she'd been right. The ride from the fort to the village was a short one. Even Elizabeth and Bessie came out to see her, so why not Quade?

She knew the answer. Once he realized she was Crooked Snake's long lost daughter, he had rethought his proposal. She'd given him a month to come to her. There was no way she would go to the fort and beg him to love her.

She double-checked the last problem before addressing the

class. Without turning around she began. "This is your assignment. Please copy it onto your slates and—"

"And you're dismissed for the day. It's a holiday, so there's no school for the rest of the week."

Hannah's heart skipped a beat before it began to pound like the drums the people played for celebrations. The voice belonged to Quade, but could she believe her ears?

Behind her, she heard the children leave the schoolhouse. As they did, she knew she was alone with the man who had dominated her dreams since the moment she first saw him arrive at the fort in Simon's carriage.

She turned, almost afraid to see Quade standing in the doorway. The uniform that had been such a part of his identity was gone. In its place was a pair of sturdy blue britches, a shirt and vest like the ranchers wore and a pair of boots that certainly weren't army issue.

"Where is your uniform?" she asked, unsure of what else to say.

He made no move toward her. "I'm no longer in the army."

"Was it because of Crooked Snake? I heard you defended him at the trial. Did they strip you of your rank for defending the enemy?"

"No, I've taken a new position with the government. I just won't be in the military."

"Oh," she said, unable to mask her disappointment. He'd come to say he was leaving Montana and she didn't know if she could stand to hear the words that would take him from her. "I hope it's something you want."

Quade took a step closer, causing Hannah to back up until she stood flush against the blackboard.

"Are you afraid of me?" he asked, a hint of sadness in his voice.

"I'm not afraid of you, just what you've come here to tell

me. I haven't seen you in a month. Is this good-bye?"

Quade crossed the short distance separating them and put his hands on her upper arms. "Do you still love me?"

Tears spilled from her eyes and cascaded down her cheeks. As much as she wanted to shout her answer, no words would come. If she professed her love she could get her heart broken. If she said no, it would be a lie. Instead she nodded.

She closed her eyes unwilling to see his reaction to her words. To her surprise, Quade enfolded her in his arms and allowed her tears to wet the front of his shirt.

"Thank God. I was afraid I'd lost you. Will you still marry me?"

Hannah's eyes flew open and she raised her head to look deeply into his eyes. "I want to say yes, but I can't leave my people. Father is dying and I need to be here to see to their spiritual needs. And there—there's..."

His lips covered hers, silencing her protests. "There is no reason for you to leave," he said once he kissed her into silence. "The job I've taken is the one that belonged to Simon. I've come to love and respect the Cheyenne as much as you do. I don't want anyone else to be here for them."

"You're—you're the new Indian Agent?"

Quade nodded.

"Do the elders know?"

"Yes they do, but I asked them not to tell you."

"But why?"

"Because you were finding your people. If one of the young men caught your eye, I wanted you to be free to follow your heart."

"There could never be another to capture my heart. It was I who questioned your love. I thought—"

He put his finger to her lips to silence her. "I never stopped loving you."

"Then why did you stay away so long?"

"George Roberts came from Denver to be the judge for both Crooked Snake and Simon. It was George who suggested I take this position. He also insisted on going to Canada with us to bring Tall Elk and Growling Bear home. There was a lot to do to move not only your brothers but also Growling Bear's family and his mother-in-law. The women and children made the return trip much slower."

"Tall Elk and Growling Bear are here?"

"Yes, along with Wind Dancer, Morning Sun and the children. They have agreed to live in peace so that your entire family can be together."

"That will put my white father's mind at ease."

"I should have asked about him before. You said he's dying. How long does he have?"

"He moves a little further away from me with each passing day. There are fewer times when his mind is in the present. He is only alert when he has something to look forward to."

Quade smiled and again hugged her tightly. "Then we'll have to give him something to look forward to. I plan to marry you as soon as we can make the arrangements. I want him to join us as man and wife."

Nineteen

Quade was pleasantly surprised to find his house completely furnished. Even more surprising was the fact that Simon's carriage, horses and wagon also belonged to him. Since the army had allowed him to keep the horse that had been his for so long, he now owned a total of three horses. With Charging Buffalo's permission, he would eventually run them with those of the Cheyenne.

As he hitched one of the horses to the carriage, he thought about the reunion between Crooked Snake and all of his children. The people had prepared a feast as soon as Quade and Crooked Snake returned to the village.

There had been tears and laugher as the people embraced those who had been lost to them for so long. Owl Woman had been especially emotional as she was reunited with the friend she had not seen in fifteen years.

Quade had decided to distance himself from the festivities. He had a lot to do to get settled into his new life and intruding on such a reunion was not on that list. It was Morning Sun who had come to get him.

"You must be with us," she said in almost perfect English.

"This is a time for family," he'd protested.

"You are now part of this family. Soon you and Hannah will

be married. It is not right that you do not share in the joy you have brought to this village."

The memory warmed his heart. Soon he would have the same kind of reunion with his mother. It pleased him that his house had two bedrooms. From what his mother told him when he'd been at the railhead, she was intent on staying with Quade for an indefinite period of time.

"Are you ready to go?" Hannah asked as she joined him at the carriage.

"I am, if you're certain you can leave Horace for an entire day."

"Owl Woman has been staying with him while I'm at school. He's comfortable with her. I'm sure Wind Dancer will come as well. She will be good company for her since Father sleeps much more than he ever did before."

Quade understood. He had seen for himself how Horace had failed. He wondered how badly his arrest affected him. It was true he was failing before any of this happened, but it wasn't as bad as it was now. It made having the wedding as soon as possible imperative.

The drive from the village to the railhead was the first time Quade and Hannah had ever been completely alone. Without anyone else around them, they stopped often for long embraces and hungry kisses.

~ * ~

Hannah had never been to the railhead and yet she knew everyone and considered them her friends. It didn't take her long to recognize Josephine McPherson and George Roberts. They sat at a table next to the piano talking over coffee.

"Quade, what are you doing back so soon?" Josephine asked, as she rushed to embrace her son.

"Hannah said yes. I've come to take you back to the village. There's plenty of room at my house, so you'll be comfortable. I promise I won't make you sleep in a teepee. We also want to invite everyone to our wedding on Saturday."

"So soon? Doesn't Hannah need more time to prepare? I'd hate to think of you rushing such an important day for her."

Hannah smiled at Josephine's comment. "I don't need time. I have an entire village preparing for our special day."

Josephine looked in Hannah's direction for the first time. "You have to be Hannah. You're just as beautiful as Quade told me you were. I know we're going to become great friends."

"You'll have to do it on the way back to the village," Quade declared. "I don't think Hannah should be away from Horace any longer than necessary. How soon can you be packed and ready to leave?"

"It won't take me long," Josephine replied, as she got to her feet to make her way to the stairs leading to the upper rooms.

Hannah couldn't miss the look that Josephine gave George. It seemed as though she was reluctant to leave the handsome major behind. It was as though something more than friendship had begun to grow in the two short days the two of them had been together at the railhead.

"When does your train leave for Denver, George?" Quade asked.

"I'm afraid I'm stuck here for another week. I missed the last train by a matter of hours. I could ride there just as quickly but the thought of spending so much time on horseback isn't exactly what I had in mind. I sent a wire to my office and explained the delay."

"Good, then you'll be able to come to the village with us. I'd be honored to have you as a guest at our wedding."

Hannah was pleased when George agreed to return to the village with them. "I have heard many good things about you," she said, as they prepared to leave. "Of course, Quade has told me of how fairly you treated my father and brothers, but they too have told me of you. I'm grateful for the mercy you have shown to my family. It pleases me to finally have all of my family with me for the first time in fifteen years. With Quade and me getting married, I am certain we will both have a lot to learn about the Cheyenne. Now, thanks to you, we can do it together."

~ * ~

Hannah knew the children enjoyed the crisp fall afternoons with no school to attend. She felt almost guilty that she was spending her time planning her wedding rather than teaching their eager young minds, but everyone assured her she was doing the right thing. In anticipation of her acceptance of Quade's second proposal, Owl Woman began working on an elk skin dress for the wedding. In looking back, Hannah knew she should have realized that the elegant garment her aunt was making was not an ordinary dress.

As soon as Hannah and Quade announced their plans, Horace rallied. He even insisted on going back to the fort with Quade and George when they went to invite the soldiers as well as Bill, Elizabeth and Bessie to the wedding.

Hannah was surprised when they returned with Quade's wagon loaded with all the treasures she had left behind and was certain would never see again.

On the morning of the wedding, Owl Woman, Wind Dancer, Morning Sun and Josephine all gathered to help Hannah dress for the wedding. "Oh dear," Josephine lamented. "We have something new, this beautiful dress; something borrowed, Morning Sun's beaded moccasins; and something blue, these ribbons for your hair, but there is nothing old."

"I have the remedy for that," Horace said when he came into the room. "Your mother wore these for our wedding." He pressed a box into her hands. "She made me promise that I would give them to you on your wedding day."

Hannah opened the box and gasped at the sight of the diamond pendant suspended from a delicate golden chain. Also in the box were a pair of diamond ear bobs. "They're beautiful, but I—I..."

"Of course you can. Your mother came from a very wealthy family in the east. She told me that these jewels had been handed down from mother to daughter for many generations. Someday they will be given to your daughter. It matters not that Martha didn't give birth to you. God made you our daughter and now He has allowed me to give you back to the people of your birth and to unite you and Quade in marriage. When I go home, I'll be able to tell your mother that I've found your people and you are happy."

The thought of her father's death, even though she knew it would soon happen, brought tears to her eyes. "Oh, Papa. I do love you so. What will I do without you?"

"You will carry on. I, like your mother, will never be far from you, and God also is with you. He gave you to us for a short time to make our lives complete. It was God who decided the time had come for you to return to your people. Love them and allow them to love you, but first and foremost, love your husband and the children he will give you."

Hannah lifted the chain and allowed the sunlight to reflect off the perfect diamond. She remembered being very young and having her mother show her the pendant. At the time it meant nothing more to her than a pretty bauble. Now she knew it was so much more. No matter who the woman was who gave her life, she was the beloved daughter of Horace and Martha Whitfield.

She allowed Horace to put on the necklace that dropped just to the top of her dress and felt warm against the skin of her upper chest. After attaching the ear bobs, she turned to survey her reflection in her mother's cherished full-length freestanding mirror.

She gasped at the reflection. She'd never considered her appearance before. Others called her pretty, but she'd paid little attention to them. Pretty was for the young white women she saw at several of the military bases they had been to over the years, it was not for her.

"I have one more thing to give you," Horace said.

"You've given me so much, what more can there be?"

"This gift is one for you to give away." To her surprise, he loosened his tie. From beneath his shirt, he pulled a leather thong. Suspended from it was a golden ring. Just seeing it, she knew its meaning. Although she rarely saw other men wearing rings, her father had always worn a wide gold band that matched the one her mother wore, on the third finger of his left hand.

"When I was a young man, about to marry your mother, my father gave me three rings. One was for me, one for your mother, and the third for my first-born son. He said it was the same gift that his father gave him on his wedding day. He had worn the ring he gave to me around his neck, the same as I have worn this ring, from the day it was given to him by my grandfather. Of course I had to find a goldsmith to make my ring smaller, but I do not think Quade will have the same problem. My father told me that the love between a man and a woman is like this ring. There is no beginning and no ending. Since I will never have a son, the ring is for Quade. On this day he will be the son Martha and I could never have."

Hannah held out her hand to receive the ring that was definitely too large for her father's slender fingers. As she touched the highly polished golden circle, she remembered the ring her mother always wore. When she died, Hannah questioned why her father didn't take it from her finger. He told her that the ring belonged with her mother for eternity.

~ * ~

Quade had always envisioned his wedding day much differently. As a young man, he thought he would be standing in a church wearing either his uniform or a suit. Instead, he would be standing in the center of the village wearing a sturdy pair of blue pants, a white shirt and a string tie. He knew he should have bought a suit, but it would have been a foolish purchase, for where would he have ever worn it again? His life was with the Cheyenne, not in a fancy town. Even if they did attend the dances at the fort, no one ever dressed up. This was not Missouri. It was Montana and people certainly didn't dress to impress their friends and neighbors.

Until last evening, he had thought there would only be a Christian ceremony, but Swimming Beaver, the tribe's shaman, came to tell him otherwise. He had planned a special ceremony to join them in the Cheyenne way. Hannah had been impressed and Quade was surprised to say the least. Such an honor meant that Hannah's people accepted him.

Early this morning his mother had given him a ring for Hannah. "It belonged to my mother," she had said. "I probably should have given it to Quint, but it was for my first born son. I knew when you were ready to get married, you would let me know."

Quade pulled the ring from his pocket and looked at the wide beautifully carved band. How had he thought he could marry Hannah without a ring? *I didn't think. I wanted her so badly; I didn't want to wait for anything.*

He heard a knock at the front door and went to answer it. He was pleased to see Bill, Rollie and George, along with Crooked Snake and Charging Buffalo waiting for him.

"The women sent us to make certain you wouldn't get cold feet," Rollie greeted him.

"Not a chance. I spent all the time it took to bring Tall Elk and Growling Bear back worried that she didn't want me. I just didn't expect things to happen so quickly, but Horace's health being as it is, we decided not to wait."

"He didn't seem so bad when the two of you came to the fort the other day," Bill observed.

"That's because this marriage is something he wants," Charging Buffalo said. "Before he knew of the wedding he spent his days sleeping while Owl Woman stayed at the house. His time to walk the earth is coming to an end. Seeing his daughter happy is making the difference."

Quade looked to Crooked Snake to see his reaction to what Charging Buffalo said. He couldn't help but wonder how the old man felt about Hannah being referred to as Horace's daughter.

"You worry without concern, my friend," Crooked Snake said, as he put his hand on Quade's shoulder. "Horace saved her life. Had he not come when he did, wild animals drawn to the village by the smell of death and blood might have attacked her. She could have also starved. I owe him a great debt, not only for keeping her safe, but also for returning her to the people of her birth."

Quade could hardly believe Crooked Snake had answered the question that only just formed in his mind. "How did you do that?" he asked.

Crooked Snake smiled. "I am Cheyenne. When you have lived with us for a while, you will learn how to read people's thoughts by looking deep into their eyes. With your sense of family, you are Cheyenne at heart."

Crooked Snake's words meant a lot to Quade. He had prayed these people would accept him and now his prayers had been answered. He was so consumed in his thoughts he didn't see Charging Buffalo step forward.

"Owl Woman told us to give you this," the old chief said,

holding out a while elk skin bundle.

"What is it?" Quade asked.

"These are the clothes you are to wear for your wedding. Owl Woman and the other women of the village made them for you. They match the dress Hannah will wear."

Quade took the bundle from Charging Buffalo, the lump in his throat too large for any words to pass. He stepped back, allowing his friends entrance into the house. Once they were all inside, he was finally able to swallow down the lump and express his thanks.

~ * ~

Hannah stood at the edge of the crowd gathered in the center of the village. Her wedding dress fell just below her knees and the high moccasins caressed her legs, covering her from knee to toe. It wasn't the white satin and lace wedding dress her mother had promised she would one day wear, but it was worth ten times the price of a white woman's dress.

The circle of people opened, allowing Crooked Snake to come forward to escort her to Quade. As he took her arm, she remembered Horace instructing Crooked Snake about the Christian wedding ceremony.

Her heart pounded in anticipation as she saw Quade. He looked so handsome in his shirt and leggings. He even wore a pair of moccasins, indicating he was not only accepting her heritage, he was embracing the Cheyenne people.

"Dearly beloved," Horace began, his voice stronger than it had been in a long time. "We are gathered here today to join this man and this woman in the bonds of holy matrimony. Who gives this woman in marriage to this man?"

Crooked Snake turned so that he could look into Hannah's eyes. "I have just found my daughter and yet for her happiness, Horace and I give her to this man in marriage." A bit of a smile crossed Crooked Snake's lips as he placed Hannah's hand in

Quade's. "You have proven that you are a brave warrior, Quade McPherson. I entrust my daughter to your care."

Hannah had no idea what Crooked Snake had planned to say. When she heard his words, tears formed in her eyes and she could hear the women behind her weeping as well. As she glanced from Cooked Snake to Horace and then to Quade, she realized she was loved, not only by the man she would soon call husband, but also by her two fathers.

~ * ~

The ring on Quade's left hand signified Hannah's love for him, just as surely as the one he'd given her professed his undying love. He'd never heard of a man wearing a wedding ring before. The customs that had been handed down through Horace's family made him even more a part of Hannah's life. Theirs would be a love without a beginning and certainly without an end.

With the Christian ceremony ended, Swimming Beaver took them to a circle of stones, where two small stacks of wood waited to be ignited. Between the two, was a large stack of wood.

"I am an old man and I have met many of my brothers from other tribes. This ceremony is an important one for the two of you. Fire purifies all it touches. With the burning of this wood, old hatreds between white and Cheyenne will be destroyed. This union between Quade and Hannah will seal the future of our people in the white world. No longer will the whites cheat us, for Quade has agreed to become one with the people."

Quade stood in awe of the old shaman. He wanted nothing more than to protect the Cheyenne from people like Simon, who were intent on cheating them.

Swimming Beaver ignited the large pile of wood. "This fire represents the Great Spirit's approval of the union between Quade and Hannah. The fire to the north represents Quade's life before coming to the Cheyenne. The fire to the south belongs to Hannah. Because of the acts of the white soldiers she was taken from us. Because of the love Horace has for her, she has returned."

While Quade and Hannah silently prayed for their happiness together, Swimming Beaver sprinkled tobacco, sage, sweet grass and corn on them and their respective piles of wood and the people sang. After that part of the ceremony was finished the small fires were lit.

"Quade, I pray to God and the Great Spirit that our union will last forever and our children will be strong and healthy," Hannah said, as she pushed her small fire into the larger one.

"Hannah, I pray to God and the Great Spirit that our love will burn brightly for all of our lives. May we and our children live in a world of peace and love." As soon as he spoke the words, he, like Hannah, pushed his fire into the larger one. They had become one just as their fires had become one.

With the ceremony completed, the people sang praises and wished them well before they spent the remainder of the day feasting on the bounty of food prepared for the occasion.

As darkness fell, Quade and Hannah made their way to Quade's house. For this night, his mother would be staying with Wind Dancer so they could have the privacy needed for the consummation of their marriage.

At the door, Quade scooped Hannah into his arms and carried her into the house. Beneath his feet a floorboard squeaked. The only light came from the moon as it shone through the windows. Although not completely full, it gave enough light to show Quade the way to the bedroom.

Gently he put Hannah down on the bed before sitting down beside her. "Do you know how very much I love you?" he asked, as he placed his hand to her cheek.

"It can't be half as much as I love you," she replied, as she put her hands on the hem of his shirt and lifted it over his head.

The cool fall air against his skin stood in direct contrast to the heat of desire that burned in his heart for her. With little effort he lifted her enough to free the hem of her dress so that he could take it off and feast his eyes on her magnificent body for the first time.

He smiled when he realized she wore no undergarments. There was nothing to hide her beauty from him. As she sat before him, he took one of her magnificent breasts in his hands. As if by magic, her nipples puckered into hard nubs ready for him to take them into his mouth and pay homage to them.

To his surprise she stopped him before he could lower her to the bed and begin to suckle. "You are being unfair. I am naked before you, as is only right, but you still wear your leggings. I long to see the man who will make my life complete before I receive any pleasure."

Even though he didn't want to tear himself away from the pleasure that awaited him, he stood beside the bed and untied the drawstring of the leggings. At Charging Buffalo's instruction, he had not worn underwear, allowing her full view of his body as soon as the leggings dropped to the floor.

"We will fit very well together," she observed, as she tentatively reached out to touch him. The feel of her fingers caressing him brought his staff of life to full attention.

"We must go slowly," he cautioned. "Tonight must be very special for you and not one filled with fear and pain."

"I do not fear you."

"Perhaps not, but I know there is pain associated with a woman's first time of being with a man. I never want pain to be part of our lives."

Although it was hard for him not to take her immediately, he refrained. He began by paying homage to her breasts and trailing kisses to the mound of her womanhood. Through it all, he brought her to complete readiness with his fingers as they massaged the heart of her woman's soul. He didn't enter her until he was certain she was well prepared to accept him.

Slowly he pushed passed the barrier between virgin and woman. When she uttered a shocked "Oh", he stopped to allow her to adjust to his length. Once he felt her relax he began to slowly pump against her until her knew she was in complete acceptance of him. Together they gave and received pleasure until the first light of dawn crept through the windows and they fell asleep in each other's arms.

Epilogue

One Year Later

Hannah took her newborn daughter to the cemetery outside of the village. The late summer grass grew tall and lush over Horace's grave.

"This is your white grandfather, Martha. He saved my life when I was a small child. As you grow, you will hear many stories about him."

A shadow crossed the grave, causing Hannah to turn to see who had joined her. "This is a peaceful place," Crooked Snake said. "I come here to speak to Horace's spirit often. He was a special man."

"Yes, Father, he was. I plan to keep his memory alive for all my children."

"Your daughter, as well as those children still unborn, will have good role models. Your brothers have adapted to living in peace and rejoice at the birth of their niece."

"You say nothing of her father. Quade is a good man, too."

Crooked Snake nodded. "I need no words to express my pride in Quade. He is a very good man. With this winter coming, our people are better prepared than they have been since the whites brought us to this land. Through his wisdom the gardens have produced good food, our braves have been allowed to hunt and no one has gone hungry. On the day of your wedding I told him he was a Cheyenne in his heart. I think he finally understands what I meant."

"What of you, Father? Have you found love in Wind Dancer's arms?"

"That is not a question a daughter should be asking her father, but yes, I have found love. Before the snow falls, I hope to make her my wife. It is not good for a man to grow old alone."

Martha's cries of hunger ended their conversation. Crooked Snake caressed the dark hair covering his granddaughter's head before Hannah walked back to the house she and Quade shared.

After her white father's passing, Quade's mother took over the mission house, leaving Quade's house for the two of them. From the whispered conversations she had heard among the women, Major Roberts had requested permission to move onto the reservation when he retired from the military. It was also whispered that Charging Buffalo, Crooked Snake and Swimming Beaver had agreed to his plan. She prayed what she had heard was correct and that she would be the one to unite George and Josephine in marriage.

In the distance she heard the shrieks of the children at play. A check of the sun told her that they had been dismissed for the noon meal. She was glad that Quade's mother had asked if she could teach the children. It gave Hannah more time for the adults as well as for Martha.

~ * ~

Quade hurried toward home. It was close to noon and he could almost taste the venison roast Hannah had started early this morning. Allowing the men to hunt had been one of the best ideas he'd implemented. By doing so, they had been able to barter fresh meat to the railhead for supplies. That, coupled with the vegetables the people grew in their gardens, made the supplies from the government less necessary.

After many letters to Quint, he'd been able to pull from his memory the farming skills he'd learned as a child. By using the corral as the garden, the poor ground would have natural fertilizer. Next year that area would be planted to grass and allowed to rest. It would be a three year cycle. Each area would be corral, garden and lastly grassland. It was a good rotation. Without Quint's help, Quade would have never thought of what to do. He'd been away from the farm far too long to implement the changes on his own.

The aroma of roasting meat assaulted his nostrils as soon as he entered the house. The silence that greeted him was unusual. He'd expected to hear Hannah singing or Martha crying.

"Looking for someone?" Hannah asked, causing him to turn toward the door. "Martha and I took a walk and lost track of time. I took her out to the cemetery to meet her Grandpa Horace."

Martha made her presence known and Hannah took her to the parlor in order to feed her.

"I can see who comes first in this house," Quade teased as he followed her. "Do you mind if I stay and watch you feed her?"

"Not at all," Hannah said.

He enjoyed the sight of her unbuttoning her dress and holding her breast close to Martha's mouth so she could nurse. It took only a minute for Martha to take Hannah's nipple in her mouth and start to suckle.

"I was talking to Growling Bear this morning," Quade said. "He told me how the young boys go on a vision quest to get their adult names. I couldn't help but think about the past ten years of my life. I've been on my own vision quest and didn't even know it."

Hannah laughed. "And just what did you find?"

"I found not only a woman I love with all my heart, but also a village of people whom I respect. They needed me and I needed them. Growling Bear told me that Charging Buffalo wants to give me a Cheyenne name. What do you think it should be?"

"That is not for me to say, but Tall Elk had the same conversation with me. We should both go on a vision quest, but I'm afraid we're too old. We both have too many responsibilities. I've been giving my name a lot of thought. I'd like to be known as Nesting Bird."

Quade smiled at the mental picture the name portrayed. In the past year he'd actually taken the time to study the creatures of nature that surrounded him. A nesting bird, no matter what the species, was one of the most beautiful things he could think of. Not only did the female never stray from the duty of hatching the next generation of young, she nurtured them until they were ready to leave the nest.

Hannah was so like those birds. She gave birth to his beautiful daughter, but she was nurturing the entire village by teaching them the ways of the one God.

"Do you find my name amusing?" she asked, as she switched Martha to her other breast.

"Not funny, my darling. That name is so appropriate. You are like a nesting bird. Instead of caring for only our child, you care for the entire village."

"And so do you, my dear husband. I think your name should be Standing Mountain, for like the mountains, you have been sent to be strong for the people."

"Do you really think these are the names the people will give us?"

Hannah nodded.

"How do you know?"

"Because those are the names my father told me have been

chosen, just as Crying Bird has been chosen for Martha. When the moon is new, there will be a celebration and we will be given these names. It is a great honor, one that is rarely bestowed upon those not born of this village."

Quade watched until Hannah put Martha back in her cradle. Once the baby slept peacefully, he took Hannah in his arms. As he smothered her with loving kisses, he realized this was exactly where he needed to be. God had sent him into the world as the son of Willard and Josephine McPherson. As an adult, God had led him to the Cheyenne and helped him to find his true people.

Meet Sherry Derr-Wille

A country girl at heart, Sherry Derr-Wille fell in love with strong frontier heroes from watching the old westerns on her family's black and white television. Sherry grew up playing games of cowboy and Indians at a one room school in LaPrairie township near the Illinois boarder.

By day Sherry is a wife to her husband Bob, a mother to her three grown children, and a grandmother to her seven grandchildren. By night she writes and writes and writes, creating new worlds for her myriad of characters. With thirty-four books in print, she feels she is well on her way to achieving her dream of becoming a well-read author.

*VISIT OUR WEBSITE
FOR THE FULL INVENTORY
OF QUALITY BOOKS*:

http://www.wings-press.com

*Quality trade paperbacks and downloads
in multiple formats,
in genres ranging from light romantic
comedy to general fiction and horror.
Wings has something
for every reader's taste.
Visit the website, then bookmark it.
We add new titles each month!*